REFORM

ALAN M MILLER

abbott press

Abbott Press books may be ordered through booksellers or by contacting:

Abbott Press
1663 Liberty Drive
Bloomington, IN 47403
www.abbottpress.com
Phone: 1-866-697-5310

Because of the dynamic nature of the Internet, any web addresses or links contained in this book may have changed since publication and may no longer be valid. The views expressed in this work are solely those of the author and do not necessarily reflect the views of the publisher, and the publisher hereby disclaims any responsibility for them.

Any people depicted in stock imagery provided by Thinkstock are models, and such images are being used for illustrative purposes only. Certain stock imagery © Thinkstock.

ISBN: 978-1-4582-1777-6 (sc)
ISBN: 978-1-4582-1779-0 (hc)
ISBN: 978-1-4582-1778-3 (e)

Library of Congress Control Number: 2014915851

Printed in the United States of America.

Abbott Press rev. date: 10/01/2014

This book is dedicated to the patients that I
have had the privilege to know and care for
and for all those to come. May they always have
a human touch at the center of their care.

The canary yellow clad technician glanced casually at the screen in front of her, and then forwarded the information down the line:

Patient: Denise Carter

Age: 57

Sex: Female

Occupation: Office Worker

Diagnosis: Glioblastoma Multiforme

Ratio of treatment cost to projected productivity: Unfavorable

Treatment plan: Refer to termination center

CHAPTER

1

Head down Michael Guidry plunged forward trying to ignore the taunting crowd as well as his own growing doubts. The number of protestors at the Med-Met Regional Center increased daily.

It was relatively quiet inside, in contrast to the noise outside. The constant soft synthetic music covered the background mechanical hum. Transport robots scuttled silently along the edge of the hallways or hovered overhead. Personnel wearing jump suits color-coded to match the hallways, hustled through the corridors. Pale blue for housekeeping, gray for computer systems and engineers, brown for maintenance, white for diagnostic technicians, mint green for treatment technicians, and finally canary yellow for the euthanasia attendants. Colleagues also referred to the yellow-clad crew as "Heaven's Helpers."

Michael arrived at his station just before eight. He touched his left sleeve and his schedule appeared on the material. The first clients would be coming through shortly. Many came just for their routine biannual diagnostics screen; sort of a preventative maintenance. Others made drop-in visits when they had specific complaints, such as a runny nose, a rash or a hernia.

He noted that several Synthotech employees were scheduled. It was one of the large corporations that contracted for regular biannual examinations of its employees. This allowed for early detection and treatment of simple illnesses, minimizing lost time from work, or expensive treatment for advanced disease. It also facilitated the early detection of incurable illnesses. This allowed Med-Met to plan early to ease the individual to their date with the euthanasia attendants giving the employer ample time to find a replacement.

Michael placed his palm on the work station, it registered his biologics and read the implanted data chip. The system came to life. He checked to see that all was functioning normally, and settled in just as he did every morning.

Clients rolled through as usual. Those with symptoms or problems stopped at the input terminal. They registered their chief complaint and answered prompts from the computer that would help lead to their diagnosis. Those coming in for routine check-ups with no symptoms to declare just moved on to the scanners.

Michael directed traffic. He determined whether a patient needed to go to the input terminal or on to the scanners. He answered any questions and handled any problems. There never were any problems. No one ever asked a meaningful question.

"Doctor could you help me?" It took Michael a second to realize that she was addressing him.

"I'm sorry," he said putting on his best Med-Met smile and courteous voice, "but, I'm not a doctor I'm a diagnostic technician. Can I help you anyway?"

A thin older woman stood in front of him, she was nicely dressed but in clothing that was out of date. She hesitated and spoke softly, "Please excuse me but this is all very new to me and a little frightening. The last time I was sick I was a young girl."

She looked at him, he held his smile and nodded for her to continue. "The last time I saw a doctor was when I had my last baby. It was in fifty. That was when they still had regular hospitals. I didn't like hospitals then and I've managed to stay away from these new places 'til now. I haven't really been sick and frankly these places scare me, so I stay away."

Michael fought the urge to hurry the woman along. His schedule was light and she seemed fragile. "Well, you're here now, so what can Med-Met do for you today?"

She shrugged, "I really don't know what I'm supposed to do. My daughter, she brought me. They made her wait outside, so maybe you could tell me what I need to do. Should I get undressed?"

He couldn't remember the last time he met anyone who was not Med-Met experienced. Children began visits at birth. By the time they were old enough to go to school most considered a trip to Med-Met a major fun event. There were holo-computers to play with, and all input was in game format. Cooperation was well rewarded with treats and prizes. By adulthood the Med-Met way was a common experience.

He didn't say anything for a few moments. There was something sweet about this woman, she reminded him of the old time grandmothers from the early vids. "No, that won't be necessary. The first thing you have to do is answer a few questions. Just sit down at one of the input terminals, and place your right palm on the pad. The computer will ask you some questions, and you just answer them." He demonstrated, holding his right hand over the table showing her what to do.

She eyed the terminal nervously and edged away. "I never really have had much experience with computers. I know that must seem strange to you, but when I grew-up we belonged to a very orthodox religious group that frowned on them. The whole community lived that way.

"As I got older there were always other people who would operate them for me. I never even used the cook-puters. My children make fun of me because I still use a stove. That's not so bad is it?"

She fingered the clasp on the old fashioned purse she carried. It was the type women used to tote before the time when identi-chips were implanted at birth. Back when people needed to carry things like money and multiple forms of identification. She looked at Michael for help.

"There's really nothing to it. All you do is answer the questions." He tried to be reassuring, but he was uncomfortable with the situation, which diluted his effort. She continued to look up at him and played with her purse clasp continuously. Her eyes spoke to him, they were soft and pale blue, not young, but with a child-like innocence. They asked for help in a deeper way than words could have.

"Why don't I sit with you for a few minutes and help you until you feel comfortable with the computer," he said in answer to her silent request.

Her eyes closed for a brief moment, and along with her voice, said thank you. He notified the registration desk that he would be tied up for awhile, and sat down at the computer with her.

She placed her palm where he had shown her. A small holographic avatar appeared on the table top in front of her. She flinched, Michael gave her hand a reassuring pat. The soft tones of the computer voice issued a greeting. "Welcome to Med-Met, I do not detect an identi-chip in your palm. I will need to ask you a few questions to get us started." It asked her the basic questions, name, address and other identifying information. She looked at Michael with each answer as if he was asking her the questions. He realized that she was looking to him for approval with each answer. He nodded and she continued.

She began in a shaky voice, "I'm Lettie, Lettie Rubin, and I'm 75 years old." Again she looked at Michael who gave another nod. "I was born in 2014 in New York City and I lived there until last year when I moved here to be close to my youngest daughter, Rachel, and my granddaughter."

Michael sat quietly in his chair giving her his full attention. When she hesitated the avatar pushed her to continue.

She gave her address and said that she lived on her own in a small apartment in a government subsidized elder hostel. She described it as "The kind of building where you care for yourself. There are nice people who work there in case you need help or for emergencies."

The avatar asked her to please describe her background and family history.

"My people are Jewish, very orthodox, they didn't take to a lot of the fancy new machines." She glanced at the avatar, which was seated cross-legged on the table top, and then turned her attention back to Michael. "I married Lou, my late husband when I was 20. We grew up in the same neighborhood and both had large families so there were always others around when it came to any crisis or event. We had each other and didn't have much to do with the outsiders."

Michael enjoyed listening to her. He hardly ever paid attention to clients as they interacted with the computer. His fixed Med-Met smile gave way to a soft genuine smile. Again the computer inserted itself and asked her about her activities and hobbies.

She no longer hesitated, but addressed herself directly to Michael, "I love to read and cook. I don't like those reading machines or cook-puters. I go to the antique shops on Magazine Street to find real books. Have you been there?"

Before Michael could answer she pressed on. "I can still see pretty well, but I have to hold the one's with tiny print farther back."

The computer was receiving more information than it needed. There was a subtle change in the tone of its programmed flexible voice simulator and the avatar stood and walked to the edge of the table as it pressed her for more pertinent information regarding her chief complaint. Michael resented the computers interruption. He had been feeling that this was a conversation between Lettie and him.

Lettie became less animated as she answered the more specific questions. "I felt fine until about six months ago then I began to have a dry cough. It wouldn't go away." At that point she made a small cough, almost to illustrate what she was saying. "At first I made some teas and they helped a little. When they weren't working so good, I bought some cough syrups, they helped me sleep. But now, they don't help so much either. I've started coughing up some thick stuff and sometimes it has red specs in it."

The computer asked her another series of questions, she continued to address her answers to Michael. She had not had any pain or fevers.

She had never smoked, it wasn't something her people did, and by the time she was in her teens cigarettes were no longer being produced. The computer asked questions about where she had lived. It had been in an older building from the time she was a child until she got married. She remembered that for some reason they closed the building down for awhile and changed all the ceilings.

She began to cough more forcibly and removed a tissue from her purse. Looking embarrassed, she demurely spit what she had coughed up into it. She held the tissue looking around. Michael realized that she was searching for somewhere to deposit it. He passed his hand over one corner of the work station and an opening appeared. Taking his cue she dropped the tissue in, there was a brief flash of light and the hole closed.

The avatar pushed her to move on, requesting information about her family. Michael positioned himself between the avatar and Lettie, telling her to take her time. "Most of my brothers and sisters have all passed. I don't know what they died from. They were all more modern than me, they came to these places," she waved her hand indicating their surroundings.

"My Lou, god rest his soul. He was never sick, he died in an accident, shortly after our youngest, Rachel, was born. We had three children. Thank god they're all in good health."

The computer thanked Lettie, when it had all the information it wanted. The avatar instructed her to move on to the diagnostics room, and melted back into the desk-top.

She looked at Michael and asked, "Will you go with me?"

Michael didn't want to disappoint her, but explained she would be helped by another technician through the next steps.

Pursing her lips tightly she took his hand. "You're a very good doctor. You know how to listen to a person. I'm glad I could talk to you, instead of that machine."

Michael felt embarrassed, both by being called a doctor again, and because he couldn't help her further. "Thank you, but I'm not a doctor."

She shushed him and squeezed his hand harder with her frail fingers, turned and headed in the direction he had indicated.

A shiver ran through Michael as he wondered whether she might be walking to her death. He wanted to call out to her, to tell her not to go. He held back, feeling helpless, his job didn't allow that.

★   ★   ★

Michael thought a lot about Lettie over the next month. He wondered if he could have done more to help her, but reminded himself that he already had gone beyond Med–Met protocol. His curiosity caused him to violate another protocol. Between clients he called up her file to find out what had happened. His breath caught as he read the last entry in her file: *Treatment Plan: Refer to Termination Center.*

CHAPTER
2

Michael headed for his break, once again thinking about Lettie. He was startled when a young woman wearing a white jump suit, identical to his snapped her fingers in front of his face. Recovering, he greeted Marsha Walsh also a diagnostic tech, as well as an occasional date.

"Mikey," she said, calling him a nickname that he hated. "Did you catch the demonstration yesterday? Those Hippies are becoming a real nuisance. Somebody should do something about them. I saw an expose' vid. It shows how these guys treat patients with these crazy medicines from the 20th century. After the people die a slow, painful death they cut them up. If that's not bad enough they dump the remains in lakes and rivers spreading the diseases that the poor suckers had."

Michael shook his head slowly, His curiosity had led him to try and learn more about the protestors that he encountered daily. He did some research and from what he read some of their philosophy didn't sound all that bad. "Really Marsha, do you believe everything you see in the vids?"

"Sure, they documented it. The narrator said that they had someone on the inside."

"Come on, you know they can put together a vid to show anything they want. I'm sure the Hippocratins, aren't animals, they---" He noticed the way she was looking at him and decided not to push it further.

Marsha jumped in before he had a chance to back track, "Well, I think they should be stopped." Without taking a breath her voice softened and she smiled at him. "Anyway, want to grab some dinner after work?"

Tired and still thinking about Lettie, Michael lied, "Sorry, Marsha, I've got plans. Some other time, okay?"

"Okay," she laughed, "but don't take any Hippie medicine."

★   ★   ★

When Michael returned to his station he had another surprise. A balding man was sitting in his chair. His black jump suit told Michael that he was from information security.

Remembering his breach of Lettie's records he began to construct a story to cover his actions. Before he could say anything the man turned and spoke to him.

"You Guidry?" The man's voice was flat and non-threatening.

Still Michael hesitated, "I'm Michael Guidry, who are you?" The man's badge was turned off.

"Doesn't matter, I just want to give you a friendly warning."

Michael wasn't sure what was going on, the man's manner was straight-forward and he looked directly at Michael's eyes.

When Michael didn't say anything the man continued, "You need to be careful where you wander in cyberspace. Do you understand what I'm saying?" He looked at Michael waiting for an answer.

Michael spoke rapidly, "I just needed to follow-up on that patient. I wasn't sure if her scans registered and I wanted to confirm."

The man slowly shook his head, "I don't need reasons, just want to make sure you understand. It isn't just the lady's records, it's also some of the research you've been doing from your home unit. Don't forget you're in a company apartment and you are on the system."

Michael felt his heart racing, realizing the man was talking about the materials he had been reading about the Hippocratins, and other alternative groups. Before he could think up an answer the man got up from the seat and walked over to him.

"This doesn't go any further, but you need to watch yourself. Next time someone else may be on duty and they won't be as forgiving," without waiting for a response he walked past Michael and down the hall.

★   ★   ★

Leaving work that day Michael was still shaken from his encounter with the security man. Despite his distractions he couldn't help notice that the demonstration had increased in intensity. Recent news reports said that the Hippocratins and the religious groups had been joined by a more radical and violent faction, the Weatherpersons or Weps.

Working his way through the noisy crowd, he stared straight ahead avoiding eye contact. Almost colliding with a woman, he mumbled an apology and moved to go around her. She stepped back into his path.

"Do you know that you are contributing to a system that denies the existence of hope?" Her dark eyes flashed, as he looked for a way to escape. He took a few steps back, she moved forward matching his retreat with her attack. "You work for a system that gives up on a person when they need the most help. A system that takes the human factor out of medicine and replaces it with all-powerful machines".

He felt trapped and wanted to run, instead he found himself parroting Med-Met advertising. "We provide a service that people want. We have the best healthcare system in history. Everyone has access and gets equal treatment."

"How naïve are you?" she said, again closing the distance between them. "Everyone is equal until they have a serious condition. At that point equality is defined by the algorithm. If the formula determines that it is economically more advantageous for them to live, they get optimal treatment. On the other hand if costs outweigh the economic benefits, it's sayonara."

As he had backed away they had separated from the crowd and now stood off by themselves. Michael didn't speak. He stared at the woman in front of him. She stood about 5'5" and had a nice body. He stared into her eyes which were as dark as any he had ever seen but sparkled as she spoke. Her breath smelled of spearmint and drifted up to his nostrils, her body radiated heat. She grabbed him with her passion and he was drawn to her.

He suddenly realized that he was now defending Med-Met, while a few hours before he was defending the Hippocratins to Marsha. "Wait a minute," he practically shouted trying to gain some control. "Who are you? What you are doing here? Why did you pick on me?"

"Reasonable questions. I'm Sara Anson, I'm here because there are people who feel that the Med-Met system is the greatest abomination of the twenty-first century. It represents the culmination of what began as the industrial revolution and has resulted in the dehumanization of mankind. It has reduced each of us to a series of scans and a battery of tests the results of which decide if we live or die. It is a system that has far out grown its limitations and has become part of our social framework. It serves the political ambitions of its managers and lines the pockets of its corporate masters, and you are part of it.

"Regarding the third part of your question," she continued. "I might tell you that it was chance, or that I chose you because I found you attractive, but that isn't the case. I know who you are, Michael Guidry, and I have been waiting for you."

He tried to ease the tension with levity, "You've been waiting specifically for me, and you don't find me attractive? I'm crushed and puzzled."

She pressed on maintaining her intensity, narrowing her eyes and lifting her chin. "I didn't say that I don't find you attractive. That's irrelevant. As far as waiting specifically for you, that is relevant. We have people inside Med-Met who look for those who seem dissatisfied with the system, who perhaps question its morality. You were identified as one such person, and we want to help you with your dilemma."

"Who's we?" He looked around to see if anyone was paying attention to them.

She smiled, "If you want to know more, join me for dinner. I think you will. My sources haven't been wrong yet."

She leaned across him, her blouse brushing against his chest, and tapped her wrist band to his. An address scrolled across the screen. "If you want answers be there at 7:30 sharp."

As she left he stood looking at the message on his wrist, wondering what he might be getting himself into. He pressed delete, the message Delete or Cancel scrolled across the screen. He paused, finger wavering between the two choices, he took a deep before breath before selecting Cancel.

As he walked off he wondered who her sources were at Med–Met. How had they known about his doubts and growing dissatisfaction? Had he been so transparent? Sara Anson intrigued him.

CHAPTER

3

Darren Walters had risen rapidly through the ranks of Med–Met management. At thirty-three he was the youngest manager in the history of the system, and his region, the Midwestern, was the largest of the six nationally. He jogged up and down the undulating forest trail, listening to birds in the trees overhead, and the sound of twigs cracking beneath his feet. It seemed so real despite the fact that it was created by his projection treadmill and that he was suspended one foot above the floor of his spacious office. He tried to concentrate on the annual budget reports due that week. Instead he couldn't shake his annoyance over the group of demonstrators he had to pass on his way to his office that morning. He was so caught up in his thoughts that he didn't notice his assistant standing off to the side. Her voice came through the background noises as if she were there in the woods.

"Boss, are you in there?"

"What, oh Suzanne, sorry I didn't hear you come in. I had something on my mind."

"Must be something pretty big. I could have moved the furniture out of here and you wouldn't have noticed until you tried to sit down at your desk."

"It's the same thing, but it keeps getting worse. Now Central is starting to breathe down my neck. The group protesting out front is becoming a real problem. They may have their rights, but that ends when they start to affect operations.

"Central sent out a memo showing that efficiency is down across the system. Ours is the worst of all. They tie a lot of this to the activity of the Hippocratins. There's a correlation between drop in volumes and the level of Hippocratin operations in each region."

He looked past Suzanne as the hovering treadmill settled back on the rug and came to a stop. The holographic trail faded out.

He pressed on as he moved to his desk. "I don't really understand what these people want. Lately they've begun to gain some sympathy from the public and that could be detrimental to Med-Met. Some employees are hesitating to come to work for fear of confrontation. There are clients out there who have received a final diagnosis and gone home to make final arrangements, but they don't come back. The main office is convinced that the Hippocratins are influencing them not to come back, and to try their brand of medicine instead."

Darren continued talking, barely noticing her, never waiting for her agreement, just expecting it. "Frankly, our friends in Washington don't like the idea of people with terminal diagnoses walking around and not getting their final treatment. Think about the drain on our resources if we have to support a bunch of sick terminals. Think of the effect on the population of actually having to deal with the infirmed, and what about the diseases they might spread."

He glanced at Suzanne who was shifting from foot to foot, staring at a holo-painting on the wall,

"This is serious Suz. These fanatics don't have the right to shout their opinion if the consequences cost society dollars, and lives and suffering."

Darren finished and nodded. He liked what he had said. He had gotten to where he was by recognizing opportunity when it presented itself. The Hippocratins, might just be such an opportunity. Suzanne stood there, just another piece of furniture.

"Get me the file on those Hippies, and any Med-Met company press releases and official policy concerning their activities. Make sure you get me some detailed information on Jacob Rokoff".

Suzanne turned and looked at him, hesitating, "Why do you need stuff on him?"

"He's becoming a folk hero. I think he's a key." As she was leaving the office he thought to himself, *If I can make an issue out of shutting them down I'll be doing a service to society and I'll have the wedge I need to get a vice presidency at the main office. I just need the right angle.*"

Before she was out the door he added, "Do me a favor and get Wil Armbrister on the link. I want him here this afternoon."

She returned shortly with some file chips and vid-recordings. Scanning the files he concentrated on the details of Rokoff's background and education. He was impressed. Rokoff came from a wealthy background. His family on his father's side contained a long line of doctors, including some who had been quite prominent. His mother's family made their fortune in the steel industry in the early part of the twentieth century. Darren smiled considering that his own forebears had been steel workers and had quite possibly worked for Rokoff's family and fought against them with the rise of unions.

Rokoff had a distinguished educational background. He received his undergraduate degree in Ethics at Harvard. Despite a decreasing public interest in medicine, and increasing hostility toward physicians, he had gone to medical school. He wondered out loud "Why would Rokoff surrender a lucrative and uncomplicated career and instead choose to practice an obsolete trade in a hostile environment? Doesn't make sense to me."

Suzanne who had been standing quietly asked if he wanted her to stay.

"Sure, in fact take notes. I may want you to tag some segments to recall later."

The miniature holo-images rose out of the table. A narrator's voice said that they were looking at a graduation at Georgetown University School of Medicine, the year 2060. A tall, red-haired young man in graduation robes received a diploma. The narrator further explained that this was the last degree conferred to the last class of the last medical school.

The scene shifted and an insert appeared showing the year 2070. At a poorly attended press conference the same man, a little leaner and harder looking, stood at a podium. Seated to his left was an older man, arms crossed.

"Thank you all for coming. I'm Jacob Rokoff. We are here to announce the formation of the Hippocratin Society. I'm sure many if not all of you know Marshall Ellis." The older man nodded and Rokoff continued. "Our goal is simple. To preserve the human side of the practice of medicine. We will assure the involvement of humans in the delivery of care, and the maintenance of humanistic ideals in the care of people.

"Dr. Ellis will outline for you our apprenticeship program, and how we plan to implement it." While the older physician made his way to the podium in the holo, there was a knock at the door. Walters put the recording on hold, the figures faded away. Suzanne turned toward the door.

Before she could take a step the door slid open and a squat dark haired figure in a late twentieth century style business suit burst into the room.

Wil Armbrister was known for his retro attire as well as for his keen public relations skills. He was also said to be a master of dirty tricks and an avid reader of anything written by or about his hero, the 37th President, Richard M. Nixon. Armbrister repeatedly said that if he had been there to handle the press the Watergate affair would have been a minor footnote in history, and Nixon would have gone down as the true political genius that Armbrister knew him to be. "Someone looking for me?"

"Wil, come on in. You know Suzanne Hartstein, don't you?"

"Not as well I'd like to buddy boy." He gave a soft laugh, focusing his gaze on Suzanne, "I guess I'm not as good a P.R. man for myself as I am for others. I can't seem to convince the lady that I'm the new and improved product, the one that no woman should be without."

Suzanne gave a phony looking smile, "Sorry Mr. Armbrister, but I always tune out when the commercial comes on."

"She's a sharp one Dar, if you ever leave here I'm putting in my bid for her." He turned his focus back to his boss, "So, what can I do for you, need some nifty commercials about our new annual executive tune up, or our family total health plan?"

"No Wil, I've got a problem that's a bit more complicated and one I think you'll find quite a bit more interesting. It's the Hippies."

"What a bunch of weirdos. It's getting worse, not only the Hippies, but the religious freaks and the Weps. The Weps are the ones that really worry me. They openly talk about violence. I had to hover all the way around back to find a place to park.

"Thought about just landing on top of them! That would have been something! It seems there are more of them every day. Who'd notice if I squashed a few?" Armbrister laughed again apparently the only one in the room appreciating his humor.

Oblivious he continued, "You think they would have quit after that old geek retired. What is he two hundred years old? But no, they've just gotten more popular the last four years."

Darren jumped in, "If you mean Marshall Ellis, he's only one hundred and one, but that's part of the reason for the increasing popularity. People look at him, his age, his health and he's never visited a Med–Met facility. They wonder if the Hippocratins have a secret fountain of youth or something. Combine that with their 'humanistic' teachings, and self determination rhetoric and they attract a lot of impressionable young people."

"So, what's the problem, your kid sign up?"

Darren waved dismissively, "No, you know my oldest is only five. The problem is that they're beginning to effect business, and that has the Central Office in an uproar. The way I see it, if we don't do something to turn it around, it will be our asses. On the other hand if we're the ones to come up with a way to handle the situation, it's a ticket straight to corporate headquarters."

Armbrister's eyes lit up and a slight smile crossed his face. "So what we've got to do is to turn people on these spacoids. We make them less popular than the diseases they're supposed to be treating.

I like it. You know, Nixon had to deal with hippies also. A bunch of long haired, bare-foot freaks, their big gripe was the military industrial complex. I see some great parallels here. Our hippies are after the medical industrial complex." Darren nodded, this is why he kept Wil around the man had talent and passion.

Wil pressed on, a small drop of spittle emerging from the left side of his mouth. "We need to learn from history. Nixon surrounded himself with some real incompetents who let the situation get out of hand. We need to shut these guys down before they gain anymore strength, and we need to avoid making heroes or martyrs of any of them.

"Play this one right Darren my boy, and we could get you elected President."

"Wil let's not get carried away, the Presidency of Med-Met is not an elected office."

"Who's talking about Med-Met?"

CHAPTER

4

Michael double checked the address Sara had given him, it was an apartment in the warehouse district. He searched both sides of the door for a communicator finding none he knocked. He put what he thought was his sly smile on his face, preparing for Sara. The smile quickly dissolved as the door opened. Where he expected Sara's eyes to be was a male chest in a tee-shirt with an embroidered snake wrapped around a pole over the left breast. He was more startled as he looked up at the man in front of him. He was at least a half a foot taller than Michael's five-ten. He had shoulder-length red hair streaked with silver and tied back in a pony tail.

Michael tried to see around him, but couldn't get a good view. He backed away debating whether to ask for Sara or just to excuse himself and leave.

"Good evening," the man said. His voice was deep, but soft. "I'm Rokoff, Sara will be back shortly. She's picking up some pizzas. Come in and meet the others."

Increasingly confused, Michael took two steps into a fairly large room that looked as if it served as a kitchen, dining room, bedroom and oddly enough a classroom. He looked back at the door it was closed.

At first he thought that this was some sort of planning meeting for demonstrations like the one held today at Med-Met., and he wanted no part of that. On closer examination he began to get a different impression. Two men and three women all in their twenties or thirties sat around the room facing in the general direction of a data wall. On the wall was the outline of a human body with various structures drawn in different colors. It reminded him of a Med-Met thermoscan. At intervals it rotated providing lateral and posterior views. Any illusions he still harbored that the real reason Sara had invited him to dinner out of romantic interest, were gone.

Each person had a data pad, as well as a variety of antique bound texts. That in itself was surprising as books had long been replaced by micro-floppies and holo-readers. The cover of one particularly old and thick volume stood out, *Grey's Anatomy of the Human Body*. All of a sudden it hit him and he gasped realizing who had greeted him.

He should have recognized him immediately, but he was too busy trying to figure out where Sara was. After all how many red-haired giants with pony tails were there. The man said his name was Rokoff.

Jacob Rokoff. Rokoff, the Heretic. Rokoff, the Witch Doctor. Rokoff, the leader of the Hippocratins. Michael was standing in a classroom where medicine was being taught. He wanted to run. He was a Med-Met technician, and this was the enemy. He turned toward the door and then stopped and turned back to the room. Frozen to the spot emotions flooded through him, fear, curiosity, and a degree of excitement. He thought about Lettie and others like her, coldly assigned to termination. But there was also his job, a good job. Just being here put that at risk.

Just as Michael was about to turn for the door Rokoff touched his shoulder. "Sara told me of your conversation this afternoon. I'm glad you could come. The young men and women in this room are my students. Apprentices if you please. Two will be graduating shortly and I would like to add at least one other. Sara seems to feel that you would be an excellent candidate."

"Well thank you, mister, ah doctor Rokoff..."

"It's Jacob, and don't thank me. I may not agree to take you on. One cannot judge a person's ability to be a physician by one brief tete-a-tete during a demonstration. Sara has a knack for forming judgments too quickly. I'll have to break her of that if she's to become a reliable diagnostician." He smiled and chuckled softly.

"If you are interested in learning about our group, I invite you to attend our sessions over the next week and then we can decide together if you are suited for this type of training."

Michael was sweating despite the temperature controlled environment. He was trying to digest what was happening. He was being presented with the opportunity to make a complete turnabout. He was being asked to consider leaving legitimate medicotechnology and enter the fringes of respectable and legal science.

Before he could speak, the door slid open and a stack of pizza boxes atop shapely legs stood in the entrance. A female voice emanated from the stack, "A little help please."

"Ah, Sara's back." Rokoff turned to help and spoke to Michael over his shoulder, "Think about it and we'll talk later."

"Sara, your Med-Met friend has arrived. We're all quite famished so get settled and I'll serve up the pizzas."

Michael stared at her as she handed the food to Rokoff, crossed the room and headed toward him. Someone else produced a pitcher of iced tea, and Rokoff joined the rest as they began to consume the dinner. Sara's dark brown hair hung to her shoulders, her eyes sparkled and a wide grin crossed her face as she approached Michael. It seemed to him that she was clearly enjoying the surprise she had sprung.

"I'm glad you came. I think you'll enjoy our group."

Michael tried to appear unfazed, "And I thought all you wanted to do was to get me alone. I don't know whether to walk out now or stick around and satisfy my curiosity."

"What did I do?" she moved closer to him, feigning innocence.

"You damn well know. I didn't know what was going on when he answered the door." Michael said pointed to Rokoff.

"Oh, excuse me. I didn't realize the only reason that you accepted my invitation was because you were smitten with me. I thought you were interested in our cause."

"I am, interested, in the cause that is. I just wish I had known what to expect so that I didn't have to stand there with my mouth open until I figured out what all this was."

"If I had told you would you have come?"

He shook his head, "I doubt it."

"But now you'll stay?"

He wasn't going to give her the satisfaction of his leaving, "I might as well, at least for this evening's session."

"Good," she said smiling and taking his hand pulling him further into the room. "Let's get at the pizza before the rest of the gluttons finish it, and perhaps after class is over we can still have that private talk." Her eyes twinkled and he bristled knowing that she was enjoying his discomfort.

"Oh most definitely, I want to learn all about your ... program."

Sara led him into the group and introduced him to the others. Michael grabbed a slice and a drink, sat back and listened quietly as they tore apart the whole system that he represented.

Rokoff began. "I heard today that Iowa outlawed Medical Clinics, that's the third state so far this year."

Between bites one of the students asked, "What's going to happen to their program?"

"Well," Rokoff answered, "I haven't spoken to them since the news, but they expected it. They're going to follow the groups in Kentucky and Alabama and go underground."

One of the others added, "That will to make it twice as hard to recruit new students, not only will public opinion be against the medical arts, but also the law."

"What about taking direct action?" Sara was half out of her seat going for more food as she asked.

"If I can assume from your usual viewpoint that you are referring to retaliatory strikes on Med–Met centers, none are being officially sanctioned. I would prefer that my students were not so quick to wish for violent actions." He paused looking directly at Sara, "If I have misjudged your intent this time, and you were concerned with legislative initiative, the answer is yes. Appeals to the state's high court have been filed as we've done in the other two states. Additionally we are trying recall movements against a number of legislators who we feel voted against the wishes of their constituencies due to Med–Met money received under the table."

Michael had yet to take a bite of his food. The end of his slice drooped forward and the cheese slowly edged off. "Wait a minute. Are you saying that Med–Met is bribing legislators to vote against the practicing of medicine?" Michael knew that Med–Met was working against the Hipporcratins but found it hard to believe that corruption was involved.

"Of course, it's a conspiracy." Sara jumped in. "Med–Met is intent on wiping out the competition. They are buying every state legislator that they can. They've even got a few Congressmen and Senators in their pockets. If we don't counter with aggressive action, they'll have us standing in line for termination."

Rokoff shook his head and finished swallowing a bite of the pizza, "Sara sees bogeymen everywhere. I think she takes this as a personal attack directed against her. However, in the Med–Met plan of things this is just business."

"I don't need to see bogeymen, Jacob," Sara snapped. "I see their damn bagman, Darren Walters. He's lurking in the corridors of Congress, ostensibly lobbying while actually doling out dollars and pimping for our noble representatives."

One of the other students, a pale blond, Earl Carter, drawled, "So what do you want to do Sara, shoot Walters, blow-up Congress, and buy our own Senator with our pizza money? Maybe you can just use your charm and get one of them to join our group."

There was some laughter, as well as a few looks in Michael's direction.

"No, not at all, but if we attack them where it hurts, the pocketbook, they may not be able to afford to maintain their pet legislators."

"Sara," Rokoff interrupted, "We've gone over this many times. We'll turn public sentiment against us by violent actions. Med-Met wants us to react irresponsibly. They're already trying to paint us as heretics and fanatics. This would only serve as fuel for their public relations machinery."

Rokoff leaned forward and slapped his knees, "That's enough politics for tonight. I wouldn't want Mr. Guidry to think that's the only thing we talk about around here. I would like you all to continue with the review of the development of antibiotics, I believe we were on the complex beta lactams. Ms. Murphy, would you kindly lead the discussion? I will be having a chat with Mr. Guidry."

Patricia Murphy, one of the more senior students began the group discussion. Rokoff ushered Michael into a secluded corner where two chairs flanked a small table.

Rokoff pulled his chair around to face Michael, "I need to know if you really want to be here. In this state we are still allowed to exist, but we certainly aren't the darlings of society. Many of your friends will avoid you like an incurable disease if they find out that you've joined us. You'll be harassed by the law, and you will most certainly lose your job at Med-Met."

Michael tried to put on a convincing smile, "You paint quite an attractive picture Jacob, what are the bad points?"

"I'm glad you've got a sense of humor. The truth is I can't compress the reasons for staying with us into any brief exchange. Why don't you tell me about why you're even listening. Why didn't you bolt through the door as soon as you realized who I was, and what our group is about?"

Michael paused before speaking, "I came close to leaving. I suppose curiosity has a lot to do with why I didn't. But it's more than that. If it was only curiosity, fear would have won out." Swallowing hard, Michael chose his next words carefully. "I've had these feelings for quite some time that something was wrong. When I trained for Med-Met I thought I would be able to give something to people. I knew that Med-Met Centers were cold and imposing places, despite how they try to dress it up. I remember as a child going for my school check-ups and vaccinations. Everything was clean and orderly, the mechanical voices directing you through the rooms and machines. All of a sudden a hum, a whir, and then the belt would move you down the line and eventually spit you out the end. The only bit of humanity would be the Tech. Much of the time they were as mechanical as the rest of the equipment, but occasionally there would be one who would sense a young boy's fear. Just say a soft word, or provide a reassuring grasp on the shoulder. They made it so much easier. I wanted to be able to do that."

Rokoff sat quietly, leaning in, as Michael ran both hands through his hair and continued. "But that's not how it is. It's the machines that we're supposed to be concerned with not the people. We're supposed to make sure the machines are always functioning, keep them in top shape. If a machine has a break down it's a major crisis. Senior techs are flown in from all over the world to solve the problem. Everyone works overtime until the problem is fixed. But what about when a person breaks down, when the machines can no longer figure out and solve the problem? Do we fly in specialists from all over the world, do we work over time? No, that's when euthanasia tech takes over. Doesn't the man at least deserve the same chance as the machine?"

Rokoff smiled warmly at Michael. "You are now the teacher my young friend. You put into simple words what I could not. What we stand for is humanity, kindness, and dignity. And one commodity that there is never too much of is hope, we try to offer hope.

"I don't expect a commitment from you now. I would like you to sit in with us for a week or two. When you are sure you will tell me. Whatever your decision I will respect it."

"What do I do about my job, my friends?"

"For the present, if you can, do nothing. Maintain your normal routine. This gives us one more friend on the inside. There are others who feel as you do, keep your eyes and ears opened." Rokoff stretched as he stood, "Come let's join the others."

Rokoff strode toward the group. Michael watched him cross the room and noticed a large metal clad door just behind the data wall. He was about to go over and look more closely at it when he suddenly felt his hand in another's. It was Sara, her hand was warm and her grip tight.

"Well, come on freshman, it's time to join the group."

CHAPTER
5

The next morning everything at Med–Met was the same, but still something felt different. Time moved much more slowly. Each minute seemed to drag on, the change of the hour was always too far away. Michael continually looked around. If a co-worker made eye contact he wondered if they were the one who had pointed him out to Rokoff. If someone looked away he was concerned that they knew where he had been. A supervisor moved slowly from station to station, chatting with technicians. As she got closer Michael tried not to look in her direction. He wiped his sweaty palms on his thighs and focused on his screens, reviewing his lists. He felt her presence as she came up to him and flinched as she placed a hand on his shoulder.

"Sorry to startle you Michael. Just checking to see how everything is going."

Michael took a deep breath wondering, *what does she know?* With a nervous chuckle he answered, "Everything is fine, just another great day at Med-Met."

"Well I'm glad to hear it. I want to let you know, people have noticed the job you're doing." She squeezed Michael's shoulder and walked on to the next station.

He had to check himself to keep from hyperventilating. What had she meant by that statement? He sensed that she had moved away but checked to see if she was still watching him. She was already talking with the next tech. He checked the time again.

★　★　★

That evening Michael made himself dinner but ate little of it. He constantly looked around, to see if he was being followed, as he returned to the apartment where he had met Rokoff. Now only Rokoff, Sara, Earl, and one other student were present. Rokoff signaled him to an empty chair and began.

"Michael let me explain the smaller group to you. Yesterday when you were here we held our weekly discussion sessions. All of our students attend those. Tonight is a basic science lecture. Only our first and second year students are required to participate in these."

Rokoff stood up and the room became quiet. "Today we will begin continue with the facial musculature. Earl, please bring in Clarence."

Earl got up, walked around the blackboard, and headed for the metal door that Michael had noticed the previous evening. Michael was staring at it and Rokoff answered his unasked question.

"That Mr. Guidry is a cold room. The temperature is 4⁰ Celsius and it's the home of Clarence."

Before he could ask who Clarence was, a long stretcher was wheeled out. On it lay the body of a man. He or it was uncovered and various parts of the limbs had been cut open, exposing the muscles. The acrid smell of some type of preservative hit Michaels nose and he jumped up from his chair, knocking it over. He felt a strange chill, probably from the open cold room door. The contents of his stomach churned and for some reason he recalled that last night's pizza had been right where the body now resided.

Pointing at the gurney Michael blurted out, "Dr. Rokoff, that man is dead!"

Rokoff quickly came to his aid, and quieted the snickers with a raised palm and a few sharp glances. "Quite dead Michael, if he weren't he wouldn't be nearly so cooperative."

"You must understand one cannot fully comprehend the structure and complexity of the human body without first-hand examination of the parts. How can one address cardiac disease without seeing the valves and arteries of the heart? How can one remove an appendix without knowing where it is?"

Backing away from the body Michael stammered, "Yes, but can't the NSU remove an appendix? It's a machine and has never seen a cadaver."

Rokoff maintained an even professorial tone, "That's true, but the original NASA-Surgi-Unit was programmed by surgeons who had seen the real thing. Over the years those programs have been passed on to succeeding generations of NSU." He paused and fixed his gaze on Michael, "Think what would happen if those programs broke down, or unforeseen biological changes occurred. Without a continuum of human medical knowledge we could reach a point where the machine was the only repository of anatomy. The loss of a piece of information might be irretrievable."

Michael had to hold his hands together to keep them from shaking. His voice was too loud for the space. Sara had gotten up and moved toward him. He ignored her and continued to address Rokoff, "But where do you get them? Do you steal them before they get to the disintegrator?"

Jacob shook his head and continued softly, "No Michael, they are willed to us. They are given to us at the bequest of those who believe in our cause, our patients, friends, family."

"Who was Clarence, your Uncle?" Michael took several deep breaths trying to calm himself. Maybe Marsha was right and the Hippocratins were a bunch of ghouls who went around hacking up their dead mothers.

"We don't work on anyone we knew, none of us could. Instead we have an exchange program with other clinics so that we all have strangers, and we all have the opportunity to learn." With that, Jacob moved back toward the group but signaled to Sara with a tilt of his head indicating that she should go to Michael. "I must return to the lesson. If you feel up to it join us."

Sara put her hand on Michael's arm, he shook it off and headed as far from Clarence as possible. Feeling light-headed, he sat in a chair focusing on everyone's ankles trying to avoid looking at the cadaver. Sara brought a chair and sat silently next to him. A smattering of what was going on penetrated his thoughts, some Latin sounding names and mentions of arteries. His mind was boiling with a gumbo of conflicting thoughts. He vacillated between a deep desire to be part of all this, to learn the art of healing, and an urge to have them all arrested for desecrating a corpse.

Sara spoke quietly, penetrating his thoughts. "I'm sorry I didn't let you know more about what I invited you to. This is a lot to digest at once. Why don't you let me take you home, and then you can think about whether this is for you."

Michael tried not to look at her, but when he did he found her large dark eyes pulling him in. "Sara couldn't you have found a better way to introduce me to all this? It feels like I was thrown into the water with no idea how deep it is and no flotation device. I'm thrashing around looking for something to grab onto to save myself."

Sara nodded, "I know, sometimes I forget that the things I know with certainty to be right are quite alien to others. I'm sorry that this has made you so upset, and I'll understand if you leave now and don't come back."

Sara's soft tone surprised Michael, it was such a contrast to his initial encounters with her. "What if I decide I want in?" His own question surprised him, two seconds before he was prepared to run.

Smiling gently and reaching for his hands she said, "You can meet with Jacob and he will put your application before the other faculty and apprentices along with his recommendation. Then we'll make the final decision."

"And if I decide to stay with Med-Met."

"Then you go your way, and I go mine. The only advice I'll give you is to stay out of the crossfire."

He wasn't sure what she meant by the final statement but it left him unsettled. He decided to see himself home so he could think.

★   ★   ★

Back in his apartment he stood before the mirror staring at the face in front of him. He clenched his jaw, watched the muscles tighten and relax. He compared the outlines of the muscles to what he had seen on Clarence. He had never before really considered what was under the skin. What it was that made a mouth turn into a smile or a frown, or how one chewed food.

He let his robe fall to the floor and studied his body. He nodded. It was in relatively good shape, not too much body fat and decent muscle tone, but he knew so little of what was below the surface. He tried moving each part of his body slowly and watching what went on, speculating, what kind of intricate pulleys must be involved to flex a toe. He ran his hands up and down his body feeling ribs, muscles, and veins touching parts that he had felt thousands of times without ever stopping to think about their intricacy.

The wonder that grew within began to wash away some of his doubts. He was not quite ready to abandon his current life but he knew that he had to learn more about Rokoff, his teaching and his followers.

CHAPTER
6

Armbrister paced back and forth, presiding over the small meeting like a kid organizing games at his birthday party. All the attention centered on him, and everyone was waiting for him to blow out the candles. Walters sat to left of Armbrister's empty chair. Suzanne Hartstein sat on the other side of her boss. To the right of Armbrister's chair sat Joel Rogers the regional office's Chief Financial Officer, and next to him Angela Stuart, Chief Operating Officer. High backed well padded leather chairs, surrounded dark oak tables, and portraits of the Med-Met founders and current directors stared down from the walls, giving the room an austere air. Armbrister imagined maps and graphs on the walls and a model of a battle field where the big oak table sat. This was the war room, he was the general and he was about to lay his battle plan out for his commander-in-chief.

"At Darren's request I have formulated a plan to neutralize the problems that are being caused by the members of the so called Hippocratin Society," he practically spat out the name. "I have looked at many potential ways of dealing with this ranging from totally ignoring them to hiring a squad of mercenaries to eliminate them. The latter is tempting, but there is too much potential for it to backfire on us. That's a lesson I learned from reading Liddy. We're not going to go that far, but we're going to get awfully close.

"We need to totally discredit them. We need to make criminals out of them. No martyrs, no heroes, just plain criminals." He placed his palms on the edge of the table and leaned in, looking from one to the next. "If we do anything short of that they will have the potential to gain sympathy and grow stronger. History tells us over and over again we must crush them or risk a final helicopter ride into disgrace"

"Wil," Angela interrupted, "What exactly are you thinking about doing? These people are within their rights? Wasn't this country was founded on the freedom of expression?"

Wil rolled his eyes and let out a breath, "I agree they have the appearance of constitutional protection, but that protection has always extended only as far as the point where it begins to infringe on another's rights and life. The classic example is falsely yelling fire in a crowded theater, and the danger that that puts the crowd in as they climb over each other in their panic to escape. These Hippocratins are hampering the operations of Med-Met, they are influencing people to refuse final therapy for terminal diagnoses. They are preventing the optimal delivery of the best health care available. They are potentially putting the population at significant risk of exposure to individuals with terminal illness.

"In summary, they are criminals. They care only for their own personal gains and don't care what that means to others or society as a whole. They believe in an obsolete practice that has been replaced by something infinitely better. It's like using leeches, like voodoo, witchcraft. We need to convince the public, and that is what Darren Walters – with our help, will do."

The room was silent, Armbrister had built to a wild eyed finish, and when he was done no one was quite sure what to say or do. All eyes focused on Darren.

Rather quietly Walters broke the silence. "Wil, can't we start out a little bit more conservatively. Perhaps an advertising campaign that points out the benefits of Med-Met over the antiquated medicine of the Hippocratins. Show pictures of a clean efficient Med-Met facility in contrast to some back street medical clinic." There was a general nodding of agreement around the table.

"No! Darren," Wil was up and pacing again. "Can't you see, we can't let people even think that they are worthy of comparison." As Armbrister spoke a his chest heaved, "If we let the public make the comparison, they begin to examine the alternative. They may find something sympathetic in that alternative. The public through their professional snoops, the press, will look deep into the hearts of the Hippocratins, and into ours. They'll do in-depth reports on the founding of the Hippocratins, bios on Ellis and Rokoff. That will provide them with the platform that they want."

His breathing had slowed and he continued, "That was what faced Nixon when he came to office, it was already too late to stem the tide. Johnson had opened the door. He had allowed the hippies and the peaceniks to hold their rallies, to March on Washington. He had allowed them to become the darlings of the press. Slowly but surely with the eye of the media on them a small group of unbathed, overeducated loudmouths became a national movement. The establishment became the bad guys, and anything the government tried to do was labeled repressive. Nixon was fighting a losing battle from day one. Once you lose the press you lose the war. The press loves to tear down the establishment and build-up the little guy. We're the establishment. We can't let these people gain a foot-hold, we can't let them be sympathetic figures. We've got to paint them as devils and witches of the worst magnitude. We've got to make it so bad that anyone who expresses sympathy for them is also going to get dirty. We make them the equivalent of polluters, child molesters, and dope dealers. No quarter can be given."

"Let's suppose for a moment that we took this approach. How in the world could we do it?"

Darren seemed to be warming to Wil's excitement and Wil was ready.

"We need a multi-pronged approach, first we use our advertising to build us up. No comparisons to the Hippies, just straight hype on the wonderful Med-Met system. Happy, healthy people getting the best care possible. We do that for six months or so, real heavy, real slick and the public thinks positively about us."

He now stood behind Suzanne and laid a hand on her shoulder. She pushed it away with her other hand and he moved on continuing as if nothing happened, "The second phase is to begin to solidify the support of our current friends in the state legislatures, here and in other states. We educate them as to the threat the Hippocratins pose to Med-Met and to society. In states where we figure we have the votes we initiate legislation to make it more and more difficult for the Hippies to practice their voodoo. At the same time we line up the best legal minds to spearhead the battle against the inevitable challenges to those laws. Through the law we begin to shut them down, and when they defy the law they become criminals, not heroes."

Angela Stuart again interrupted, "Logical so far, but what is to stop the public from making martyrs out of these guys?"

Wil smiled at her as he would a child, "That Angela is where our boy Darren comes in. As the new laws begin to be passed, Darren will take a leave of absence from Med-Met, putting you in charge by the way." Darren who had been reading quickly looked up concern on his face. Wil continued, "Darren is then free to become the visible leader of the move to eliminate this menace from our society. Through speeches, press releases, glad handing, and careful manipulation of the media, Darren becomes the protector of the nation's health, shielding the public from the dangerous and sinister witches of the Hippocratin Society."

Darren put up both hands palms forward, "Hold on Wil. I'm taking a leave of absence? What am I supposed to live on? I've got a mortgage, private preschool tuition for the kids, not to mention a wife with rather expensive tastes, who, is used to the salary of a Med-Met regional director."

Wil quickly jumped in, "The question is not how you are going to live, but how we are going to live. I'm planning to resign my position to head the public relations efforts of the Committee for a Healthy America, the CHA. Long before we make that move we will have formed the CHA and have begun to stock a financial war chest through the contributions of our good friends. Mainly those individuals and corporations whose financial health depends on a strong and unchallenged Med-Met system. The CHA budget will include salaries and fringe benefits for its Chairman and the Director of Public Relations that are commensurate with our current positions."

Darren didn't appear convinced, "Do you really think we can raise that kind of money, with enough for an operating budget, travel, advertising, office staff, etcetera?"

Joel Rogers spoke next. The quiet efficient number cruncher sat up straight in his chair to get the most out of his slight frame. "Darren, Wil already has asked me to analyze the financial needs for this type of operation, and our potential sources of contribution. The way I see it the number of people who depend on Med-Met for their financial security is immense. There are thousands of corporations whose only client is Med-Met. If we demonstrate to them that the Hippocratins are a threat to the financial welfare of Med-Met, they will contribute whatever it takes to the CHA to secure Med-Met.

"I'm sure enough about that to volunteer my services as treasurer until we've raised enough to begin fulltime operation. Once we can afford it, I too will resign from my job to become the fulltime treasurer of CHA."

Darren sat back, seemingly more relaxed and trusting Roger's assessment, "If we organize this committee, and it doesn't take off as you expect, what do we risk losing?"

"Nothing that I can foresee." Wil was glad to have the floor back. "We initially set this thing up with some of our well meaning friends in the leadership positions. Our names stay out of it. I work quietly in the background raising money, but the rest of you just carry on business as usual here at Med-Met. When the war chest is deep, and the political climate is right we begin to participate in

CHA activities, and then logically and as planned our friends invite us to assume leadership of the organization.

"If by some fluke things don't go well, and this thing doesn't get off the ground we remain safe and secure at Med–Met. Don't forget, you will only take a leave of absence, you can always step back in."

"You sound pretty sure of yourself Wil."

"No Darren, not sure of myself, but sure of the public. After all that's what a good P.R. man is paid to do."

CHAPTER
7

The other first and second year students were drifting in when Michael arrived. Rokoff called Michael over to the side and pointed to a large cardboard box on the floor. "Those are yours," he said smiling.

Inside were six or seven large and musty books. Michael noted a stale, old aroma. Jacob spoke from behind, "Vidicomps can provide the same information, but there is something about a book that they can't match. With a book it's like you're holding the knowledge or information in your hands." Rokoff delicately held one of the texts and flipped its pages as he spoke. "It's not only transferred to you by what your eyes see. It's absorbed through your finger tips. I suggest you find some old fiction pieces in their original printed form. When you read them your mind interprets the writer's words. With the author's guidance your mind imagines the characters and situations that the words convey. It's a personal relationship between you and the author. With Vidicomps there is a middle person who interprets for you."

The box contained volumes on anatomy, pharmacology, physiology, biochemistry. It was amazing. "Where did these books come from?" Michael wondered out loud.

"As medical schools closed down our members and friends went to all the liquidation sales and bought up everything we could. It hasn't been too difficult or expensive because nobody else wanted the stuff. We have several warehouses in major cities where we store our materials. Additionally we have four regional medical libraries, one is here in New Orleans. Later on when you need to delve further into a subject I'll take you there. It's complete right up to the point that they stopped printing new books, and most of the medical journals went out of business. Of course we keep up to date on the two remaining journals, *Annals of Humanistic Medicine*, and *The Hippocratin*. Let's go, it's time for school."

Michael couldn't recall ever really telling Rokoff that he would be continuing on as a student. He just kept showing up for class. That evening there was no visit with Clarence. He learned that the weekly curriculum was fairly structured. One evening would be anatomy, another pharmacology, etc. That night's topic was physiology. Rokoff directed him to a text in his box on human physiology. The others referred to it as "Guyton". He felt a hand on his shoulder, and looked up into the big brown eyes of Sara Anson.

"I see you made it back. I hope Clarence didn't give you too many nightmares." She was smiling widely. When he tried to avert her teasing eyes, he found himself staring down her modest but most inviting cleavage. She gently lifted his chin with her index finger, pursed her lips slightly and slowly shook her head no. "Time to pay attention to physiology, anatomy was yesterday."

Rokoff was at an image board. As he spoke a hologram of a pumping heart appeared. Next to the heart were several graphs. They learned about Starlings forces, afterload, preload, and the basis of cardiac dysfunction. It was amazing how complex it all was, and how beautiful in its complexity. The fact that anything so tenuous in construction could function so reliably was incredible. As they watched the images he could hear soft sloshing sounds in the background, it was like the sound of the ocean rushing to the shore, except that it had a regular pattern to it. Rokoff explained, "What you are hearing is a Doppler, or echocardiographic recording of heart sounds. The harsh sound you hear at regular intervals is a result of a sclerotic aortic valve which impedes the flow of blood out of the left ventricle. This results in turbulent flow that is picked up as the harsh sound, or echo. At this point the problem is not severe, and the individual feels no ill effects. If the process progresses and the valve continues to harden, the patient may experience easy fatiguability, shortness of breath and perhaps chest pain." Rokoff went on to describe various forms of heart failure and their manifestations while Michael sat fascinated.

"You will need to review the cardiac physiology chapters in Guyton before next week.

Also for relevance I would like you to review Harrison's chapter on heart failure. Those of you who do not yet have a copy of Harrison's can either look at a copy from one of their classmates, or use one of the two copies that I keep here. That will be all for this evening." With that Rokoff ended the formal portion of the evening's session, and members of the group broke off into informal discussions.

Michael leaned over to Sara and whispered, "What's a Harrison's?"

"Harrison's Textbook of Internal Medicine. Used to be one of the main textbooks. Rokoff gives each student a copy when they complete their first year. You can borrow mine if you'd like."

"Thanks, I may take you up on that. Right now I've got to concentrate on getting this pile of books home, they must weigh 100 kilos."

"Want some help. I could ride with you, and help you get this load home."

"Thanks, and for a reward I'll treat you to a cup of actual brewed coffee. It's a tradition passed down in my family. Even though everyone says the synth-coffee is identical to the real thing, my father maintained nothing could compare to a cup of coffee brewed from freshly ground beans. As each of us left home he would present us with a coffee pot and bean grinder. One of the few luxuries I allow myself is to import beans from the few remaining plantations in South America."

"Sounds like a good deal. Lead the way."

They divided up the books and placed them into two plain boxes to avoid strange looks and questions. The trip took only a few minutes. It seemed much longer to Michael because of the feeling that that people knew what they were carrying, and because Sara was coming back to his apartment. He tried unsuccessfully to remember whether he'd picked up his socks that morning. He couldn't help wonder if this might lead to more than a cup of coffee.

As they arrived at his residence complex he remembered the sign in the lobby. He wondered how Sara was going to react to the raised gold letters proclaiming *Med-Met Residential Center 117*. It didn't take long to get an answer.

"A company flat. Someone's been a good boy, haven't they?" she asked mockingly. It was well known that company subsidized living accommodations were offered as a reward for high performance ratings. The subsidized flats were less expensive than equivalent private housing, and allowed one to have a little more luxury within their means.

"Hey, what're you implying? Can you fault a guy for getting to work on time, having a good attendance record and a clean nose."

Sara looked around the well decorated lobby, "Sorry, didn't mean to hit a nerve."

They arrived at his door which opened in response to his thermal patterns. He placed his box of books on the floor and took the box from Sara and placed them along side. "Would you like to see how they used to make coffee?"

"Absolutely, you know I'm a student of the ancient arts."

Michael ceremonially took the small bean grinder from the cabinet and delivered the right amount of beans from the serving unit. Sara watched as the small blades whirled grinding the beans to a fine powder. She was very close to Michael. "You are about to experience one of the great lost aromas of the world," he said removing the grinder lid with a flourish, and holding it near her nose.

"That's incredible, I never imagined coffee could be that vivid," her chest swelled as she inhaled deeply and closed her eyes. Michael nearly spilled the coffee down the front of her blouse as he watched her reaction to the bouquet.

Struggling to regain his composure, he took out the ancient electric percolator and connected the adaptor that allowed interface of the two pronged plug with the power pad on the adjacent wall.

"Now we wait, that's another thing about coffee the old fashioned way, it takes time."

"I'm in no rush," she answered. "What did you think of tonight's class?"

"It was fantastic, I cannot believe how intricate and complicated the heart is. It's totally amazing that it can function as well as it does for as long as it does. I'm really looking forward to being able to learn about the physiology from the vidicomps and books, and to actually see the heart when we get to it in Clarence."

"The heart is truly amazing," Sara replied as she moved closer. "It never rests. Reading about and seeing the cadaveric heart are useful but one can only truly appreciate the heart in its dynamic beating form." She took his hand and placed it below her left breast. There was nothing beneath her tunic to impede feeling her pounding heart, however his own heart pounding out of his chest confused the issue.

"What about the coffee," she asked as he slid his hand upward.

"I'll make some fresh in the morning," He answered pulled her close, making a mental note to check Guyton to find out how in the world erections happen.

CHAPTER

8

F ew in the room knew the real names of any of the others. It was this way for their protection. They called each other by code names. That way if anyone was arrested they couldn't reveal the identities of the others. The meeting location was always changed, and announced in a coded classified memo in the daily vid-chip.

The Weps, short for Weatherpersons, had formed about a year earlier. Its members were drawn from the more radical elements of a variety of organizations including organized religions, the Hippocratins, and the Demo-Republicans. Sara was among the first to join, she had been approached during a demonstration at a Med-Met facility. She was known to these people as Curie.

"Each of you must continue to work within your parent organizations to continue to dissuade people from accepting the final solution, to maintain the peaceful demonstrations and keep the pressure on Med-Met. In the meantime we continue with our activities to disrupt operations in more dramatic ways. I'm sure you've heard, our East Coast chapter successfully infected the computer at the New York facility with a virus. The diagnostic programs rapidly discovered and purged the virus, but not until it had eliminated the current list of terminally ill at that facility. It will take weeks to reconstruct that list. It's felt that several individuals will probably escape for the time being." The man called Plato did not appear the radical type. He was always well dressed and groomed. Sara guessed that his primary affiliation was with the Demo-Republicans, perhaps he was a lawyer. By appearances one would expect him to prefer to combat his enemies with well thought words, but he clearly had no aversion to more violent methods.

"What we need," Plato continued, "is an insider at our regional Med-Met center. We need someone who knows the layout, and can provide us knowingly or unknowingly with the means to disrupt the operations, in a major way."

"How do you propose we get someone in there? I mean after all we just can't waltz up to their employment office and say, hey I'd like a job that will give me access to sensitive information that will help me blow this place up." Spiderman was one of the few in the room who disguised his appearance as well as his name. Perhaps they were more paranoid, or perhaps they would have been easily recognized. Spiderman wore a red hood-like mask on his face, apparently copying a literary figure from earlier in the century. He was quick to criticize, but rarely added constructive comments.

"No," Plato answered. "I don't suppose that we could do that. It would take years for us to infiltrate and have someone rise to a level of trust with access to critical components. I think we need to get to someone already in such a position, perhaps someone that one of us knows and can influence. We might be able to get the information from them without their ever knowing they helped our cause. Curie you had your hand up."

"Plato, what type position would this person need to hold in order to gain access to the necessary information?"

"There are probably several different types of Med-Met personnel who could help us. Most definitely any of the computer personnel could provide us with critical information on how to get into and disrupt the network. The people involved directly in patient treatment could help us to disrupt the flow of patient processing and information and let us know where the critical elements are in the unnatural death system. If anyone knows such a person, please talk to me about it at the end of the meeting and we can begin to plan strategy."

A man known as Alpha stood to speak, "I believe we need to reopen the discussion of what to do about Walters. The man is gaining momentum and power daily. Every time you insert a daily vid-chip he's in it. You walk down the street and people are talking about what he has to say. They're buying his bullshit, flies and all. One of my co-workers told me that all the Hippocratin doctors had sex with their female patients as part of their therapy. People are eating this stuff up."

Alpha was one of the major advocates of violence in the group. Plato asked him, "How do you suggest we address the Walter's issue?"

"I'm not quite sure. I wouldn't rule out assassination, but it might only serve to create a martyr. I think it would be better if we could discredit him. We need to get some dirt on him, something serious enough that we can either blackmail him into silence, or make him look like a joke. I'll tell you this, no one climbs as high and as fast as Mr. Darren Walters without a little lying, cheating, back-stabbing, or buddy- humping. If we can find someone who has been flattened by the Walters juggernaut, maybe we can get the info we need."

"All right Alpha, why don't you put together a three person team and sniff around the Walters organization. Be on the lookout for someone who was passed over for a promotion, or who has fallen out of favor with his holiness. I've got to warn you, this guy is slick. He buries his mistakes, and you're going to have to dig deep."

"What if that doesn't work?"

"If it doesn't work, we'll reevaluate. All options remain open."

As the meeting was breaking up, Sara lingered, waiting to get a moment alone with Plato. She wasn't sure whether she should tell him about Michael. She doubted Michael would ever go along with providing information on how to sabotage Med-Met. He was already scared enough with what he was doing, and was just adjusting to the idea of being associated with the Hippocratins. He would never understand the Weps."

"Curie, is there something I can do for you?"

"Plato, I think I know someone who has the Med-Met access that we need."

"That's wonderful, when can I meet them?"

"I don't think I can get him here. He doesn't know about my involvement. Although he is disillusioned with Med-Met I don't think he would approve of some of our methods."

"Well, do you think you might be able to get him to give you the necessary information? I could help you with the appropriate questions."

"I think I could do that, I believe he trusts me. If my questions come off as simple curiosity, I'm sure he'll tell me what he knows."

"I want you to understand this information is crucial to our success. We need you to use all your resources to get this information, you can't do this halfheartedly. Do you think you can do this?"

"Of course, the cause is the most important thing. What do we need to know?"

CHAPTER
9

M ichael needed a break from the gas exchange formula he'd been studying in his medical physiology book. He wasn't surprised that people had readily let computers take over figuring out diffusing capacities, and flow loops rather than having to do the calculations themselves. Rokoff insisted that one could not understand disease until one truly understood the normal physiologic processes.

He closed the heavy book, and inserted the daily vid-chip into his monitor. Instantly, a holo appeared across the room. The scene showed a barren rocky landscape strewn with rubble, and derelict equipment. Two robotic salvage units picked through the debris, following the lead of two individuals clad in modified twentieth century space suits. The announcer, safely in his studio, was superimposed to the right of the main action. "What you are observing," he droned, "is the first phase of the lunar salvage project. The project engineers are the first visitors to the moon since the disaster at Sheppard City in 2050. Space travel beyond Earth orbit has been banned since shortly after the great disaster in which over 2 million lives were lost. Although the government reports that this project is solely to retrieve any resources or documents of value, it is hoped by many that this will open the door for renewed space exploration and settlement."

Michael knew relatively little about the history of the lunar colony. His father used to tell him about the golden age of space exploration in the late twentieth and early twenty-first centuries. The first permanent colony outside of Earth was established on the moon in 2030. A large dome had been constructed and a full city built inside. Huge financial incentives from companies who wished to quickly develop and exploit the lunar resources drew over two million people to Sheppard City in less than ten years. And then late in 2050 disaster struck. The huge dome, composed of reportedly indestructible polymers, cracked when hit by a small but high velocity meteorite. A number of fail-safe systems failed, including the highly touted deflector system, and the back-up sealant system. In a matter of minutes the artificial atmosphere escaped into space, the dome collapsed inward and two million men, women and children perished.

The reaction on Earth was enormous. Accusations of faulty construction, substitute materials and sabotage filled the media, conversation, and courtrooms for years. In reaction to the magnitude of the disaster, space travel beyond earth's atmosphere was outlawed, and technology began to look inward toward Earth rather than out toward the stars.

The scene shifted to New York where a crowd stood outside the United Nations building carrying signs and shouting slogans. By remote the announcer interviewed a young man in the crowd. "We are here," the man shouted over the crowd noise, "to put an end to the illegal and immoral activities occurring on the moon. No good can come when we leave the boundaries of the Earth. It has been clearly demonstrated that this can only lead to disaster. If we don't heed the lessons of our past, we will have no future."

The crowd evaporated and the announcer was now alone in the studio, "we will return after this message from Med-Met, the only medical care you will ever need." The announcer dissolved and was replaced by a scene quite familiar to Michael. The bright corridors of a Med-Met diagnostic clinic filled the holo. Happy smiling people were greeted by a neatly clad Med-Met technician. Laughing children played one of the input games at the computer terminals. In the corner of the scene a distinguished well dressed man appeared. "Hi, I'm Darren Walters, Midwest Regional Director of Med-Met. It is a pleasure for all of us at Med-Met to offer you the most comprehensive and advanced medical care in the history of humanity. At Med-Met we are with you for life." The scene shifted to an obstetric robot passing a newly delivered, but already cleaned and swaddled baby to the beaming new parents, and then melted away.

A giant weather map appeared at the far end of the room, Michael let go a deep sigh, and disengaged the vid-chip.

CHAPTER
10

S am Chen jumped at the chance to join the lunar salvage team. He had been involved in several salvage missions in near earth orbit, including the dying Lev II space station, before its fiery disintegration in Earth's atmosphere. The lunar mission however was a salvagers dream. Virtually an entire city waited to be reclaimed, and his father's salvage company had won the exclusive rights to the project. The contract with the United Nations Space Council was simple. Chen Salvers financed the entire mission, retrieved the critical documents and energy sources for the U.N., and then was entitled to anything else they could salvage and transport back to Earth. There were twelve on the initial team including Sam, his brother, Georgi, and their father Thomas. Their job was to assess the situation, determine the extent of the damage, and decide what equipment would be needed to complete the job.

For the past week their time had been concentrated in the area along the eastern boundary of Sheppard City, close to the base of the dome. This area had little physical damage to the structures, as the vertical portion of the wall still stood for 50 meters or more and curved above this portion of the city protecting the buildings below. Just as they reached what they had thought was the eastern limits they found a small road heading further east toward the base of the dome.

The road didn't appear on any of the maps but was there, none the less. Sam lifted his enhanced binoculars and peered down the road. Approximately two kilometers ahead a wire fence blocked the road. Sam gunned his rover, and headed down the road. The vehicle was amazingly similar to those used on the early Apollo lunar missions over a century before. The fence was six feet high and appeared to head off into the distance at angles that would intersect the dome at both ends. On the sliding gate that blocked the road was a small sign. The message in permapaint was still quite legible, "Infinity Research Laboratory. No Trespassing. Trespassers will be fined, and permanently exiled from Sheppard City and all lunar territories."

Sam thought about going further but decided he needed to discuss this unexpected finding with the rest of the team, and get advice from his father waiting back at Chen Salvage Station I.

★   ★   ★

Thomas Chen had not built the largest and most successful space salvage company on, or more precisely off, earth by passing up opportunity. The uncharted facility that his son had discovered needed to be explored. He saw no need to consult with the U.N. Space Agency before proceeding. His contract gave him salvage rights to all of Sheppard City. Why risk being denied access by asking.

The salvage team gathered in the main room of the prefabricated building that served as the operations base for the mission. The geodesic structure had been set-up just outside the remains of the shattered city and would eventually house one of the four twenty-four member salvage teams. The main room was octagonal and located in the center of the structure. This room served as dining room, recreational facility and meeting room. On each of the eight walls was a door leading to surrounding rooms. Four of the doorways lead to sleeping quarters and bathroom facilities for six crew members each. One led to the kitchen facilities and two others to workshops for processing and cataloging the materials collected on the salvage mission. The eighth door led to a series of airlocks and changing rooms which allowed the crew to change into their spacesuits and exit to the lunar surface without losing atmosphere, or disturbing the temperature inside.

The senior Chen nodded to his two sons and the others. "As you know, Samuel made an unexpected discovery earlier today while exploring the outer fringes of sector 21. It is somewhat puzzling that we have no record of Infinity Research Laboratories, but several possibilities exist. Pure oversight is one explanation. The records we have are the best that were available to the space agency, however, they may not be complete. There was much confusion at the time of the great collapse, and if this laboratory was relatively new it may not have made it into the permanent records."

"A second possibility is that the Space Agency purposely withheld this information from us. I find this unlikely in that sooner or later we would stumble across it. A third, and to my mind more intriguing, possibility is that the existence of Infinity was unknown to the Space Agency by design. If that is the case then what we find may be of unmeasurable value to us.

"No matter the reason, if we are to undertake further exploration of Infinity, I must count on you all for total secrecy, even from our other teams. I chose this group for the initial exploration because you are my family and my most loyal employees. I am not sure how the Space Agency will react to this unforeseen event. They might seek to restrict us, or to claim that it is outside of our contract as it was not included on the original plans. In addition to the secrecy aspects, there is an element of unknown, perhaps danger in proceeding. For these reasons, in addition to your agreed upon contract, we will split equally any profit gained from our investigation of Infinity. Does anyone have any questions?"

Everyone looked toward Sam Chen. As Thomas' oldest son he was the most comfortable questioning his father. "Dad, why would a research laboratory be kept secret from the Space Agency? After all, didn't they administer Sheppard City?"

Thomas tented his fingers and appeared to be in thought before finally speaking, "I can't answer that for sure Samuel, remember it was long ago and I was just a young man at the time. What I know is partially from the stories I heard in school, and on the news, and partially from the rumors of the day. It seems that in the years prior to the great collapse there was a growing move for independence in Sheppard City, a desire to be autonomous of the United Nations Space Administration, the predecessor of the current Space Agency, which controlled the city. It was rumored that many clandestine industrial ventures were established to avoid the large taxes levied by the Space Administration. Perhaps Infinity was one of those, and its existence remained unknown to the Space Administration."

Georgi jumped into the conversation, "Don't you think exploring this place is risky?"

"I really don't know. There may not be any risk or there may be a great deal. Normally, when we go into a salvage operation we have plans and inventory of what to expect. In this instance we have no idea. Now I think we should all get some rest, tomorrow we explore Infinity".

After their father had retired to his quarters, Georgi pulled his brother to a corner of the common room where they couldn't be overheard. "I don't know about this Sam, there's tons of stuff just waiting to be scooped up, without going into this Infinity place. Why bother especially if there's possibility of danger."

"You can't always follow the easy path. Sure there's plenty of stuff out there but you know the Space Agency has rights to the currency, precious metals, and important documents. Most of the mechanical equipment is in disrepair. Infinity being an unknown presents us with the opportunity to keep whatever we find, because it's unaccounted for on the Space Agency ledgers. If these people were trying to hide their assets, there is a possibility of precious metals or stones which can't be traced."

Georgi looked down, avoiding his older brother's gaze, "I still don't like it, but as usual when does my vote ever count."

CHAPTER
11

"Is this where I take my clothes off?"

Michael spun around at the sound of the familiar voice, and at the question. He wasn't unaccustomed to Sara sneaking up on him, nor was he a stranger to her undressing. In the three months since he had invited Sara to his apartment for a cup of coffee, they had continued to see each other socially. Occasionally it led to spending the night together. Neither of them appeared to be in a rush to make anything more permanent or regular of it. Sara treasured her independence and was always running off to meetings and rallies for one cause or another. For Michael holding down a job at Med-Met and keeping up with his studies was consuming enough. Sara's intensity was also a little too much to take in large quantities. She was certainly the most exciting woman he knew, but he still kept his options open and dated others as well. What surprised him was not Sara, or the question, but where they were. He was at his post at Med-Met.

"What are you doing here?" He quickly looked from side to side to see if anyone else was around and then stood there with his mouth wide open. Sara gently lifted his chin to shut it.

"I came for an annual complete health appraisal. See that's what this little chip is for isn't it? Now, is this where I take my clothes off?"

"What do you mean you're here for a health appraisal. You get all your medical care at the Hippocratin clinic, and furthermore you hate this place."

"I know, but I wanted to get a good look at what the competition has to offer. And besides, I thought it would be fun to see where you worked."

"Well, I don't think it's fun. I have a job to do here."

"That's right technician, and I paid for a complete health appraisal. Now, do I start undressing or not?" She gave a slight smile, raised one eyebrow and began to undo the top of her jumpsuit.

"Stop that right now."

Sara smiled an impish grin, appearing delighted in his discomfort. "What's the matter Michael, you never stopped me from undressing before. As a matter of fact you usually help me."

"Sara, what do you want? Do you want everybody to find out about my studies with Jacob, or do you just want to embarrass me?"

"Neither Michael, I really just want a look around. To size up the competition, `know thine enemy'. I figure the best way to do that is go through the usual routine. I was just trying to have some fun with you. Sorry if I over did it." Sara let her lower lip go into a pout. "You will show me around, won't you?" She touched his arm and a shiver ran through him.

"Yes, if you promise to keep your clothes on until I tell you it's time to take them off."

"Goody, I thought you had lost interest."

"Behave yourself or I'll throw you out. I'd better take you through the whole process myself. Who knows what havoc you'd wreck with the other personnel. Let me have someone relieve me here." He explained to one of the other technicians that his girlfriend had come in for an assessment and that he wanted to show off for her. The friend graciously took over the post, noting that he had a similar situation, and it really scored points when she saw how important his work at Med–Met was. Michael knew he had the wrong audience for that but wasn't about to explain Sara.

Sara followed Michael through the steps of the Med–Met's annual complete health assessment. She asked questions about everything. At the input terminals she wanted to know where the data went, how it was stored, how it was transferred to the other regions so that you could show up at any of them and they would have your full records. He explained the satellite uplinks and data transfer, and all the subtleties to the extent that he knew. The knowledge available to a technician, even to one who was curious and inquisitive, was still limited to what they really needed to know.

As they walked to the diagnostics sector Sara took his hand and stayed close by his side and whispered, "If I'm your girlfriend, we should act the parts."

Blushing, he said, "I didn't know you were close enough to hear that."

"I wasn't, I can read lips, but I think it was cute. Am I really your girlfriend Michael?"

"Cut it out Sara. I know your teasing, you've told me many times you don't want to get caught up in traditional dating rituals, and I agree with you. What we have is a friendship with physical aspects to it, and that's fine. I used the girlfriend excuse because the other techs would buy that and let me take you through the whole process."

"To impress me?"

"Yes, to impress you. You know many girls are quite honored to be in the company of a Med-Met technician. It's a very prestigious position, and we're considered to be quite a catch."

"Oh sir, I am in awe. I might just swoon."

They both broke into laughter as they walked hand in hand swinging their arms as they went. Michael began to sing, "We're off to see the Wizard..."

"What are you singing?"

"Just an old tune I remembered. Seemed appropriate. I'll teach it to you some time if I can remember the rest of the words."

They were expected when they arrived at diagnostics. Michael was glad it was Sil Campano that greeted them, and not Marsha Walsh. He didn't think that he was socially adept enough to deal with two women that he dated, together at the same time. What Sil added next made him doubly happy that it wasn't Marsha on duty.

"Word's come down the line that this is a special guided assessment." Sil pulled Michael over to the side. "I saved you the exec check-up suite, no big-shots are scheduled for the next hour so you two can take your time. But a little advice from old Silvano. No physical exertion until after the scans have been run. I heard one of the managers went through the scans after a hard work-out with his secretary, and the thing went crazy. Between the rapid heart rate and the high adrenalin, damn thing diagnosed him as having a pheochromocytoma and almost shipped him to the surgical unit. By the way, this one's got Marsha beat by a mile."

"Thanks Sil, you're a real pal." He saw no sense in denying anything at that point, because Sil would believe whatever he wanted anyway. He knew however that with the Med-Met rumor mill in full gear that chances of future romance with Marsha or anyone else at the center were pretty well shot.

The executive check-up suite was built for those who could afford a little extra. The healthcare was the same, but the amenities were different. Instead of a small curtained cubicle for changing, there was a well decorated changing room. Instead of cloth gowns to be worn after undressing, there were plush robes. One was able to enter each of the scanners directly from a door in the dressing room, so that no waiting needed to be done in public areas and one could sit and view vids, listen to music or read while waiting for their turn in the appropriate scanners.

"Oh, very nice. Just like we have at the Hippocratin clinic. You haven't been there yet, Michael, but I can assure you it's just like this."

"Well, everyone doesn't get this kind of attention you know, but with you being in the medical profession and all, consider this professional courtesy. Now my dear, if you will step behind the screen over there, it is the time to get undressed."

"Wait one minute." She stood with her hands on her hips, "I paid full price for this and I don't expect to have to undress myself. I mean you technicians must get paid for something."

He started to protest, but knew Sara wouldn't let up, and also knew Sil had them covered. "Alright, but after that it's right to scanner one with you, we have a schedule to keep."

"Yes sir, I wouldn't want to violate, the schedule, and I wouldn't want to be diagnosed with a pheochromocytoma." Sara gave him a great big smile and her dark eyes flashed with amusement. "By the way am I really prettier than Marsha?"

"Damned lip reader!"

Sara got out of her clothing, with a little help from Michael, and proceeded to scanner one. "Aren't you coming in with me?"

"No the scanners are designed for only the patient. Other signals in the room might confuse the sensors. All you need to do is go in and lie on the table in the outline of the figure. All additional instructions will be given to you once you're settled in. Oh, and don't be scared of the needles, it's just a little prick and won't hurt."

"I bet you say that to all the girls."

After about two minutes Sara returned to the dressing room, parading naked through the door rather than using the robe provided. If her purpose that day was to unsettle him she was certainly succeeding. "So what was that one for?"

"Scanner one," he explained, "monitors vital organ function, and metabolic status. It's kind of a combination of a physical exam and full laboratory work up, including a full battery of blood tests, electrocardiogram, and electroencephalograph." Next you go to scanner two, which will have a look at your insides. It utilizes the most recent developments in micro-magnetic resonance imaging, and electron spin resonance imaging. When the blood samples were drawn you were also injected with the magnetic contrast material."

"Well let's get it over with," and she marched off to scanner two.

Sara returned after the second scan, and asked what was next.

"Nothing, that's it. By time you get dressed and ready to leave all the data will be analyzed. If everything checks out okay you get a certificate of health and go home. If something is wrong and requires immediate treatment you'll be sent on to the therapeutic sector and if anything requires follow-up you'll get a return appointment."

"Very neat. Doesn't anyone sit down and review the test results with me."

"That would be quite irregular. It's one of the things about Med-Met that started my doubts. You blindly follow the instructions, but never get a chance to ask questions."

"Well you remember that when you're a real doctor because listening to our patients, and helping them deal with their fears is one of the greatest services we can give to them.

"Hey what happened to my clothes?"

"Did you forget, this is the executive treatment. Your clothing is being cleaned and pressed, and will be ready for you when you finish your shower."

"This decadence is too much. I want you to do two things for me. First never tell anyone that I allowed myself to enjoy this luxury."

"That's fair enough, what's second?"

"Scrub my back."

After some preliminary soap play they began making love in the shower, and finished on the couch in the changing suite. After, they relaxed, and waited for her clothing to reappear.

"Michael, all the data from the tests and scans, how is it analyzed and how are the decisions made as to who is healthy, who is not, what treatments to give, and who winds up in the terminal group?"

"Gee, Sara it was really great for me too." It wasn't that he needed to be reassured, but Sara had an annoying habit of moving on as if she was between bites of a hamburger.

"Alright," Sara said mockingly, "the earth moved. Now will you answer my question?"

"Sure, if you put it that way. You know it's all handled by the computers. First they compare the findings with a range of norms for someone your sex, age, size, etcetera, and against any old data that is stored from your previous visits. If everything fits, nothing further needs to be done and the health certificate is drafted.

"If anything out of the ordinary shows up the data is analyzed further. If it appears that it might be a transient abnormality that needs to be followed for trends, you get a return appointment. If it is more complex the pattern of abnormalities is checked against the medical files, an appropriate diagnosis is made and treatment planned."

"What if the symptoms don't fit a pattern, or what if a new disease comes along."

"The system's programming is flexible enough to deal with a broad range of variation within a known disease entity to be able to deal with the heterogeneity of expression of disease manifestations. As far as new diseases, you know from our teachings with Rokoff that there are no new diseases, just old diseases manifested differently, or diseases that were around for centuries but not really recognized. Remember, Jacob used the examples of Legionnaire's and AIDS."

"Maybe that's true, or maybe we are being short sighted. Do you mean to tell me that every computer at every Med–Met facility stores information on every disease ever known? Not only that, but keeps a broad enough symptom base to detect all the possible variants."

"No, that would overload the capacity of even our most modern systems. The computers at the regional centers are designed to dump from its memory any disease that has not been reported in over thirty years, this helps to keep things from getting too cluttered."

"Then what happens if one of those diseases reappears, does anyone who gets it automatically get terminated?"

"No, when the information is deleted from the regional computers, it's transferred to the archives computer. If a disease shows up that is not in the local computers, the archives are accessed, and when a match is found that disease is then reprogrammed to the regional computers. The archives are located at the Baton Rouge facility. When I was in training we were taken there and given a tour. One of the interesting things is that we are still connected to Baton Rouge by the old fiberoptic network that used to connect the Universities in the state, rather than by satellite."

"It seems pretty shaky having only one location. What if the system were damaged?"

"I think you're getting out of my field. We've been assured that the system is well backed up. It has to be, if the archives were destroyed the system would be in chaos."

"This is all pretty interesting, but it doesn't come close to a cold stethoscope and a warm smile. Interested in another shower?"

"There's nothing I'd like better, but my colleagues are going to get tired of covering for me," he glanced at his sleeve, "And there is an exec due in this suite shortly. Your clothing should have been returned by now." Her jump suit hung neatly in the closet where it had been returned by a conveyor system. Also hanging from the conveyor was an envelope which contained Sara's certificate of health. As they left he was about to thank his friend for his special arrangements but instead received an icy stare from Marsha Walsh who had relieved Sil.

CHAPTER
12

Thomas Chen rarely went out into the field these days. He was physically able, he had just turned sixty and was in superb shape. Unfortunately, administrative duties usually demanded that he remain at the base camp dealing with the paper work. Chen thought about the term "paper work". It was interesting because it had been at least forty years since paper had been used with any degree of frequency. Chen enjoyed the collection of engineering books that he had accumulated over the years. They lined his library back home on Earth. He had brought his most recent acquisition with him, an original of the work of Buckminster Fuller describing the concept of the geodesic dome. From this work Chen devised the lunar station from which they currently worked. The book had been a gift from his old friend Jacob Rokoff. He had known the doctor for the past twenty-five years. It began when Rokoff had cared for his late wife, and helped her deal with the pain and dying from her incurable cancer. Chen appreciated the dignity that Rokoff had given his wife, and they kept in touch after her death. Over the years they became close friends although they might go for a year or more at a time without seeing each other. They shared among other things their love for books. Whenever either found a volume they thought their friend would appreciate, he would acquire it for him. Over the years Chen had been a generous financial supporter of the Hippocratin movement, helping to make it possible for them to continue their work.

This day however Thomas Chen would leave bureaucracy behind, and join his team in the exploration of the Infinity Research Laboratory. Thomas and a team of four, including Sam, headed off to Infinity in their rover while the others continued surveying Sheppard City. Their lasers quickly dispatched the chained gate at the entrance road, and they proceeded down the unpaved path until they came to a low curving building, hugging the base of the dome.

"Interesting construction, Dad," Sam said. "This is the first building I've seen that has used the dome as part of its structure."

Thomas scanned the lunarscape. The glint from the sun on the remnants of the dome caused him to squint his almond shaped eyes, which wrinkled his weathered skin. What he viewed was full of contrasts. Infinity was a crisp angled long low building. The exterior was a windowless light brown sandstone-like material, reminiscent of the architecture of the old Southwest United States. Around the building was level ground of crushed rock, characteristic of the developed portions of Sheppard City. It was now devoid of the covering of soil and plants that had thrived under the dome. The stark but man-made plain surrounding Infinity was sharply contrasted by the craggy uneven lunar surface on the outside of the dome remnants, beyond the back wall of the mystery building. The remains of the dome rose from the rear of Infinity and ended in a ragged edge above them, and then there was the blackness of space.

"Yes Sam, it's quite novel. But why is it here, and why didn't we have any information about it. Perhaps we'll find the answers inside, let's try to find a door."

Finding the door was no problem, but getting through it was another matter. The door appeared to be rough hewn wood consistent with the overall architecture, however it was an impervious material and had a finger print and DNA sensing locking device. As those whose data were encoded in the locks memory were long dead, another way to open the door was needed. This problem was the senior Chen's specialty. Never one to favor pyrotechnics, Thomas instead chose his trusted chemical methods. Although old fashioned the proper combination of acid and other corrosives did the job of weakening the structure surrounding the locking mechanism. After that one well-placed concentrated laser blast was enough to leave a hole where the lock had been. A loud high pitched rushing noise immediately followed along with a blast that knocked down Keri Davis who had been operating the laser, and causing the gravel around the doorway to kick up and cloud the area. In a few seconds it was over.

The three teammates looked to Davis who was slowly raising herself to a sitting position. "What the hell was that?"

Thomas was relieved to see that his crew member was relatively unhurt. "I'm not sure, but I think it was atmosphere. This building may have had a self maintaining atmosphere, and has been sealed for the last 40 years."

"But how could the pressure have been maintained over all this time Dad?"

"Another good question. Either this place was perfectly sealed so that no leakage at all occurred or there is still a functioning reactor that has maintained the atmosphere."

"If that's the case Boss," Davis was now standing with the group again, "We may have a perfect base of operations for the rest of the mission."

Thomas started forward, "We won't know if we don't move ahead."

It was totally dark inside the building. The salvage team quickly set-up portable lights revealing a room about 16 square meters in size. A large console desk sat in the center with a bank of vid screens facing the chair behind it. Several built in seating units were along the walls. The walls were adorned with prints of the famous Gowalski lunar vistas. A full set of the six classics hung around the room. Sam, the art expert of the team, quickly moved to inspect the works.

"Dad, you're not going to believe this, we're just in the lobby and we've already hit pay dirt. Not only are they signed, but they're the complete set of twos."

"What does that mean Sam?" Rob Krantz was a technical expert and had not spent much time in the appraisal aspects of the salvage business.

"What it means is that these things are worth a fortune, and they are all ours. Gowalski only made 50 sets of numbered prints, and only numbers one through five were signed. Sets four and five are in private collections on Earth, set three is hanging in the Smithsonian. Set one was displayed in the Lunar Museum here in Sheppard City. As we have already seen nothing remains of that building or its contents. Until three minutes ago no one knew the whereabouts of set number two. We will be able to name our price. I can't wait to see what else this place has to offer."

There was a single door behind and to the left of the desk. There was no apparent way to open the door but Krantz quickly began to examine the console at the desk. "I'll be damned if this isn't a security desk, and there has to be a door release somewhere."

Krantz pressed numerous buttons with no response, he reached under the console pressed a rocker switch and the board lit up. A moment later the room was bathed in lights from above. "Bingo, there's no doubt now, this place has got a live reactor."

The discovery of the Gowalskis, and now of a functional reactor had Thomas Chen as excited about the job as any he had been involved in for at least twenty years. This building was in superb condition, and promised to hold a great deal of reward for the salvage company. "Do you think you can get the door opened?"

"Shouldn't be too much of a problem, now that the boards lit up, everything's labeled. All I need to do is push the button marked door."

"Nothing happened."

"There's a warning light on the panel, it reads *Entry depressurized. Pressurize before opening inner door.* It must be a safety mechanism. We need to seal up this room and get the atmosphere reestablished before that door will open. We probably only let out the air from this one room. Otherwise we would have really kicked up a storm and Davis might have been blown back to Earth."

Krantz and Davis quickly patched the blown-out lock, placed an anchoring rope, with a suction attachment, to the inside of the front door and pulled the door tightly shut. Krantz then pushed the flashing button labeled pressurize and a hissing sound was heard and dust began to rise up from the floor. In five minutes the message on the board was replaced by *Pressure normal, proceed.*

Krantz pressed the door button once again, it slid silently open revealing a narrow well lit hallway with doors and corridors randomly spaced on both sides. A large set of what appeared to be high oak doors were at the far end.

"Well done," Thomas said. "Now take some readings on the air in this place."

Krantz anticipated his boss and had already taken out his atmospheric sampling equipment." Ambient temperature 25 degrees Celsius, air composition nitrogen, oxygen, and carbon dioxide, all in the proper ratio. No trace of toxic materials. Just like home."

Thomas led the way and opened the seals on his helmet, and removed his bulky space suit. He and his team had been burdened by the relatively primitive equipment that they were using on this job. The ancient space suits and vehicles were a result of a forty year gap in technology. As no extraterrestrial body was allowed to be visited, there had been no need to improve on the apparatus since the disaster. Thomas planned to work on some modifications when they returned to Earth to recruit a full complement of workers and to prepare for the major portion of the salvage operation. It would be much easier to explore Infinity in their fatigues.

The doors on the two sides of the corridors led to a variety of offices, what appeared to be laboratories, utility and storage rooms. The corridors off to the sides were equally nondescript. The doors were all the same, and just marked by room numbers. The exceptions were the large oak doors at the end of the main corridor and the last door on the left hand side of the hall immediately prior to the oak doors. The door to the left was broader that the average door and appeared to be forged of high grade steel. This last finding was unusual in itself in that it would be extremely heavy and cost a tremendous amount to transport to the moon. There was no pressure plate to open this door as there were on all the others. A sign on the door proclaimed "Corridor A, Security Area, Authorized Personnel Only."

Sam approached the door and a smooth mechanical voice sounded from a speaker in the ceiling above him. "State your name and identification number, for voice pattern verification."

Sam was startled, but quickly blurted out his name and universal identity code. "I'm so sorry," the voice returned, "that is not a valid combination. Access denied, please see the Chief of Security to obtain clearance."

"I doubt if I can find the Chief of Security at this time." Sam answered to the ceiling. "Rob, do you think you can get us through that door."

"Not with the equipment we brought up on this trip. We didn't anticipate that anyone would have high grade steel up here, and the Space Agency didn't give us voice code tapes for this place. We'll have to get the proper gear when we go back down to Earth."

"Alright then," Thomas was anxious to proceed, "let's forget this door for now and find out what's behind these big oak slabs."

Next to the oak doors was a small brass plate with the inscription, "Executive Offices, Infinity Research Laboratories". The door presented no problems. All it required was a twist of an old fashioned brass door knob. What greeted the salvage team was again unexpected. The decor was very different from the standard functional design of the rest of Sheppard City. The floors were solid marble, and the walls covered in high quality decorative papers. What appeared to be sections of the trunks of real trees were built into the walls and branches and leaves sprung from them but were really a part of the wallpaper. The sofas were plush and covered in what looked to be real leather. A large crystal chandelier hung from the high ceiling in the center of the room. A receptionist's desk was centered by a semicircle of office doors on the wall opposite the door from which they had entered.

"This is amazing," Davis was fingering the walls, "these are real sections of tree trunks, and the floor is Carrara marble. These Infinity chaps must have been exempt from the weight restrictions. This stuff is incredibly heavy, and if I remember our briefings everything shipped to the moon had to be functional and not waist space or weight.

"And look how well preserved it all is. No cracks in the leather, and no yellowing of the wall covering. The environmental control in this place is unreal for everything to have remained so pristine."

"Wait a minute," Krantz said, looking around. "If everything else is so well preserved, and the environment has remained intact, what happened to all the people."

"As you know the great disaster occurred in the middle of the night and most of the residents of Sheppard City were home in their beds." Thomas Chen looked perplexed as he continued, "it has troubled me however that we have not even seen any sign of security personnel. Perhaps we will still find their remains. Maybe they stayed here until they ran out of food and water, or perhaps they went insane when they learned what happened and ran out into the open, or perhaps the answers are in Corridor A.

"Right now I suggest that we explore the other rooms in this suite, let's start with the central door. The space between it and the doors on either side suggests it's the largest. I'll probably want to make it my office on the moon."

Again the door presented no problem. It slid open as Thomas stepped on the threshold. As with the main lobby, and with the central room of the office suite the team was totally unprepared for what they saw. The room was four meters deep and eight meters long and slightly curved both along its length, and from the floor to the ceiling. The dominant feature in the room was the far wall which was transparent and revealed the stark lunar landscape. Although the team knew that the back wall of the building was up against the dome, they hadn't expected it to be so dramatically incorporated into the architecture.

"Good lord, I don't believe what I'm seeing." Sam broke the spell created by the window to the moon.

"Yes, it is an incredible use of architecture. To be standing indoors yet to have the feel of being part of the lunar vista is quite remarkable."

"No Dad, that's not what I mean. Look behind you." The wall to the left of the entrance door was dominated by a large painting. It was an oil painting of Sheppard City under construction. Sections of the dome were in place and buildings were being erected under temporary enclosures. The lunar visage once again offset man's attempt to claim and tame a portion of it. The Earth hung as a blue jewel over the edge of the open dome, highlighted by sunlight that also glittered off the edge. "I think it's an original Gowalski oil, and I don't think this one is in any of the catalogs or records. Also it appears to have been painted before Sheppard City was completed, which means it may be Gowalski's first work on the moon. This is the mother-load, the prints up front were valuable, but this ..."

"This, my son, is our future. All of us now have our retirements secured. This is a find of a lifetime for us and for the world of art. Picture Gowalski, an itinerant artist of little note who had signed on as an architect's assistant with the Sheppard City construction project. His job was to do sketches for the building facades.

"On weekends he would take a small portable dome, some food, a sleeping bag, an easel and a palate, and camp out on the lunar surface painting his surroundings. His most haunting works were those that contrasted the raw beauty of the moon with some sign of man, a derelict land rover from the Apollo missions, or the simple beauty of a lone sunflower in an experimental dome garden. He painted in solitude and became the first, and sadly only great artist of the moon. Just as his work began to garner acclaim he perished in the Great Disaster. Most of his work was also lost here on the moon. That which had made its way to Earth increased in value incredibly, and surpasses that of even the great masters. This painting should set a new price standard for a single work of art."

The rest of the tour of the accessible areas of Infinity was less rewarding and less exciting. There was little available in terms of readable records to give any clues as to Infinity's purpose. The records they were able to locate were all on protected memory strips, and attempts to break the codes were frustrating. It was decided to wait until they were back on Earth with all their resources available.

Some industrial quality gems were found in the laboratories, none of which were of any great value except for one large ruby that was part of some type of optical focusing system. The laboratories were all rather standard in appearance equipped for either biological, genetic or physical experimentation. In some of the laboratories locked safe boxes of sorts were found, these were all of high grade steel, and had security locking devices that appeared explosive in nature.

That evening back at the operations base Sam briefed the rest of the crew on the Infinity findings, and basked in the opportunity to unveil the Gowalski prints and the original oil to the rest of the group, all of whom would soon be quite wealthy.

After much speculation on the prices the works would bring, and how much one twelfth of that would be, Krantz asked, "What do you think is in the blow up boxes, Sam?"

"I'm not sure. Two of them were in the room where we found the ruby and the other gems, so we are hoping perhaps that there are more or better stones inside those boxes. One that really has me puzzled is the box that is obviously refrigerated. By the gauge on the outside appears to be at -140°. We had to disconnect it from Infinity's reactor to move it, but we've already hooked it into our ship's reactor to maintain the temperature."

"Well why don't we crack them open and see what we've got?"

"I'd love to Georgi, but once again we have encountered materials and technology we did not expect and did not come prepared to deal with. This stuff is going to have to wait until we get back home or we risk harm to ourselves, or the contents of the boxes. I'm afraid Infinity will not give up her secrets easily."

CHAPTER

13

Wil Armbrister again presided in the conference room. In addition to the usual officers were several new faces from outside of Med–Met. "I am happy to report that the first six months of our campaign have gone extremely well. Our war chest is considerable. As I anticipated our friends have been quick to contribute to the cause once they understood how their own financial futures are tied to the success of our venture.

"Darren's public relation campaign has been well received. The polls that I have taken show him to have an extremely high name recognition level in this region. Visits to our regional center have picked up significantly. This has not gone unnoticed at the national level. After the first few months of running our ads here, national picked them up Darren Walters and all. So Darren now has national exposure.

"An interesting recent development has been that pro–Med–Met counter demonstrations have begun. People have actually come out and begun to wave signs and shout at the Hippies for interfering with access into the facility."

"Wil," Darren broke in, "what's the current political situation."

"Things are moving along well. Kansas has recently become the fourth state to outlaw the barbaric medical clinics. Our people tell us that things look promising for South Dakota, and Mississippi to follow shortly. There are several Congressman and Senators who we have easy access to. The Technocrat Party has been quite friendly to us, especially since we have contributed to the campaigns of several of their candidates."

"What about the Hippocratins?" Darren asked.

"Well, as you know they continue to function openly and flagrantly." Shaking his head Wil continued, "Our efforts in this state have not been as fruitful as in some of the other states. This continues to be a problem for us. Rokoff is still a popular figure, and our people tell me his clinic is full."

"It appears then that from all aspects we are prepared to move to the next phase." Walters was no longer the passive follower he had been in the early stages of Armbrister's planning. He had quickly begun to take command in his efficient managerial style, leaving little doubt as to who was in charge. "With Wil's agreement I have decided that it is time to take a leave of absence from my position as Regional Manager and to accept the Chairmanship of the Committee for a Healthy America. I would like to thank my friends," nodding to the new faces at the end of the conference table, "who have been the visible leadership of the CHA until now.

"On Wednesday the Committee will hold a press conference and announce that they have invited me to chair the organization, and that I have accepted. I will then read a fire and brimstone speech that Wil and the writers have prepared, and accelerate our war on the Hippocratins.

"Angela and I have been making plans for her to take over as acting Regional Manager. This has already been discussed with Med-Met National who agreed to my leave and Angela's appointment. Angela, do you have anything to add?"

Angela bit her lip and looked around at each person, "Well, we face a hard period of adjustment. Not only will Darren be leaving, but Wil and Suzanne will be going with him." Nodding toward the CFO she said, "Joel Rogers is going to stay on for the next few months to help me with the transition, before he leaves to join the others. I will need all of your help in keeping this facility operating at the superior level that it has achieved under Darren.

"I do have one important question. How have the Med-Met corporate offices reacted to all these changes, and do they know what's really going on?"

Ambrister was quick to answer, seeming to want to recapture the spotlight. "They have taken it quite well. I don't believe they know for sure what's going on. They suspect we are up to something but seem happy with the results. One good indication is that they have given a substantial contribution to the Committee for a Healthy America. Coincidentally that contribution came out to roughly the annual salary and benefits of a Med-Met regional manager."

CHAPTER
14

Jacob felt uncomfortable. He was unsure if it was the dark business suit he wore, the austere paneled offices, or the stares he was getting from the several strangers who knew him only by reputation. The only familiar face was that of Georgi Chen and who had not glanced up from his knees.

The youngest son of his closest friend looked pale, lacking sleep and unkempt. Georgi looked the way Jacob had felt since receiving the news two weeks earlier. Less than six months after the initial expedition, Thomas Chen had put together a larger crew and headed back to continue salvage on the moon. Shortly after leaving earth orbit, something went wrong. The ship exploded. All on board including Thomas and Samuel Chen had been killed. The news had stunned Jacob and now he sat here in this pompous law office listening to the reading of Thomas' last will and testament.

Two nights before the ship's departure, Jacob had been with Thomas and his sons. He had toasted his dear friend's fortune and basked in the amazing beauty of the Gowalskis. Thomas had wanted Jacob to see them before they left for France and the Louvre. From the generous donation that the Chen's had presented to the Hippocratins Jacob had no doubt that Thomas had been well rewarded for his find.

Thomas and Sam had entertained Jacob with descriptions of the sharp contrasts of the moon, the ravishing destruction and the stark beauty. Georgi behaved rather sullenly throughout the evening. When he did speak it was only to complain that he was being left behind to continue recruiting salvage teams and would not join his father and brother for another month or two.

Thomas' attempts to explain the importance of Georgi's job in recruiting as well as in cataloging the acquisitions from the initial mission did nothing to soothe the younger Chen's hurt feelings and bruised ego. Jacob wondered how much of Georgi's current angst was grief and how much guilt that he had been spared while the others perished.

Jacob had never cared for Georgi, but he knew that he owed it to his friend to reach out to the youngster at this difficult time. Georgi had always seemed so lazy in contrast to his father and older brother. He was frivolous and tended to spend his money on clothing and status symbols and loved to be seen with show business types. Despite this, as far as Jacob knew, Georgi was now all alone. Jacob planned to talk to Georgi when the reading of the will was completed. He wanted to keep in touch and provide whatever help he could for the young man.

"And to my dear friend, Jacob Rokoff," Jacob was startled to alertness by the sound of his name being read in the nasal voice of the senior partner of the law firm. "My dear friend Jacob with whom I could truly share my thoughts and dreams and love for things of age and value, I leave my library. In those books reside the true riches of the world. In addition I leave to Jacob the value of one third of the remainder of my assets and worldly possessions to be used to further the practice of medicine and the goals of the Hippocratin Society."

There was an expression of general disbelief from around the room. Georgi finally looked up from his knees and toward Rokoff, but his eyes still remained emotionless. Jacob could not tell if Georgi had any feeling regarding his father's bequest. Georgi himself was more than well provided for with the bulk of the remaining two thirds of Thomas assets, the third that was to be his and the third that would have been Sam's. Additionally, by prior agreement as the sole survivor of the first lunar mission, Georgi acquired the rights to all the salvaged material they had brought back. This variety of valuables and junk still sat in the Chen warehouse waiting for inventory. The various acquisitions from Infinity were stored in a separate room in the warehouse.

Jacob sat in shocked silence trying to realize what Chen's bequest would mean to the Hippocratin movement. As he thought of the clinics they could build the medications they could provide and the students they could teach, he nearly failed to notice everyone filing out around him. He rushed out to the hallway hoping to catch Georgi before he left the building.

He didn't have to look far. The reporters surrounded Georgi like a pack of hungry dogs. The young man stood silently as they barked questions and aimed holo-cans at him from all directions. Rokoff quickly moved to Georgi's side. "Please, you must excuse Mr. Chen. He has been through a very difficult morning and his grief is still quite fresh. I'm sure he will issue a statement when he is ready." With that he quickly led Georgi out of the crowd and out toward the door. Just as they reached the door he heard a shout from behind, "Hey, that's Jacob Rokoff," and with that the temporarily docile press pack came shouting and running toward them. Jacob grabbed Georgi's arm and led him away.

"Thank you, Dr. Rokoff," Georgi spoke for the first time. It was a lifeless monotone. "I appreciate your intent, but I was perfectly fine. I just didn't have anything to say to those people."

"Unfortunately I have become all too familiar with the press of late. Even if you say nothing to them they are likely to misquote you. I was overwhelmed by father's generosity to me and my organization. His gift will be of tremendous value to our work in a very difficult time. I hope you didn't find the size of his gift inappropriate."

"No, Dr. Rokoff I understand my father's strong friendship for you and his belief in your work. I have been well provided for and will live very comfortably. Some of the others, the distant relatives and hangers on who were hoping for a bigger piece of the pie may resent both of us however. I'll be going now doctor thank you again for speaking at the memorial service."

"Wait, Georgi." Jacob put a hand on Georgi's shoulder as he turned to leave. "What will you do now? Do you plan to continue the business, the lunar mission?"

"No, the business was never my interest; it was my fathers and Sam's. I was part of it because it was expected of me. As far as the lunar project goes I want to put as much distance between myself and anything related to it as I can.

"I have received an order to cease all operations involving the project, pending an investigation. The reports on the news suggest a lot of support for closing down space travel again," he shrugged. "Maybe they're right and the moon is cursed. I have no real plans right now. Maybe I'll travel a bit on earth, I've never been a tourist. After awhile I'll think about what to do, there's no rush."

The emptiness in Georgi's voice startled Jacob. There was no sadness, no conviction, just nothing. "Georgi, please keep in touch. I want you to come visit and see what we do with your father's gift.

"Don't hesitate to call on me if you need anything. Your father and I were closer than most brothers, so think of me as family."

"What could I need, Dr. Rokoff? I have more money than I could ever spend, I have homes and cars and even planes. What could I need?" With that Georgi turned and disappeared into the thickening crowd.

CHAPTER
15

Walters shut the vid-chip reader and as the holo faded he spun in his chair and shouted into the communicator on his desk, "Get Wil in here now!"

It only took minutes for Armbrister to come puffing in from his own office down the hall. "What is it chief?"

"What is it? Did you see the news about the money that Rokoff and the Hippocratins inherited? With that kind of money they can become a much bigger problem than we imagined. They can build more facilities, advertise, and contribute to politicians. What are we going to do about it?"

Armbrister wiped the sweat from his brow and hitched his pants up below the overhang of his belly. "Is that what you're fired up about? You need to calm down. One of Nixon's problems was that he always got fired up before getting the complete picture, and then his people would hop around like scared rabbits. I've got this one under control. When I watched the news I noticed some not too happy faces coming out of the lawyer's office. I tracked down a couple of disgruntled cousins who are anxious to contest the bequest to Rokoff. We've got some top legal people working with them."

Walters sat back in his chair listening. The vein that had been bugling in his left temple had subsided and his reddened face returned to its usually lightly tanned appearance. "Okay, what grounds do they have for the appeal?"

"Simple, it's one that a lot of people will go for and will help our side at the same time. They're claiming that Rokoff treated the old guy in his clinic and used drugs to affect his mind and get him to change his will. It promotes the voodoo image of the Hippies, and will keep the money tied up in the courts for years."

"Very nicely done Wil. What do the cousins get for all this?"

"Well for one thing the hope of winning the suit and getting very rich and in addition a small allowance from us to help cover their legal and other expenses."

Walters leaned over his desk and quietly asked, "Can it be traced to us?"

"No way, Darren no way."

★　★　★

Standing silently she could only see the back of his head and beyond that the large picture window. Far below the penthouse office the twisting curves of the Mississippi River carved the landscape that gave New Orleans one of its nicknames, the "Crescent City".

The man in the high-backed chair spoke in a soft but commanding voice. "Your people have done well. The Space Council is expected to forbid any further lunar travel and once again the Infinity chapter will be closed."

"Thank you sir, there is a general consensus that the explosion was an accident. Other than the Gowalskis there has been little interest in what the first expedition found. The speaker a woman in her early thirties stood at military attention as she addressed the back of the chair. She wore a nondescript coverall with no markings or insignia, and had the appearance of a hardened combatant.

"You cannot imagine the concern I felt when I saw the Gowalskis on the nightly news and realized where they came from." The chair swiveled slightly and he continued, "What about the loose ends? What about the son and the remaining material from the first expedition."

"The son appears to be no threat, sir. He is unmotivated and just drifting at the present. We are keeping tabs on him. In that he poses no immediate threat it's my feeling no action needs to be taken. If anything were to happen to him it could reopen the investigation of the explosion. As far as the remaining salvage Chen has placed it in one of his warehouses and ordered it locked and sealed."

"Very well, and your opinion on whether they entered Corridor A?"

"Negative sir. From what we know of their equipment they did not have the technical capability. Furthermore, if they had entered Corridor A we would have heard the repercussions."

"Thank you Captain. One more thing. Have some people look into what Darren Walters is up to. His recent notoriety concerns me."

CHAPTER
16

Michael walked quickly toward the exit, his shift was over the next beginning. Others hustled in both directions. He reached the door and was shoved backward, falling over a co-worker who had been coming up behind him. "Everyone back inside," a voice blared over a bullhorn. Next there was a loud crack and a smoky substance drifted up from the hedges toward the entrance.

"Close the door close it! It's tear gas!" Michael tried to get up and close the door as others from the outside tried to push their way in. The group forcing their way in included a mixture of Med-Met personnel and protestors, from both sides, trying to get away from the billowing gas.

Before the door could be closed, a mixture of stumbling bodies and irritating fumes continued to invade the entrance hallway. Michael tried again to close the door as the opposing protestors fought the choking fumes and each other. Again he attempted to seal off the doorway with the assistance of some co-workers who had now sorted themselves out of the confused and disoriented crowd. Just as the door was about to catch, it once again burst inward this time followed by a squad of helmeted and gas mask wearing security police.

At least twenty officers in full riot gear entered, quickly sealed the door and began to separate the wrestling and writhing protestors from the easily identifiable Med-Met personnel in their color coded coveralls. The ventilation system rapidly cleared the gas from the area allowing the squad to remove their protective masks. Michael noticed three figures in the middle of the group not in uniform.

Two of the three established a clear area and set-up a holo-cam while the third went about straightening his clothing and smoothing out his hair. It only took moments before supporter and foe alike recognized the familiar face of Darren Walters.

"Alright he shouted, let's get the lighting set-up. How do I look? Did that mask leave any marks on my face?"

"I'd like to leave more than a mark on your face Walters," one of the anti-Med-Met faction half yelled and half coughed just before a security officer slammed a stunner across his lower back driving him to the floor.

"Get those damn hippies out of here." Walters shouted as the security force tried in futility to sort protestors from counter protestors.

The winter had been mild, even for Louisiana. The temperature had only been in the 40's two or three times and the usual spring rains had yet to begin even though it was already April. The unusually good weather had encouraged the frequency and intensity of protests at the Med-Met facilities, but with a difference. Counter protests were occurring at almost all the facilities, particularly the South Central Regional Headquarters in New Orleans. The fire of the emotion on both sides had been stoked by the ever present images of Walters on the vid-chips, bill boards, holo-news and public appearances. Since taking leave of absence from his position with Med-Met, and accepting leadership of the CHA, Walters had become a vocal and dangerous opponent of the Hippocratin movement.

The CHA through its public campaigns and the use of political muscle had managed to get Hippocratin clinics and the practice of medicine outlawed in three additional states and clearly battle lines were being drawn both figuratively and literally. The protests which had been peaceful at first became more vocal, and then marked by occasional violence. The violence came from both sides. In Seattle at the Western Regional Center a bomb had gone off in the terminal suite severely damaging the section of the facility and killing two A.O.D. Apparently a terminally ill client had smuggled plastic explosives in inside his body and acted as a human bomb. He was subsequently linked to the Weps. Violence against protestors was becoming increasingly common and now demonstrations by Med–Met supporters were regularly occurring at Hippocratin clinics.

Michael was amazed at how quickly the security personnel and the other Med–Met workers jumped to Walters' commands considering it had been several months since he had stepped down as Director. The security force picked out anyone apparently hostile to Walters, sorted them out of the crowd and whisked them to another area. Additional security teams from within the building joined in the process and two other media types mysteriously appeared to assist the holo–cam crew. An assistant whispered to Walters's, who looked in Michael's general direction and nodded.

Before anyone clearly knew what was happening lights glared and three holo–cam remotes hovered in a triangle around Walters who had a microphone in hand. "This is Darren Walters head of the Committee for a Healthy America. I am in the lobby of the New Orleans Med–Met Center. You have just witnessed the horror unfolding outside where a gang of lawless Hippies have attempted once again to disrupt our ability to deliver the best health care possible. I know that several have been injured and I hope and pray that no one was severely hurt or killed. The only way that we are going to end this wanton violence is once and for all to stop these so called humanistic doctors who are only out for their own glorification. They seek to turn back the clock to the days of leeches and surgery performed by shaky handed old men rather than precise fully automated Surgi-units."

"These supposed defenders of your right to choice want to allow terminals with contagious diseases to wander among us spreading their germs and pestilence. They want us to watch as our loved ones suffer in pain and wither and rot before our eyes, rather than go on to their well deserved final therapy. We are not going to let that happen. Good people like you and me are not going to stand by and let these Hippies tell us that we are going to go backwards rather than forwards.

"Look around me and what do you see? Here in the entrance of this marvelous state of the art facility are the shocked and stunned faces of our clients and our dedicated Med-Met personnel. Many of them trying to reach the facility or to go home at the end of their hard but rewarding day were met by violence and repugnant treatment by that disgusting rabble outside.

"I myself was nearly severely injured and managed to reach the relative safety inside the building where I witnessed the actions of our dedicated staff in securing the building against the onslaught of those thugs. I recognized Michael Guidry a dedicated diagnostic technician as he fought to protect his colleagues and clients. Michael would you please join me for a moment?"

The holo-cam spun toward Michael the lights and remotes hovered to triangulate him. He was caught with a look of total shock, as he was pulled up and to Walters's side. He had never met Walters personally, although he had been introduced to him when Walters was still director and made inspection tours of the center. Michael stood in the glare of the lights, his mouth open and a blank stare."

"It is obvious that Mr. Guidry is in near shock over what has been occurring yet he had the presence of mind to act in this crisis." Walters had his arm around Michael's shoulder as he spoke, "Michael Guidry is an outstanding example of what Med-Met is all about. He has been with Med-Met for almost four years and currently serves as a diagnostic technician. He has been commended for his service to his clients and consistently receives the highest ratings for efficiency and courtesy.

"Michael I know that this must be a difficult time for you, but can you tell us what you are feeling right now."

Still shaken by the violence and tear gas compounded by this unexpected turn of events Michael stood for what seemed hours without speaking. Just as Walters was about to pull the microphone away Michael took a deep breath and looked directly at Walters.

"Well, Mr. Walters as you've said these are very difficult times. In difficult times we need to make decisions. They are not always easy decisions to make. Sometimes they involve sacrifice and pain in order to achieve a higher goal. I hope that I have what it takes to do what is right."

"Beautifully put Michael." Walters beamed at Michael and tightened his fingers on his shoulder in a fatherly gesture. "We need to follow Michael's lead, make the hard decisions, and do what's right." Walters looked into the camera and raised his hands the second and middle finger of each making a V as Armbrister had suggested. "Alright cut. That was beautiful. Mr. Guidry sorry about the surprise but we needed to act fast. You were outstanding. I'm sure we will be hearing more from you in the future."

CHAPTER
17

"So captain, what do you have to report on the activities of young Mr. Chen?"

Once again she stood at attention and faced the back of his chair as she reported. "He has been quite active on the social scene, always in the company of Hollywood types. He is favorite of the starlets. They consider him good looking, and he does have all that money. He wears all the latest fashions and makes the scene at all the hot clubs. He frequently rocket jets to Europe and Asia. He has also been sending occasional gifts to Rokoff. Seems he is really annoyed about the cousins who challenged his father's bequest. He has been giving Rokoff funds for legal expenses and to keep his clinic going."

"Interesting, there may be more to him than I have given him credit for. Has been talking about what happened on the moon?"

"All the vid talk and interview shows have been trying to get him to talk about his lunar experiences but he has rejected all offers to date."

"Why has he turned them down?"

"Our people have two operating theories. The first is that he is still deeply upset by what happened, and feels guilty that he survived while the others died."

"And the second?"

"The second is that he is being lured by his Hollywood friends to make a holo-film about the Chen expedition. They have told him it will be bigger if there is no information until the holo-film comes out. He does not appear to need the money that a movie would make, but he is enamored with the whole show biz world."

The chair shifted slightly, "We need to know if he has any plans to make the film. You said that the starlets find him attractive. What do you think of him Captain?"

"Sir?"

"I mean as a young woman, do you find him attractive?"

"I hadn't thought about it, but I suppose I would classify him as above average in terms of physical appearance."

CHAPTER
18

That evening Michael arrived late on purpose. He had debated with himself whether to show-up at all. He knew they all would have seen the report on the previous evening's news. The CHA had managed to get their reports slipped in as paid segments between the real news. With the journalistic style that Walters employed, few made the distinction between the two. Michael hoped that he could slip quietly in the back and then maybe slip out before the end of class. It was Tuesday, which meant that Rokoff would be lecturing on the history of medicine. Recently, he had been covering the events at the end of the twentieth century that had precipitated the development of Med-Met.

"If one change can most directly be said to have led to the Med-Met phenomena, it was the institution of comparative effectiveness. Can anyone tell me why?"

Michael tried to shrink into his chair as Earl who was sitting directly in front of him, raised his hand. Everyone looked toward him, and Michael. "Well," Rokoff bellowed with a smile on his face, "it looks like we have a celebrity among us."

With that the session fell into disarray. Questions and comments assaulted Michael from all sides. Somehow out of all the voices, Sara's came through the clearest as she imitated Walters modulated tones,

"What we have is an outstanding example of what Med-Met is all about." Sara grabbed a banana from the fruit bowl and held it like a microphone as she worked her way toward Michael. "Tell us Mr. Guidry what does a fine upstanding Med-Met droid like you do with your evening? Perhaps you sneak some loose hippie sluts up to your luxurious and subsidized company flat for some gross anatomy. I know that's what I would do. There are still some things people do better than machines. Eh, son?"

"Very cute, I knew I was going to have a tough time tonight, I almost didn't come."

Rokoff moved toward Sara and Michael. "Enough Sara, I thought we all agreed we weren't going to harass Michael. I'm sure he was not a party to that spectacle. By the look on his face when the camera turned on him I take it he didn't have any warning either. Michael, I know your colleagues are eager to hear what actually went on."

"It happened so quickly I wasn't sure what was going on. I was getting ready to leave for the day and apparently the demonstration outside had gotten pretty heated."

"That's an understatement," Sara interrupted, "we were just marching with our signs and chanting and those CHA goons started throwing rocks and shouting, 'Stone the witches'. The next thing I know someone swings a sign at one of the rock throwers and then the Gestapo charges over the hill and begins shooting gas canisters into the crowd. Then I see a bunch of the uniformed jerks surrounding this small group and all of them heading for the main entrance. I had to get out of there because the gas was heading in my direction."

Michael resumed his account. "At that point we were trying to get the door closed and keep the gas out. This crowd of people pushed their way in, including what must have been the group Sara just described. I was on my back. I think I had fallen over someone. I crawled back to the door and pushed it closed. While the gas was clearing from the area Walters and his group set up their cameras and got organized. It looked pre-planned."

"And so how did he pick you out?" Sara's sarcastic tone seemed to give way to her natural curiosity.

"Again I'm a little fuzzy on details," Michael furrowed, his brow. "I remember that he was looking in my direction. He said something to one of his assistants who whipped out a pocket device. It looked like he pulled up some data and handed it to Walters, who looked it over just before he began his little sermon. The rest is what you saw."

Rokoff was leaning against the wall, arms crossed. He appeared to be listening intently. "From what you're saying it sounds like Walters still has access to Med-Met information, and Med-Met personnel are still doing his bidding."

"That's how it looked to me."

"That's very interesting considering he is supposedly totally independent of his former organization, while on leave. They claim that in no way do they support the CHA. Michael, do you think you could snoop around a little, find out just how tightly connected to Med-Met he still is?"

"No, Jacob I can't." Michael said firmly.

Jacob appeared surprised by Michael's answer. "Why not? I don't want you to do anything risky, when you go back to work just..."

Michael held his ground. "I'm not going back Jacob. You remember in the interview how I talked about decisions and doing what's right? Well, this is what's right. I can't go back there anymore and be part of misleading people. I've been here ten months now and I know what I want."

Sara hugged him and mussed his hair. She faked a sniffle, "I'm so proud. The little tyke is growing up."

Jacob frowned at her and spoke softly to Michael, "You're sure this is what you want?" Michael looked up into his teacher's eyes, "Absolutely, there is no longer any doubt."

Jacob stared at Michael, not saying anything for a few moments. Michael watched a small smile appear on his teacher's face before he finally spoke. "Well that gives me an idea, if I can just get a hold of a little money." Jacob paused, "Do me a favor. Finish out the week at Med-Met and don't say anything. I'm sure you'll be quite a hero tomorrow. I need to work on something, and we need to find a place for you to live. Now, if it's alright with everyone, let's get back to tonight's topic.

"As I was saying, comparative effectiveness started with good intent. That is if there was more than one treatment available for a particular condition, and they were equally effective, the maximum payment would be capped at the price of the least expensive. In a large part it was necessary and beneficial to the extent that costs had been spiraling out of control. Each new medication was more expensive than the last. The public demanded the newest, even if it had not been proven more effective. In principal comparative effectiveness required that if two treatments were equally effective, you would opt for the less costly. Unfortunately it was used in other ways that led to decision making that has become the heart of Med-Mets cure or kill philosophy. Earl, I think you had something you wanted to add."

Carter quipped in his slow soft drawl, "Well Jacob I think you've taken all the good stuff. What happened is that it got out of control. Initially when a patient presented for treatment algorithms were created to determine if treatment should be given. That included curative intent or palliative options. As the algorithm evolved, decisions were based on the cost per year of life saved. Expensive treatments would be used if cost efficient when spread over the potential lifetime of the patient. The potential productivity of the patient was added. They factored in whether the individual could resume their previous occupation, pay taxes, etc. Slowly more was added until we get to the current algorithm, where the cost of treating an individual and keeping them alive is weighed against their potential productivity. If they can be expected to contribute more than the expected cost of their treatments they live. If not they get an appointment with the A.O.D."

"Could you give us an example?" Jacob asked.

"Sure, let's say there's a school teacher and a Med-Met executive. Same age, same disease, but he makes four times as much as she does. Now when they plug his numbers in, it turns out that he will produce twice the cost of the treatment. Unfortunately she projects as a losing proposition. Final result, he lives, she dies."

"Crude but correct," Jacob said. "Students I think that is plenty of food for thought for tonight. I will see you all tomorrow. Patricia, I would appreciate it if you could take over the clinic tomorrow morning. I have a few things to arrange."

CHAPTER
19

"Looking at things from all angles the campaign is clearly going according to plan." Armbrister was pumped up with his successes as he addressed the CHA board. Darren Walters sat beaming, as his henchman went over charts and diagrams.

"Wil, can we have the recent Med-Met statistics."

"Let's start with the average daily visits. As you can see there is a consistent upward trend since the campaign began. Additionally, if we look at the percentage of terminals completing therapy, there has been a complete reversal of the earlier decline. We also have figures for the Hippocratin clinics. They are only estimates, but they are almost the inverse of the Med-Met statistics. Next, Joel Rogers will give the financial report. As you know Joel's joining CHA is in itself a reflection of our financial growth. We're now able to afford to hire a fulltime administrator."

"Thank you Wil. I want you all to know how happy I am to be here." Rogers didn't sound convincing as he stood straight and stiff with a tight fitting collar. "As Wil suggests we are in excellent financial shape. Let me just..." As he started to display the spread sheets Suzanne Hartstein rushed in and whispered excitedly in Darren's ear. Darren shook his head a few times, but she persisted. He leaned over a whispered to Armbrister.

Armbrister shook his head slowly as he stood to speak. "If you could all excuse us for a few minutes it appears there is a matter that needs our immediate attention. Joel will continue to brief you on our financial status. We will return shortly, and Darren will brief us on the upcoming schedule of events."

Suzanne led Darren and Wil into Darren's private office. Armbrister's face was bright-red, as he spoke. "What the hell do you think you are doing disrupting a board meeting? These are important people? Do you think what you have to tell us is more important than their time?"

"I'll let you tell me after you see this." Suzanne stood her ground, "Wil, you better get a drink for yourself and one for Darren."

Darren seemed to realize that it was serious when he saw how Suzanne brushed off Wil's bluster and continued with business. "What's going on Suz?"

"This vid-chip just came across, and I think you'd better see it."

Hartstein placed the vid-chip in the reader and it sprung to life. The image of Walters at the Med-Met facility after the previous week's riot appeared. "Michael Guidry is an outstanding example…."

Wil interrupted, "What the hell are you doing, this is old news. Can we get back to our meeting?"

Suzanne stared defiantly at Wil, her own anger beginning to show. "Wil, please be quite and pay attention. Darren please make him shut-up. You need to see this."

Darren raised his hands in a stop sign. "Wil, please be quiet. Go ahead Suzanne."

The vid-chip resumed." …Michael, I know this must be a difficult time for you, but can you tell us what you are feeling right now."

"Well, Mr. Walters as you have said these are very difficult time. In difficult times we need to make decisions. They are not always easy decisions to make. Sometimes they involve sacrifice and pain in order to achieve a higher goal. I hope that I have what it takes to do what is right."

The scene shifted to Darren, arm around Michael, "We need to follow Michael's lead make the hard decisions, and do what's right."

Darren faded out and Michael Guidry appeared alone, "What you have just seen happened a few days ago. At the time I was a Med-Met technician. I spoke then of the need to sacrifice and make difficult decisions. I hoped that I would have the strength to do the right thing. I have thought about that for some time as my frustrations have grown. This has resulted from the lack of humanity of the Med-Met system."

"Son of a bitch," Wil hissed.

Guidry's image continued. "So I will make the sacrifices and follow my convictions." He slowly unzipped his Med-Met jumpsuit. "I am resigning from my secure, well-paid position at Med-Met and giving up my comfortable company apartment." He now stood in a pair of slacks and a tee shirt, over his left breast was the symbol of two snakes entwined around a pole. "For almost a year now I have been attending medical classes. Starting tomorrow I begin fulltime study with Jacob Rokoff and the Hippocratins. I hope someday I may earn the title, Doctor."

The scene shifted back to the image of Darren with his arm on Michael's shoulder. "We need to follow Michael's lead, make the hard decisions, and do what's right." The vid faded to black.

"Goddamn, motherfucking, son of a bitch." Wil had gone beyond red to purple. "I'll destroy that little shit. He can't do this to us."

Darren sat silent and still with his eyes shut. "Easy does it Wil, remember you told us that kind of anger was the downfall of your twentieth-century heroes. Besides, the kid is not the one to take it out on. Number one he is not bright enough or experienced enough to do this on his own. Number two, as you're well aware, the spots cost plenty just to produce and still more to run on a national prime time vid-chip. The who is easy, it's Rokoff. Rokoff got to this kid. He convinced him that the Hippocratin way was the truly noble way, and turned him against us. The difficult question is where did the money come from? Wil, is the inheritance still blocked in the courts?"

Armbrister had faded back to a mild crimson, "Absolutely, won't even have a hearing date for months. Maybe it's the Chen kid."

"Possible, but I doubt it. We know that he has been contributing some, but just small amounts. He is too fond of his jet-set lifestyle and lavishing money on his Hollywood friends to really get involved; at least that's my reading on him."

"Well we need to be aware of him. He's a wild card in the game."

"Indeed, but right now we have to figure out how to break it to our friends in there. If we don't, they'll find out for themselves soon enough. Maybe together we can figure out a way to control the damage."

CHAPTER
20

"Georgi baby, I'm tellin' ya this will be the biggest thing to hit the holo-cinema in decades. The whole idea of space and the moon has got everybody talking. One third believe that there truly is a curse, one third think the whole things a conspiracy to keep us from progress, and the rest think the space agency is incompetent. We can play up any of those angles and have a great plot line. That's if we even need a plot line. With the images we can project based on your descriptions and the writings of the others on that expedition, we'll have 'em lining up just to be able to see and feel what you experienced on the moon."

"Listen Sid, I know that you're a great producer, and my friend, but the death of my father, brother, and the others is still fresh. I don't want to cheapen their memory by sensationalizing what we did."

"You know my work Georgi. I won't dishonor them, I'll honor them. No cheap shots. What all of you did was great and everyone should know about it. I'm telling you it will be spectacular."

"If you're going to do this I want to have some kind of advisory role. If there is something I don't like, I want to be able to veto it or have it modified."

"Whoa, you're asking for a lot. Sid Lescher never gives away that kind of authority."

"I feel strongly about this and I'm not going to change my mind. If you agree to my terms I will guarantee you exclusive rights to the story."

"I thought you were just a party guy, seems like you know your way around business. I just might go along with this if you do one more thing for me."

"What's that?"

"Give me access to the artifacts, all that stuff you've got in that warehouse. I want to use them in the holo-images, I want to display some of them in the theaters and in travelling exhibits."

"Sid, that warehouse is full of invaluable items. I'm not just going to sign them over to you. It would take years just to catalog and appraise the contents."

"I don't want title to the stuff, I just want to be able to use it. We'll catalog it for you. After we're done it all goes back. I'll let you decide if any items can't be used, and I'll pay well for the rights to use the stuff."

"Well, I guess that would be okay. Why don't you draft a contract and I'll have my attorney review it. If she says the basic principles coincide with my wishes then we can talk dollars."

"Beautiful, I knew we could make this happen. Listen, why don't you drop by my place tonight. I'm having a little get together, the usual crowd, and there's this one girl that's dying to meet you. Told me so herself, and baby she's a knock-out."

CHAPTER
21

Sara's apartment was small and cluttered. It wasn't that there was that much in it, but there had been no attempt at creating order. You entered through a small food preparation center. It was actually a corridor with one wall containing cabinets above and below a counter level work area. On the counter was a basic reconstitution and microwave unit for rehydrating and heating the variety of prepackaged meals that most people referred to as cuisine. To the left of that was a small sink with a standard water faucet as well as a sterilized and purified faucet. Closest to the door was the disposal and recycling unit which was capable of separating reusables from small the amounts of true waste material. In one of the lower cabinets was a cooler-wave used for quick chilling those items which were preferred to be served cold. Nothing needed refrigeration since everything was stored in dehydrated form. The counter was littered with opened and unopened food packages and recyclable dishes that had been dirtied, but not yet put into the recycler.

Michael pushed aside a portion of the mess and made a spot for his bean grinder and coffee maker. He shook his head as he surveyed the general disarray and clutter. Compared to his former kitchen, which he had managed to rig for "real cooking", this was like a tight shoe. He began to doubt his wisdom in accepting

Sara's offer to move in, at least as she put it, "until he got a better offer."

The next room in the linear apartment was a small living area on one wall was a couch that could fold out to a bed. Several large pillows were strewn on the floor and a holo-vid unit sat in the corner. Sara's medical books were scattered around the room as was an odd item of clothing. Beyond the living room was the bedroom and bathroom. Michael figured he could squeeze in a small dresser and get a few of his things in the closet. He didn't really have much of a wardrobe. Until recently he only needed his jumpsuits for work and kept a few things for outside activities.

Michael wondered what it would be like living with Sara. They certainly had developed a close relationship in the year since he had first met her. They studied together, verbally spared, and when the mood was right made love, but they had always maintained their separate residences and identities. The longest time they had been with each other exclusively was a three day week-end they had spent in Destin. Other than that it was rare that they spent more than a single night together, each going their own way in the morning.

Michael was surprised by how many things about Sara he still didn't know, and certainly many things he didn't understand. He knew little of Sara's family or her childhood. He didn't really know what she did with her time when they weren't with Rokoff, or together. Tonight for instance she was out and had told him to get settled and not wait up because she would be late. He knew she went to some "philosophy group" which she told him wouldn't interest him. When he said he might like to come once to see what it was like she had gone crazy, telling him that she needed to have some things in her life that were hers alone and not do everything together. She had been so adamant that he decided to drop the whole thing, but figured it must be something political and involving her friends who were participating in the demonstrations.

★　★　★

The Weps meeting that night was in the back room of a quiet restaurant in what once was called the Garden District. More recently it was referred to as the Garbage District. The once proud mansions that lined St. Charles has fallen into disrepair as the wealthy fled the crime in that area in the mid-twenty first century and moved to the now more fashionable North Shore and Westbank. The restaurant was considered somewhat trendy by those who now were venturing back into the district as attempts at revitalization began. The streetcar was once again running as far as Washington Avenue. No longer did they clatter on the tracks as in previous times, but rather hovered slightly above the neutral ground as they slid along St. Charles Ave. The crowds still were relatively sparse and the owner was happy to have the group meet in his back room since they ordered food and paid in cash. He didn't ask questions when they stipulated that once the food was served that they be left alone. He happily filled the beer pitchers when one of the group brought them out. He refrained from asking why one of them wore red and blue pajamas with a mask over his face.

The meeting as always was run by Plato who began with an update on recent actions.

"The CHA has at least for the moment been dealt a set-back. As you know Walters popularity had been soaring as he manipulated the media at every possible turn. At least until he stumbled with that stunt at the Med–Met center. I must say I was quite surprised by the Hippocratin maneuver and counter advertising. I didn't think they had the creativity or the funds. Someone must be supplying them with the money to keep those spots on the air. As a result of these spots the Hippocatens have made major gains in the opinion poll, and this Guidry character is a major celeb. All the talk vids are after him for interviews and people are lining up at Rokoff's clinic to see the "Vidi-Doctor".

"Any chance we could recruit this guy?" A woman in a green dress, that Sara had seen at a few of the meetings, was speaking. "He could use those talk-vids to really push our agenda."

"I think it would be risky to approach this young man. We have done some research on him and the move from Med-Met appears to have been a difficult decision for him, I don't think he's quite ready for some of our methods. In addition he is being quite useful to us at the present and my sources tell me he may have already helped us in other ways." Plato was clearly looking at Sara as he finished his discussion of Michael. "Now the next item is to determine how we proceed with our disruption of Med-Met."

Alpha quickly jumped to his feet, "I still think that we need to get rid of Walters. Without him the heart is cut of the CHA".

"Alpha, don't you ever have anything else to say." Spiderman had been leaning against the wall in the corner. The bottom of his mask was curled up so that he could sip his beer. "Plato has explained over and over that Walters is just a figure head, a poster boy, and that things would still go on without him. Secondly, if he were killed they would have a martyr and things would be worse."

"I wish for once you would tell us what to do, rather than what not to do." Alpha pointed his finger in Spiderman's face and flicked at his mask, causing Spiderman to spill his beer as he pushed the hand away. "Anyway, if that's the case then why don't we get a martyr."

"I'm not sure I follow you." Plato addressed Alpha as he tried to draw his attention away from the conflict with Spiderman. "How do we get a martyr?"

"It's simple the CHA puts out a contract on somebody like Rokoff, or the Guidry kid. At least it looks like a CHA hit. After all, they've got plenty of reason to be ticked off at the Hippocratins right now."

Sara jumped from her seat, "Listen, I am not opposed to action, but what you are proposing is murdering an individual from a group that has some of the same aims and beliefs that we are fighting for. You think that's going to help us?"

"Hey, don't jump down my throat. Sometimes there needs to be some sacrifice in order to obtain the objective. In those cases the end justifies the means. If you've got a better idea I'd love to hear it."

"Alpha, I think Curie may just have some information that can help us." Plato once again attempted to take control of the meeting. "Curie has provided me with a report that provides us some crucial insight into the Med-Met operations. If she would be so kind I would like her to summarize the report for the group."

"Well, I'm not sure how the information I have gathered will help, but I will summarize the parts that Plato feels is the most important. As you know, the New Orleans Med-Met facility serves as a regional center. As a regional center the main data storage for about one-quarter of the country is here. The active memory contains all the patient records for this region, as well as all the information regarding diseases, infectious organisms, surgical procedures, etc. Back-up is provided each day by transmitting a copy of the files to the main national storage bank. This allows records to be available on a patient no matter where they go in the country. The only thing not transferred is the current terminal patient list. This is, or was before the New York incident, considered to be a relatively short term list not needing duplication. When the system was first set-up memory capacity was far less than our current equipment. In order to keep the regional systems from getting overloaded they set-up a procedure where the records of any patients not seen in a ten year period are purged from the regional system and only kept in the main national storage system. Additionally, any disease that is not seen or reported to a Med-Met facility in a thirty year period is deleted from the regional centers and only stored in the back-up. Interestingly, despite the tremendous advances in storage capacity they have continued to use these timed information purges Older data is only stored on the national system. This back up data was what allowed the New York facility to get back on line so fast. All they lost was the list of active terminals, and as you know that list is now backed up daily."

"So what you're saying," the lady in green interrupted, "is that the best we could do locally is muck things up for a few hours. It would seem that the ideal thing would be to get to the main storage. Do we know where it is?"

"That's an excellent point," Sara continued. "We do know where it is. It is right up the road in Baton Rouge. Although I'm not quite sure how we can get access to it."

"Thank you Curie, I'll take it from here." Plato once again took over. "After receiving Curie's report I consulted with some of our sympathizers who are well versed in computers and computer sabotage. They were the ones who designed the virus that infected the New York system. With our new information they believe we can get to the main system. While the other three regions are linked to Baton Rouge by satellite New Orleans is still linked directly by fiber optics, part of the old LONI system, thus making it much easier to transfer a virus. A similar virus to the New York strain will be introduced here in New Orleans. If our colleagues are correct in their design it will infect the main system as well."

The group began to show increased interest and there were numerous side conversations. Someone else asked how the virus would be introduced into the system.

"Well actually, it is rather simple. Each of us has our individual data chip. That is our initial link to the Med–Met computer system. These chips provide basic demographic information so that the system can then track our records and have our necessary history, billing information, and other pertinent data. These chips are supposed to be read only, and cannot be altered without destroying them. Our friends have found a way to change them, without disabling them and can encode the virus such that when the chip is accessed the virus is transferred. In order to get it to reach the main system we will use a person who has not been at a Med–Met facility in over ten years, and then when the main data base is accessed the virus will be transferred to Baton Rouge."

There was a general sense of approval in the room as the meeting broke up. Small groups continued discussing the pros and cons of the plan. Alpha and few others had their doubts and still wanted a bolder plan, as they left they continued discussing the martyr option.

CHAPTER
22

"Georgi Chen, I'd like you to meet Alexandra Hemingway. Alex is a big fan of yours, Fascinated by the whole lunar thing."

Georgi who had become accustomed to the Hollywood scene was used to seeing beautiful women by the dozen but was still struck speechless by Alexandra. She was taller than he, with straight golden hair that rested on her perfectly tanned shoulder. Her shoulders, arms, back, and legs were perfectly cut giving an image of health and power. This was countered by large blue eyes and soft full lips highlighted by pink lipstick which appeared to be the only makeup she wore or needed. Georgi just stood there and stared.

"Hello Mr. Chen, I have really been looking forward to meeting you."

"Uh, yes Ms. Uh…"

"Alex, call me Alex."

"Oh sure, and please call me Georgi. Wow, you are gorgeous. Are you an actress, have you been in any of Sid's films? No, that's not possible I wouldn't have forgotten you."

"No, I'm not in films, but thanks for the complement. I'm afraid I'm too self-conscious to go before the camera."

"Well, would it be impertinent to ask what you do?"

"Not at all, I am in the security business. I provide security for people who need it, or want it, but do not want the appearance of a traditional body guard. When I'm walking with a man people don't usually assume that I am there to protect him. It has its advantages. Enough about me, there is so much I want to ask you."

Sid had quietly slipped away as Alex and Georgi became absorbed with each other. After all, with the type of money she had mentioned investing in his next project, he could accommodate her in this simple request. He wasn't sure what she wanted with Georgi, she didn't appear to be a gold digger; she seemed to have plenty of money of her own. Maybe she was just one of those moon groupies.

"I'm not that interesting. Everything about me has been all over the news and vid-chips. You know, *'Lucky son stays behind, avoids space catastrophe'* and *'Moon heir finds happiness amongst the stars, in Hollywood'.* There's not much more to it than that, just hanging out and taking it one day at a time. No big whoop."

"Well Mr. Chen, I am not going to let you get away so easily. I plan to find out for myself if there is more than the vid-chip image. I have a feeling that the real Georgi Chen is hiding and I am going to find him."

"What makes you think I'm more than a rich, spoiled loser? That's what everyone else is saying."

"Let's say I have my hunches, and I have my sources. So, how about we slip out of here and I treat you to dinner?"

"You treat me? That's quite a change; I was beginning to think my name was, 'Georgi will get the check'. Let's get out of here Ms. Hemingway; I'm in the mood for some fresh air."

Later that night as Georgi lay spent and asleep in Alex' bed she slipped quietly into another room and made a call. "Contact initiated, proceeding with assignment." She then quietly slipped back to bed and joined Georgi beneath the sheets.

CHAPTER

23

Walters took the call at his CHA headquarters, "Angela, how is my successor doing?"

"Terrible Darren, there has been a major disruption in the computer system, all signs point to sabotage. The entire list of active terminal clients is gone. Not only here but in New York, Chicago and Seattle as well."

"Angela, get a grip. Sounds like the same thing that happened in New York the last time, it took them less than twenty-four hours to download a copy from Baton Rouge. Looks like the hippies managed to coordinate hits at all four regionals. All we need to do is replace the data, fire the damn computer security firm and hire one that knows what they're doing."

"It's not that simple, we haven't been able to get anything out of Baton Rouge."

"What do you mean?"

"Just what I said, we sent a computer inquiry for the back up and all we get is a blinking cursor and an error message. We tried to call them and there is no answer. Frankly, Darren it's got me worried."

"All right, order up a hover limo get a hold of Biggs from I.T. and pick me and Wil up at CHA. We'll take a quick trip up to Baton Rouge."

When the limo pulled up at CHA Walters and Armbrister were waiting outside. As the door opened they quickly slid inside. The door sealed and the limo zipped off for the 20 minute ride to Baton Rouge. Inside were Angela and a huge man, 6"4" and over 300 lbs. Darren greeted Angela and then introduced the large man to Armbrister. "Wil Armbrister, Biggy Biggs. Biggy knows everything there is to know about the Med-Met computer system. As head of medical records it's unlikely that he would have had any reason to need your P.R. services."

"Yeah, but I sure couldn't miss seeing him around. Nice to meet you Biggs."

"Call me Biggy, it really beats Horace."

Walters jumped back in, "Okay Biggy what's the scoop. Give me your analysis of the situation."

"So far it looks pretty bad, our local records are wiped. The terminal list gone, all the work-ups in progress gone, and our client's records gone. No damage to the computer system, but the memories basically empty. It's like the last virus to hit New Your, but a more complete job. It got around the anti-virus installed after New York. Kind of like it developed a resistance gene."

"And Baton Rouge?"

"We still don't have a clue, no contact. The computer doesn't respond and we don't know if that's a problem up there, or coming from our end. Can't get them by communicator, but that's not surprising as the communications systems are linked through the computers, and the place is shielded against external signals. We won't know till we get there."

"So, what's the worst case scenario?"

"Worst case, Baton Rouge is wiped and we have no back up. The terminal list is gone and if one of the designated doesn't return, we have no way of getting them back. The work-ups in progress are lost and people will have to have their studies done again. The only medical records will be on an individual's identi-chip. That can be accessed when they next come in. Except for some basic childhood data like immunization, all the stuff more than 10 years old is gone. A patient who hasn't been to Med–Met in the past 10 years basically has no records. The archives and the historical information is gone.

"The good news is that the operating systems and diagnostics were untouched and ready to go immediately."

The scene at the Baton Rouge center was pure chaos. People ran through the corridors pushing carts full of equipment, co-workers argued and computer screens showed nothing but blinking cursors. Biggs led the group directly to the main control room where the activity was the most feverish. A small neatly dressed gray haired woman set in the middle of the activity vainly attempting to get a response from the system.

"Jane, what's the situation?"

"Oh thank goodness you're here Biggy, I can't get any response from the system. Nothing, nada, zippo. Do you have any idea what happened?"

"Well it looks like an infection, its hit all four regions. It seems to be a coordinated attack. We know from the New York incident that it can be brought in by a client, but that doesn't explain how it got in here. We need to think about an inside job, where's your security chief?"

"He's around somewhere, but everyone here has the highest clearance. Do you really think it could be someone on the staff?"

"After Guidry in New Orleans, we can't be sure of anyone."

Walters leaned in, "What now?"

"It's going to take some time to figure this one out Mr. Walters, Jane and I have a lot of work to do. First task is to reestablish communications with the regions so that we can get a good handle on the sequence of events. I don't think there's anything you and Mr. Armbrister can do here. You might as well head back down to the Easy."

Armbrister butted in, "We're going to have to say something to the public, not to mention our own personnel. Anybody have anything for me to go with?"

The system manager, Jane Melancon jumped in, "We can't say much, because we don't know. I would just say we have run into technical difficulties that we are working on, and that operations at Med–Met centers should proceed as normal. Our dedicated staff is working around the clock to determine what occurred."

"Not a bad start," Armbrister said. "In the meantime I will work on the spin as to how we can use this to our advantage. How to make this into a terrorist act that has threatened the very health and welfare of our citizens. You all take care of this cyber–mystery, I'm going to find us some villains. Even if I need to manufacture them."

CHAPTER
24

M ichael and Sara watched the evening news intently. "Med-Met sources announced today that there have been technical problems with the computer systems, however they are sure that all will be fully restored shortly. In the meantime they want to assure the public that all health services will be provided in an uninterrupted manner.

"At CHA headquarters spokesman Wil Armbrister issued a statement on behalf of chairman Darren Walters." The image of Armbrister appeared.

"We have reason to believe that the difficulties experienced throughout Med-Met are the result of a malicious attempt by unknown saboteurs to endanger the very health and welfare of our citizens. Fortunately the Med-Met systems have multiple layers of security, and normal services are continuing. If you are not feeling well, or are due for your regular maintenance physical go to your Med-Met facility and you will get the care you need. We at the CHA will not rest until these low life have been hunted down, exposed arrested and convicted."

"Wow," Michael said as Armbrister faded out. A commercial for Coca-Cola came on explaining how their recent attempt to change the classic formula had once again yielded public rejection, and that the old favorite was back, as good as ever. "Somebody really threw a wrench in the computer system, old Darren's got a major thorn up his butt."

"Michael, how bad do you think the damage to the system is?"

"Well, from the fact that there were remotes from all four regions and Baton Rouge, it seems like there had to be a coordinated attack on the system. All the sites had to be hit almost simultaneously. If it's like the New York hit, then the lists are lost altogether."

"That's great," Sara gushed, "all those people have been given a reprieve maybe some of them won't go back." She glanced at Michael and noticed he wasn't sharing her joy.

"What's up pre-doc? You look as though you're not happy with what happened. Didn't you want those people to have another chance?"

"Of course I did, but I'm worried about the other things that were probably wiped out. Any new diagnoses requiring treatment will be lost and people may not get the appropriate follow up. People's medical records and histories are wiped out and will have to be manually reconstructed. I don't give a damn about Med-Met, but those people aren't Med-Met. At least it sounds like the diagnostic and treatment systems are functioning, if not there would be total chaos. We don't have enough trained doctors to take over if that were to happen."

"But, sometimes drastic action has to occur before real change can be affected. In any revolution there has been hardship to endure before freedom could be achieved. It looks like this was a pretty surgical strike."

"It does this Sara, but you can never predict which parts of a system some of these viruses can affect. It's a crap shoot. Anyway we're probably going to have a busy day at the clinic tomorrow. A combination of new patients who are going to use this as an excuse to jump from Med-Met, and harassment from the CHA as a backlash. Let's get some sleep."

The next morning Sara awoke before Michael. As per her usual routine, she checked the classifieds in the morning vid-chip. There in the help wanted section was a short, but clear, message, it read, *WANTED: Traveling companion, must be able to leave on short notice. Contact Mr. Plato.* Sara quickly withdrew the chip threw on a pair of sweats and rushed out the door.

Sara wove her way down Bourbon Street, through the mixture of early morning people on their way to work and those left over from the night before. The past and current heartbeat of New Orleans emanated from the central street of the French Quarter. A sanitized version now existed where once jazz clubs, strip joints and tee-shirts shops lined the lower floors and original wrought iron balconies the upper decks. The Quarter had been recreated to resemble what had stood for over two hundred years, but now was a computerized version built by Disney Louisiana after the first version began to crumble in the early years of the 21st century. As she passed Al Hirt's the robotic image of the great trumpeter stood in the doorway blasting out a classic Hirt rendition of "When the Saints Go Marching In". A sidewalk bar advertised "Original Hurricanes". The current version contained lots of fruit juice but less alcohol than its namesake. As she passed through the doorway of the Voodoo Museum, she thought it quite ironic that this was the location chosen for emergency meetings. Considering how she and her Hippocratin colleagues had been accused of witchery and voodoo.

Sara barely noticed the shelves of plastic voodoo souvenirs, incense and books on the history and practice of voodoo. In the back room of the narrow museum a mannequin of a gypsy shuffled tarot cards, a velvet cord separated it from the rest of the room. After checking to be sure no one was watching, Sara crossed over the rope and quickly slipped behind the robotic gypsy, who continued to slowly scan her cards. Behind the curtain was a dark narrow space. As Sara's eyes adjusted to the dim light she was able to make out the outline of a door. She knocked gently heard a faint whir and knew she was being scanned. The door slid back to reveal a small windowless room, Plato and Spiderman sat at a small table. "Sara, thank god you made it. As far as I can tell we are the only ones who have not been arrested." Plato was visibly shaken. "By reviewing their video tapes at the regional centers at the time the system went down, Med–Met has been able to identify the individuals who planted the virus. Apparently their private security forces used CIA type interrogation methods, including truth drugs to extract whatever information they could. Although we had done everything possible to hide our identities even from each other, some people were still recognized. Most of us knew who you were for a long time Sara. You've been seen with Rokoff. Once they broke the first person it led to others and things began to fall like dominoes. Apparently some of our members here and elsewhere secretly took pictures at the meetings, and used them to buy their own freedom. Only those like Spiderman here are safe, unless of course he parades around in those togs in public."

"What the hell are we supposed to do now, and being that you know me, who are you?"

"One thing at a time. First of all my name is Richard Dietrich, I once worked for NASA and invented the chip which allows the Surgi-unit to perform precision movements. It was intended to facilitate continuous upgrading in order to have ongoing improvement in surgical technique and disease treatment. When Med–Met took it over they halted all development, they were satisfied with things the way they were. For the past ten years I have been Med–Met Manager for Surgi-Unit maintenance. I guess I don't have to put up with that crap anymore.

"As for what we do now, there is a ranch in at a secret location that has been prepared for this eventuality. Only a few of us know its location, and as far as we can tell, the location has not been blown. The plan is for the remaining members of the groups that have been exposed to go to ground at the ranch."

"How much time do we have to get ready?"

"Sorry Sara, I don't think we have any. If you return home you're likely to be arrested. I have a car waiting in the courtyard, we'll wait another hour. If no other members show, we're out of here."

"But what about my things, my friends?"

"You'll have to do without your possessions, as for as your friends its best for them if you stay as clear as possible. They are probably going to have to go through a lot of grief as it is for having known you. They will be under suspicion."

"Spiderman is going to stay behind and remain our local contact. He can get a simple message to your friends, but please nothing about where we are going." Just then a buzzer sounded, a look at the vid screen showed Alpha at the door. "Alpha made it. Better write your message, we need to get rolling."

CHAPTER
25

Sid Lescher hit the speaker button on his phone, "Sid, its Georgi. Man, I really want to thank you. Alex is incredible. She's the best thing that's happened to me in ages, I feel alive again."

Sid smiled to himself, "Fantastic, so now you owe me. Are you ready to make a movie with me?"

"Could be Sid, but there are a two conditions."

"OY, more conditions. I already told you that you could review the content and have say over which artifacts we us. What kind are we talking about now?"

"First there's money, not that I need it myself, but I want to establish a foundation to honor my father, brother and the members of the lunar expedition. The foundation will support two main loves of my father, the preservation of literature in book form, and the art and practice of medicine. So even though I'm already a rich man I'm not going to let you off cheaply."

"Alright we bargain, like mensches. I say one number, you have another and we go back and forth until we find a number we can both live with. But you said two conditions, what's the other?"

"Alex has to have a major role. She can be one of the women on the expedition, we'll embellish her part, attribute more of the activity to her. I think she has star potential and I want her to be part of everything I do."

"Does Alex want this?"

"Oh yeah, I talked with her before I called you. She is ready, willing, and I do believe able."

"Well, if looks and confidence count she's got it all. I promise we'll put her in the movie, but how big her part is has got to depend on her acting ability. If she can handle it she'll be a star. After all I am Big Sid, star-maker and dream-king."

★ ★ ★

Across town Captain Alexandra Hemingway reported to her superior. "Yes sir, they are proceeding with the film, and I will be part of it."

"Good, that should put you in proximity of the materials brought back from the moon. Despite all our resources we have not been able to get close to the warehouse where the stuff is stored. If they go ahead with the movie they're going to want to use a lot of the real goods in the film. That will be a big promotional angle. This will give you the opportunity to find out just how far they've gotten, and if anything they brought back is of danger to us."

CHAPTER

26

Michael was tending to a ten year old who had gotten a large shard of glass in his palm. The boy had fallen holding a jar of bugs he had collected to gross out his sister. Michael had removed the glass, scrubbed the wound with betadine and was finishing the last of five stitches when he noticed a disheveled man limp into the clinic. The man was dirty, his clothes torn and his left foot seemed to turn inward and drag as he walked.

Michael called the nurse over and asked her to finish dressing the wound while he went and dealt with the man. He patted the boy on the head, shook his good hand and walked over to the man. "Can I help you, Sir?"

The man grunted again and pointed to the curtained partition. "You want to go over there?" Michael asked.

The man gave a half nod and started across the room, dragging his foot. Michael walked along at his side. He noticed something wasn't right, but he wasn't sure what it was. The man looked like the typical "garbage district" derelict. He looked sixty and was probably no more than fifty. His hair was in total disarray, his face and hands covered in grime, his clothes tattered and far too large for him. As they moved into the enclosed space Michael prepared himself for the expected odor of the unwashed street dweller, and then realized that was what was wrong. The man didn't smell bad. Before he could make anything of it the patient thrust a wadded piece of paper at Michael and made another grunting sound.

As he unfolded the paper, Michael recognized Sara's handwriting. He began to read and didn't notice as the man quietly slipped out of the cubicle.

Dear Michael,

I don't know how to start. By now I have left New Orleans. If you don't yet know why I'm sure you will soon. To put it succinctly I have been a bad girl. Remember those meetings I used to go to? Well, I have been part of a group that hasn't been satisfied with the pace of change. We have been working to make things happen, and one of those things was the crash of the Med-Met computer system. We thought we couldn't be traced, but obviously we were wrong. They identified several of us, myself included. The man who delivered this note was a member of our group, but he had always been in costume and not recognized. Stay well and study hard. Please tell Jacob that I am sorry.

S

CHAPTER
27

Wil addressed the CHA. "Here's the latest. The police have managed to arrest several of the Weps who were involved in the sabotage of the other regional centers. Unfortunately they haven't done as well here in New Orleans where as you know the main virus was entered. They have apprehended the individual who planted the bug, but she has not been able to give them any leads on where the others may have gone. As you know Dietrich, Anson and Jeffers have not been located, and there was also some clown in blue and red pajamas whose identity we don't know."

"Any leads on catching the others?" Darren asked.

"Well, nothing yet, but if we lean on the Hippies we may be able to get a lead on Anson. That bastard Guidry was living with her. I think that explains his motivation for screwing us. One good screw deserves another. Our friends at the police are looking for Guidry now, if he knows anything they'll get it out of him.

"Okay, next order of business. The elections are just a year away. I think it's time to get the push going to elect friendly candidates. Initially we line up our friends and financing. We can use the current events to emphasize the need to eliminate all forms of alternative health care. Anson's association with the Hippocratins will make it easy. We infer that the Weps and the Hippocratins are just two arms of the same octopus, and that we need to kill the entire beast. Not just cut off an arm or two. We point out that they've demonstrated no concern for the health of the public, or else they never would have jeopardized the Med–Met patients by damaging the computer system."

★   ★   ★

Michael arrived back at Jacob's shortly before the others were due for class. Jacob greeted him at the door. "There are police here; they're waiting inside for you."

Two stereotypical detectives in poorly fitting suits, one white, one black, were waiting on the couch, staring at the door to Clarence's refrigerator. They turned as Michael came in, got up and turned to face him.

"Michael Guidry," the older and fatter of the two addressed Michael, "we would like to ask you some questions."

Jacob stood up to his full height and stood between Michael and the detective. "Should Mr. Guidry have an attorney, detective ah, I didn't catch your name."

"It's Beatty, this is my partner Sergeant Jackson. As far as needing an attorney, only if he's guilty of something. We just want to ask some questions."

"Well, go right ahead Detective Beatty. Class doesn't start for another half hour, until then we're all yours."

"Dr. Rokoff, if you don't mind we'd like to talk to Mr. Guidry at the station. Also we'd prefer to not have you present, we may want to speak with you separately, later."

"In that case I feel obligated to advise my student not to answer any questions until our attorney arrives. I'm sure you gentleman understand. There are some who think that there is something criminal about our practice of medicine. I just want to make sure that Mr. Guidry isn't held accountable for things he hasn't done, just because of his associations."

"Yeah sure Doc, don't worry we sent our rubber hoses out for repair."

"Very well," he turned to Michael. "I'll call Mr. Mandel and have him meet you at the station."

The detectives hustled Michael out. They didn't exactly man handle him but they weren't courteous. In the cruiser on the way to the 'Vieux Carre' station they tried their best at "subtle" questioning.

"I saw some pictures of the Anson woman." Beatty turned to look at Michael and winked. "Good looking girl doesn't look like a terrorist. You been living with her for a long time?" Michael sat staring straight ahead, not responding to the detective's question. "Come on, I mean just because you're doing it with the girl doesn't mean you're a radical creep too. I can understand it if you pretended not to see certain things in order to keep a good thing going. No one would blame you. And she's gone now, you got to move on. Best way to do that is come clean. Clear things up for yourself, and then you can start over. I mean you don't need lots of hassles for some babe who left you to take the heat. Right?"

Michael continued to stare ahead and when he spoke it was just to ask how long this was going to take, and would he be able to get back to class. The detectives finally gave up and just drove. At the station house they once again tried unsuccessfully to get Michael talking. They finally gave up and placed him in a bare room with a wooden table and four chairs to wait by himself, until his attorney arrived.

Mandel showed up about an hour later. He was around forty, in good shape with sandy hair and a receding hairline. His suit was well pressed, and he didn't look at all put-out about coming out at nine in the evening. The detectives began to follow him in to the room, but Mandel turned on them and politely, but firmly said, "Gentleman, I need a few moments alone with my client."

When they were alone, Mandel spun one of the chairs around and straddled the seat leaning forward on the chair back. "So Doc, we meet again. The boys gave me an earful on the way in. Say they got a good case on you for conspiracy. They say they found your stuff all over her apartment, and how you already got a history of causing trouble for Med–Met. With that televised resignation and all. Kind of intimated that if you didn't play ball with them they were going to hold you.

"So, how much of its true, and how much is fertilizer?"

Michael was red faced, "This is all a pile of crap. I didn't have any idea what Sara was doing. I knew she was hot headed, but I never knew she was into that stuff. We were classmates, friends, and lovers, but she kept it all a secret."

"If you say so, but they're going to have trouble buying that. They figure you're doing it with a woman, living with her, you know what she's up to."

"Well I didn't damn it. I can't believe it myself."

"I think they're going to try and hold you unless you give them something. If they don't have any leads on her they'll keep you to show that they aren't just sitting on their hands. Walters is putting pressure on them. It looks like his group really wants to make a big deal out of Sara's being a Hippocratin student. Their mouth piece Armbrister has already been all over the vids implying that the Weatherpersons are a sub-group of the Hippocratins. They can't get to Rokoff, so they are going after you.

"From my perspective, if you know anything you should tell them and then they can let you go. They get to make a statement, say they're making progress and the heats off them. So if you have any idea which direction she went, where she kept her secret papers, anything, it could help get you out of here."

"Look, I don't know a thing. I have no idea where she went, and I didn't know anything about this group. If I did know anything, I doubt if I would tell them anyway."

"Well, we better let them in and get this questioning done with. I think Jacob is already working on bail."

CHAPTER
28

The man in the chair gazed out his window. The captain, Alexandra Hemingway, had reported that all was progressing as planned with Georgi Chen. He had certainly become infatuated with her and was beginning to trust her. He had opened up to her about what he and his colleagues had seen at Infinity. Importantly, he was asking her advice on the movie project.

The man, Justin Riser, was also known as "The General". He had been responsible for designing and overseeing the security systems at Infinity. He was one of the few living people who knew all of Infinity's secrets, including what was behind the high security door in Corridor A. The others were all highly placed officials of the government and the industries that had conceived and funded Infinity. By design and necessity, they remained anonymous and only the General knew who they all were. Board meetings were held by vid-link and identities were concealed. Infinity might more aptly been named Phoenix, for the General knew that it was only a matter of time before it would rise.

★   ★   ★

Georgi sat at his desk staring at the video screen reviewing a concept enactment of "The Last Mission", the story of the Chen Lunar Salvage Expedition.

Alex stirred in bed covered by a sheet except for a long perfectly sculpted and tanned leg that lay exposed and inviting. Georgi looked over, "Oh, you're awake. I hope I didn't disturb you. I wanted to check out the latest concepts that Sid sent over. I think it is coming together, but I want you to look at it after and give me your thoughts."

"I'll be happy to," she said as she rose from the bed wrapping the cover sheet around her. "Did you ever notice in the vids when a couple has been in bed together, when the woman gets up she gathers the sheets around her, or the guy somehow manages to pull on boxers before the camera does a full body shot?" As she said this she walked toward him and let the sheet fall from her perfect body. "Well, don't," she said as she came up behind him, her breasts pressing on his neck and she leaned in and whispered, "Let them do that in our film."

★　★　★

It was one in the morning when the police finally quit questioning Michael. Following Mandel's advice he had given up the note from Sara. It gave no clue as to her whereabouts, and pretty much cleared him of complicity. His description of the derelict who delivered the note gave them, and the computer reconstruction artists, something to work on, but would be unlikely to lead anywhere.

Beatty and Jackson left Michael and Mandel in the interview room. "So Jacks, what do you think? Do we charge him?"

"I don't think so. The letter seems to make it pretty clear that he wasn't involved. Let's run it by the Lieutenant."

Lieutenant Andrew Livingston listened intently as Beatty and Jackson reviewed the interrogation, and then he read Sara's letter. "I tend to agree with Jackson, the letter makes it seem like he was ignorant of what she was doing."

Beatty jumped in, "sure, but what if the letter is bogus? What if they had set it up to provide cover? I'm tellin' you Lieutenant if we can book this hookey pookey "Dr." Guidry and lean on him, he'll give her up."

"Did you say Guidry?"

"Yeah, Michael Guidry, one of the hippie doctors."

Livingston put down the letter and focused on his detectives, "Let him go."

Beatty looked incredulous, "Lieutenant you just want us to cut him loose?"

"Yes, even if we charge him the judge may let him walk without bail, based on the letter. You can keep an eye on him and if there is further contact you might be able to track down the rest of them. But, I don't think that will happen, Guidry is a good kid."

"You know him?"

"Not personally, but do you remember my mother-in-law?"

Jackson jumped in, "you mean Lettie? Sure, all the guys knew her. She was always baked stuff for us. Only person I knew who still baked from scratch."

"Well, you remember when she got sick, and all she talked about was her doctor."

"Oh yeah, the way she talked about him he must have been some kind of saint. I would like to meet that guy some day."

Livingston smiled, "You just did. That young man you are holding is 'Saint Michael Guidry'. He gave Lettie two good years that she wouldn't have had. He made it real easy when her time came. Unless you've got more, he walks."

Michael and Mandel sat in the interview room and when the door opened, rather than Beatty or Jackson, a tall graying gentleman in a well tailored suit walked in.

"Mr. Mandel, Dr. Guidry, I am Lieutenant Andy Livingston. First let me apologize for having kept you so long. I have spoken with Detectives Beatty and Jackson and you are free to go.

"Here is my card. If you are contacted again by Ms. Anson or any other members of the Weps please contact me directly."

Michael was dumbstruck, Mandel took the card and stared at Livingston. "Just like that, no more questions. What's up?"

"Nothing is up Mr. Mandel, it's just that character counts in my book." He opened the door and escorted them out.

"That was weird." Michael said when they were safely in Mandel's car. "Did you notice how nice he was? He even called me doctor none of the other cops did."

I know Mike, and that thing about character, sure you haven't met him before?"

"Not that I remember and I am pretty good with faces."

"Watch yourself Mike, because they sure as hell are going to. Keep your eyes open and try to avoid contact with Sara and her people, for your sake as well as theirs"

CHAPTER
29

On a deserted ranch in East Texas, Sara, Plato, Alpha and Spiderman were being joined by increasing numbers of Weps from other areas of the country who had slipped by the national round-up. It was a slow process as all previous group-wide communication methods had to be abandoned for fear of leaks from those arrested. A tedious back-up of individualized contact was initiated. Slowly, more and more members arrived.

Plato as the highest ranking member not arrested assumed leadership of the assembly. Factions however were quickly forming. Alpha was among those gravitating to the fringe that advocated for violent action. Sara chose to stay close to Plato and those who felt it best to keep a low profile and rebuild strength.

"Are we just going to hide out and lick our wounds?" Alpha addressed the group gathered in the converted barn that served as a meeting hall. "If we don't do something, something dramatic, they will think that they have won. That they have cut our hearts out."

A small group of his supporters shook their fists and made hooting sounds. Plato rose, "You're right on one point, they will think they have won. They will be complacent and eventually lower their guard. In the meantime we can gather strength, resupply, find more members and formulate a solid plan."

"Plato makes sense," added a tall balding man from New York, who was just called Bob. "I know that there are others from my chapter who are still out there and need to make their way here. If we take action now and lose anyone else we will never recover."

Alpha and his group were on their feet, "what a bunch of old women," one said. "Pussies," another shouted as they left the barn.

As the rest of the crowd dispersed, Plato stood with Sara and Bob. "They worry me. They aren't thinking clearly. I just hope that they don't do anything that jeopardizes the rest of us, and helps our opponents in the process."

★   ★   ★

In the months since Sara disappeared Michael concentrated on his studies, and other than Jacob and his classmates, kept to himself. Eventually, after the police had finished with Sara's apartment, he was allowed to move back in. They had confiscated everything including his books and coffee maker. He was just getting home when he noticed movement.

She came out of nowhere, and suddenly she was there. About 5 feet tall, a little over 100 lbs. light blond hair flowing all over and what appeared to be an endless supply of energy.

"Hi, are you Michael Guidry? I'm Lacy, Lacy Livingston." She said as she stuck out her petite hand to shake.

Michael took it noticing that it was warm, soft and dry. Despite its size the hand shake was firm and confident. "Um, do I, or should I know you?"

"You don't, but you should," she quickly answered. "I have wanted to meet you for a long time, to thank you, for everything. I didn't know where to find you. I mean I had seen you on the Vid. It was so cool how you quit in front of everyone. That Walters nearly shit himself.

"But, to get back on track, I didn't know where you hung out, and I didn't want to bother you at work, so I didn't get a chance to say thanks."

Michael just looked at her trying to figure out what this adorable bundle of energy wanted. He barely began to open his mouth to ask when she jumped in again.

"Finally, I realized that my dad could tell me where you lived. So, I pestered him until he gave me your address, which of course he shouldn't have, but he can never say no to me." Michael wondered if she ever stopped to take a breath, "So I figured if I hung out you would eventually come home from work, and maybe you would want to get something to eat."

He felt dizzy and wasn't sure what to ask her first. "Lacy, that's what you said your name is, right?" She smiled and gave him a nod.

"Lacy, I am not sure what this is all about. You say you want to thank me, but I have no reason why you should. You mention your father and some story about getting my address, but I have no idea who your father is. Please start again. Please, please, please, go slowly."

She sighed, "OK, my dad is Andy Livingston, Lt. Livingston. Since those dorks Beatty and Jackson arrested you he has been really sorry that they had kept you for so long and treated you poorly. Especially, after all you had done for our family. That's why I had to find you and thank you."

He massaged his temples, "That gives me something to start with, but I still don't know why you want to thank me, or for that matter why your dad was so nice to me."

She frowned and furrowed her brow, "Because of Bubbie of course."

"Bubbie?"

"Bubbie, my grandma, it's a Jewish word."

"So you're Jewish?" Michael asked.

"Half, my mom is, so her mom was Bubbie, and that's why I want to thank you and why dad helped you."

This wasn't helping, the confusion mounted, "So, I know your grand... er, Bubbie?"

"Didn't dad tell you? Sometimes he gets me so mad, he never says anything."

Michael wondered if he ever got a chance.

"Anyway you did know my Bubbie. She was Lettie, Lettie Rubin, and she never stopped talking about her wonderful doctor. You gave her two great years, and she even got to come to my graduation from Tulane. She wanted me to marry you."

Michael blushed and then remembered Lettie. She had been his first patient and a significant factor in his leaving Med-Met.

Her work-up had diagnosed advanced lung cancer. The Med-Met analysis and cost benefit review assigned her to a "final visit." She had received her letter to report but when she arrived and learned that Michael wasn't there she had left and never returned.

Then when she had seen Michael in his now famous resignation Vid she took herself down to the Hippocratin clinic and confronted Rokoff.

★   ★   ★

"I want to see the doctor," she stated directly.

"Well, I am a doctor, Doctor Rokoff," Jacob answered with an amused smile. This woman reminded him of women of an earlier generation, of his mother and grandmother.

"I have heard of you, they talk about you on the Vids. They say you're a witch doctor. I don't believe them."

Jacob raised his prodigious red eyebrows. "Thank you, but can you tell me why you don't believe them."

"Two reasons, no three. First you look like my sister Charlotte's boy. Second, your name is Jacob, Jakov, a good name. But, the most important reason is if you weren't a good man, he wouldn't have come to work with you."

"He, who is he, maam?"

"The other doctor, the young one. The one who quit that no good shyster Walters in front of the whole world. My doctor, Doctor Michael."

Jacob tried hard to suppress his grin, "I see, would you be referring to Michael Guidry?"

"Yes, can I see him?"

"Well Mrs., er I didn't get your name."

"Rubin, Lettie Rubin."

"Well Mrs. Rubin, Michael is one of my students. I wonder if you would mind my seeing you along with him?"

"That would be fine Dr. Yakov as long as you understand that Dr. Michael is my doctor."

That had occurred shortly after Michael had joined Jacob. As a freshman he had not yet started seeing patients. Jacob left Lettie in the exam room and found Michael in the classroom studying with his fellow students.

"Dr. Guidry," Jacob bellowed as he entered the room, "Might I have a word with you?" All the students stopped and stared. Jacob never called the first year students doctor and Michael was the newest of the bunch.

"Yes, Jacob."

Jacob continued to play it straight. "Yes, I need your help with a patient. A lovely woman named Lettie Rubin. Apparently, she will only see her doctor Dr. Michael, but, she has agreed to allow me to assist, because I look like her sister Charlotte's boy."

"Jacob, that's the woman I told you about. The one who came to Med-Met, for the first medical care in her adult life, and insisted on calling me doctor. No matter how hard I tried to convince her that I wasn't a doctor she persisted."

"Well Michael, sometimes it isn't the diplomas on the wall that define an individual, but rather their actions. Whatever you did, for her it was what she thought a doctor would do. Come on, let's go see what is going on with her." He stopped and looked at Michael through narrowed eyes, "Don't get any big ideas though, for at least the next year she will be your only patient."

Michael and Rokoff confirmed that she had a Stage III non-small cell lung cancer. Over the following two years symptoms were controlled and her disease progression slowed by radiation and biologics.

The Med-Met economic analysis would have determined that the costs of those treatments exceeded her economic productivity. She would have been (and was) assigned to euthanasia.

Instead, she had two quality years with her family, and when the treatments no longer were effective, she died peacefully at home with the help of hospice care.

★ ★ ★

"Of course I remember your grandmother," Michael told Lacy, "she had a major impact on my decision to leave Med-Met. I even remember her talking about a granddaughter and that I should call her."

"Why didn't you?"

"Well, most importantly I was already involved."

Lacy's smile evaporated, and her chatter slowed, "Oh, you mean the girl that disappeared, the one the police are looking for. Did you guys have something special?"

"I thought we did. Now I wonder if I really knew her. I mean she had a secret life, and I was clueless."

"Listen, I don't want to make you feel uncomfortable. I understand it has only been a short while but do you want to get something to eat, or coffee, or a drink? I want to thank you, for Bubbie."

"Thanks, but it's too soon, plus I've got a lot of studying to do. Maybe another time." Michael stuck out his hand to shake hers and say goodbye.

Lacy didn't seem ready to let go, "Okay, I have another offer. Come to the house for dinner on Friday. It won't be a date and mom will get a chance to thank you also."

Michael was opening his mouth to beg off when Lacy jumped back in.

With an impish smile she said, "If you say no, I will tell my father to arrest you again. You'd better believe that my daddy gives me what I want. So, it's your choice, Friday night dinner with us, or with a hairy guy named Monk in the parish jail."

Michael felt steamrolled and speechless. He was pretty sure that if she wanted she could get him arrested. Also, the thought of seeing her again was not totally displeasing.

"OK," he sighed, "what time and where?"

"Six o'clock, here's the address." She flashed a message from her wrist band to his, stood on her toes, kissed his cheek and then bounced off down the street.

CHAPTER
30

In another part of the city Darren Walters was meeting with his leadership team. "Alright, someone give me an update on the current situation."

Joel Rogers, the treasurer of CHA, and former CFO of Med-Met moved to the front of the group. "Let's start with Med-Met volumes. Since the computer crash visits are off thirty percent in some regions. When patients are contacted, and asked their reasons for not showing about two percent are for the usual reasons. Transportation issues, things that came up with their kids, you know the stuff. About one third of the no shows are a result of the patients not getting normal reminders twenty-four hours in advance, due to system problems. The majority however said that they had lost confidence in Med-Met. If the systems could be damaged that easily who knows what might happen, diagnoses switched, treatments messed up and maybe even incorrect final diagnosis. It is hurting the election campaign as well. Most of our candidates have dropped several points in the polls."

"Wil," Darren said, "How are we going to counter this?"

Wil Armbrister addressed the group slowly and thoughtfully, in sharp contrast to his usual blustery style, "Right now we have a situation where Med-Met is perceived as incompetent. Instead of focusing on the culprit, the public is focusing on the victim, and not in a positive way. We need to turn that around. We need to get the public focused on the real enemy"

Rogers asked, "You mean the people they've arrested, and the few that still remain at large?"

"Yes, they are obvious, but they aren't necessarily the best villains. They come from many walks of life, people in all different professions. A good many of them actually worked for Med–Met. The public looks at them and sees themselves and maybe begin to wonder, 'what did they see that we're missing.' Besides that they are already behind bars and the trial is a long way off, best that we don't focus on them.

"Instead," Wil continued, "we have to shift the focus to another group, and gain another advantage in the process. We need to move the blame to the Hippies. That will not only take the pressure off of Med–Met, but also damage their growing popularity."

"That sounds good, but do we have evidence that the Hippocratins were involved?"

Wil smiled, "Well, we know that the Anson woman was involved, and some of those that were arrested have Hippie ties. We don't need evidence, we just need insinuation. We point out the few individuals who have ties to both the Hippies and the Weps, we show how visits to Hippie clinics have gone up and Med–Met down since the attack. We imply," dragging out the word, "That it looks awfully suspicious. Also, we create a villain that people can focus on. Maybe those arrested may seem like regular people, but Dr. Rokoff certainly doesn't. He looks like some giant red–headed big bird who could have been a descendant of Ivan the Terrible. We paint a picture that suggests that he is the brains behind this whole thing. He led the Anson girl astray. He had her seduce Guidry and get him to believe in his voodoo, and then used him to publically humiliate Darren with that resignation."

"So what – another ad campaign?" Rogers asked.

"No, I think it's time to shoot the big gun." Wil held his hands as if holding a bazooka. "I think it is time for Darren to come out smoking. Begin immediately to infer that he has information that suggests that what happened to the computers is part of a far bigger conspiracy, and that he will continue to gather information and be able to show who was really behind this. Then we begin to slowly develop the picture. One by one we 'discover' the connections between the arrested hippies and the sabotage. We release statistics that showed the immediate drop in Med–Met visits and rise in Hippocratin visits. Darren asks the question. Was this a coincidence? And lets the people draw their own conclusions.

"At the same time we continue with our legislative efforts to outlaw medical clinics. I have asked Angela Stuart to join us to give us an update on those activities. Suzanne, can you ask Angela to come in."

Angela Stuart, interim Director of the Med–Met region came into the room with Suzanne. "Darren, Will, Joel, good to see all of you. I am sure that Wil has filled you in on the problems we're currently facing."

"Yes Angela, and it is good to see you again." Darren said, stretching. "Wil tells us that you are going to update us on the legislative situation."

"Certainly, as you know since our success three years ago when Iowa outlawed medical clinics, we haven't been able to get many other states to pass restrictive laws. The Demo-Republicans still have enough votes in most states to block Technocratic initiatives. That's certainly the situation at the Federal Level where they control both houses. We know that the Northeast with their intellectual snobbism and the West with the combination of new age individualism in California, and the 'don't restrict anything' attitude in the Northwest are not good targets." She paused and looked at around to see if she still had everyone's attention." We need to concentrate on strong Technocratic states, where we have good friends. We are going to focus next on Arkansas, and Oklahoma. We think those have potential in the next session. Also, we think that Wil's plan to have Darren demonize Rokoff and the Hippocratins will feed our efforts."

"That sounds like a good approach," Walters injected, "by why not right here in Louisiana, and next door in Texas?"

"We thought about those, but the timing isn't right. Rokoff has too big a following in Louisiana, and Texas is just too darn big for right now. If we can get Arkansas and Oklahoma, and then go after New Mexico, we can surround Texas and then go after that big boy."

Joel Rogers raised his hand and spoke, "Angela, how are things going with reconstructing the data base?"

"Slow Joel, some things have been easy to put together but we are still having trouble with the schedule. People show up that we aren't expecting and other times we have huge gaps between patients. The terminals list is completely gone and all we can do is hope that those who received letters show up. If they don't we figure we will recapture most of them when they develop new symptoms. Of course we believe some of them will migrate to Hippocratin and other medical clinics."

"Is that it?" Walters asked.

Angela hesitated before speaking, "Not quite. There is one other thing that worries me. We have noticed that certain medical information is missing or incorrect."

"Like what?" Darren asked, a perplexed look on his face.

"Things like diagnoses that no longer pop-up. There have been instances where the computer defaulted to an earlier version of the software. The techs believe it involves those diagnoses that were undergoing their annual update at the time of the crash. We aren't sure what kind of problems, if any, that this will cause, but we are monitoring it closely."

CHAPTER
31

Georgi monitored the activity in the Chen warehouse. Teams from the film production crew sifted through the salvage materials from the lunar expedition. Part of Georgi's demands was that all the contents would be inventoried and cataloged regardless of whether they were used for the film or not. Occasionally one of the crew would bring an odd piece to Georgi for identification. Contents of Infinity had been kept separate since the expedition had returned from the moon. Alex had strongly supported Georgi's decision to exempt those materials from that available to the film company. Possibly the idea had come from Alex, but she was subtle enough that Georgi didn't realize it.

A large man in studio coveralls approached Georgi carrying a large twisted piece of metal, "Hey chief, any idea what this thing is?"

"I think I do, Spikes" Georgi replied as he read the man's name tag, "Take a look at this picture." Georgi had a large book of pictures taken in Sheppard City when it was still intact. The item in question appeared to be the center piece of a sculpture that stood in front of the Allen B. Sheppard Museum of Space Travel. It was a large replica of the golf club and ball that Sheppard had used during his lunar walk. In the picture it showed that it had been cleverly constructed so that the club was in its follow through motion and the ball was beginning what was then the longest golf shot in history. "When we found it we were near the site of the museum. We were pretty sure that it is the golf club, although it is somewhat mangled. Do you think it's useful for the project?"

"I've got no idea, chief. Supervisor said bring back anything that looks interesting. This looks interesting. I'll let the higher pay grades decide if it's interesting enough."

★　★　★

As Georgi spoke with Spikes another of the workers drifted unnoticed away from the main warehouse area toward a door that was clearly marked "Private Do Not Enter". Brian Marino knew that they were not supposed to touch the materials in this room, but that had only made him more curious. He tried the handle and found it locked. He then tried the key card that each member of his team had been issued to access the authorized parts of the warehouse. He was pleasantly surprised to hear the door lock click into the open position. Marino entered tentatively, closed the door gently behind him and touched the light pad illuminating the room. Slowly he scanned the room getting his first glimpse of its contents, and let out a slow whistle.

★　★　★

Michael wrapped up his class work on Friday, showered and dressed to keep his appointment for dinner with the Livingstons. He wasn't sure why but he was nervous about seeing Lacy again. Clearly, he wasn't looking for another relationship. Even if he was how could he possibly want to get involved with that high energy bundle of chatter. He felt exhausted just thinking about her. She was cute, and seemed bright. He knew she had a degree from Tulane, but no idea in what. Well, make the best of it he thought. Her father seemed like a nice guy and had really helped him out that night at the prison.

Andrew Livingston greeted him at the door. He wore jeans and a pull-over shirt and Michael was impressed how un-cop-like he looked. "Good evening Lieutenant, it is nice to see you again."

"Please Michael, call me Andy, it's good to have you here at our home. Come in, but quietly, Lacy and my wife are lighting the Shabbat candles. Even though Rachel married a non-jew, she still observes some of the rituals of her faith, and Lacy seems intent on continuing the traditions."

"I remember your mother-in-law, Mrs. Rubin, was very much into tradition. She frequently spoke of the way things were when she was growing up. I think she would be very happy to see that her granddaughter is still carrying that on."

Through the opening to the next room Michael could see Lacy and her mother facing a table on which sat a pair of silver candlesticks. Both had their heads covered with white lace and their hands were over their eyes as they quietly mouthed prayers. Rachel, Lacy's mother was only slightly taller than her daughter with light brown hair. Michael could see a resemblance to her late mother, Lettie. Michael recalled that she was the youngest of Lettie's three daughters. He thought that she might have occasionally accompanied her mother to her treatments at the clinic, but had remained in the waiting room. Other than a greeting, she and Michael had never spoken. When Lettie died Michael had received a very lovely thank you note signed by Rachel and her two sisters.

The women finished their ceremony and as Lacy removed her head covering she noticed Michael. "Hey, you made it. I was worried I might have scared you and you wouldn't show. What's that?"

Michael looked at his hand remembered that on Rokoff's advice he had brought flowers for Rachel. "Oh, I'm sorry," he stepped toward where Rachel stood and held out the bouquet. "Mrs. Livingston, thank you for having me for dinner, I hope you like these."

"Michael, it is nice to see you again. Please call me Rachel." She had a soft warm smile. "When Lacy came home and told us that she had invited you to dinner we were a little surprised. We shouldn't have been, by now we should know that when she sets her mind to something it usually happens."

"Wine?" Andy asked as he held out a bottle of Chardonnay. He poured four glasses handed two to the women first and then to Michael.

"Nice home you have," Michael said as he took in his surroundings. "Very warm."

"Thank you for saying so," Rachel answered as she turned to her husband "Andrew, could you help me in the kitchen?"

"If you don't mind Rach, I would like to talk with Michael."

"I do mind. I need your help. God!"

Michael found himself alone with Lacy, she sat down on the sofa and patted the seat next to her. Michael instead chose a seat facing her, not so much to avoid sitting next to her, but rather to allow him to better hold a conversation. "You know," he started, "This is kind of crazy. I mean a few days ago I didn't know you and now I am in your home having dinner with your family."

"Not really, even though you didn't know us you have been a part of this family for a few years now. Do you realize how much what you do can impact a family? We all used to go to Med-Met for all our medical stuff. When we saw how you affected Bubbie, how much more you provided than the machines, we all became dedicated believers in the human practice of medicine. Michael, you're our hero."

Michael blushed and turned away, "I'm not a hero. I'm just someone who was a happy Med-Met employee, who through a series of circumstances and discovered that there might be something more. Rokoff's a hero he has fought the odds, the establishment and done everything he can to not let the true practice of medicine die."

"Well," Lacy said, curling her legs under her and giving Michael a little smile, "you're my hero."

Needing to change the subject quickly, Michael said, "You know a lot about me but I don't know anything about you. I do know that you graduated Tulane, but I don't know in what, or what you do now."

"Fair questions. My bachelor's degree is in social psychology. Let's be honest, not much demand in the market today. So anyway, I am now working on my Masters in Disasterology."

"In what?"

"Disasterology, I know it sounds really weird. It is a fairly new field and it really began at Tulane. Following Hurricane Katrina in 2005, Tulane began to have courses relating to major natural disasters. After the Great Lunar Disaster it evolved to a full blown graduate program. We learn about the impact of disasters on the individual and on society. We deal with preparation, recovery, and if possible prevention. It's really interesting."

"So, you're going to be…."

They simultaneously blurted out, "A Master of Disaster," both doubling over in laughter.

CHAPTER
32

Marino waited until the week-end, when there was no work going on in the Chen warehouse, before returning to further explore the contents of the locked room. After checking carefully to be sure that no one was around he used his key card and once again the locks opened without difficulty and without triggering any alarms. He now had time to carefully examine the contents of the room. The room was small, no more that 3 by 4 meters. Crates and large boxes lined one wall. Across the room were shelves that contained smaller boxes and loose items. The boxes were all labeled Chen Lunar Expedition 1: Site – Infinity, followed by numbers. It was some of the loose items that had caught Marino's eye on his first visit. There were various art objects including vases, small statues, some paintings and a jar that appeared to contain a variety of colored gems. Some looked like rubies and emeralds and even some diamonds. He was no gemologist and had no idea if they were real or had much value but figured he could find that out later as he filled his pockets.

He took his time going through the boxes. Many were filled with papers, personal photos and holo images and relatively mundane office stuff. Some of the boxes contained a good deal of protective packing material and in these he found more art objects. He chose the artwork that he thought might have the best value and carried those outside to the vehicle that he had hidden behind the building, until he had all that he could handle. He knew people who would know how to find someone who could appraise the value of the things he had taken, and to sell it so that it couldn't be traced.

He did his best to close all the boxes and leave things appearing as close to the way they were when he arrived. He spread out the remaining objects on the shelves to leave no obvious gaps. He left some gems behind and arranged them around some wadded up paper so that it looked as if the jar was still full. He had worn gloves so was confident that he had not left fingerprints. He turned off the lights and just as he was about to close the door he noticed something blinking in a corner of the room behind some furniture. He moved an old desk out of the way and found a heavy metallic box that was hooked to the power source. On top were a series of lights and number keys. He had no luck in trying to open it and figured he would take it with him and work on it when he had privacy and tools available. He disconnected it from the power source, tucked it under his arm, locked the door behind him and left.

★   ★   ★

Georgi didn't go into the Infinity storage room very often. It was officially off limits to everyone else. It wasn't until several weeks later, when Alex asked him to show her what was there, that anyone realized there had been a break-in. At the door he stopped abruptly and held out his hand to signal Alex to stop.

"Is something wrong?" she asked noting his hesitation.

"Something seems off. Let me look from here before we go further. I haven't been in here in a while, but it just feels different." Georgi was used to observing, it was one of the tools a good salver needed in assessing a site. He pointed at the shelves, "Look over there. Do you notice how there are some clearings in the dust in spots where there are no objects? Also, look at the lids of the crates, there are some gaps. Those were all secured tightly and hadn't been opened since we returned."

"Who besides you has been in here?" she asked as she followed his descriptions.

"No one should have been, the room is off limits and should only be accessed by my key card or the head of security. Let's back out and get security up here now."

Al Bronson, the Chief of Security for the warehouse was there in a few minutes. After Georgi described what he had seen Bronson ordered a check on the security system. He got his answers quickly.

"I have some bad news Mr. Chen. Apparently the restriction of the codes to this room was never implemented. Instead of just you and I having access, anyone with mid-level or higher clearance was able to open it. Three weeks ago on a Saturday, one Brian Marino an assistant manager on the inventory team used his key card to gain access and spent several hours in the room."

"Well, get Marino down here now."

"I asked for him but found out that Marino hasn't been seen since that day."

Alex excused herself and headed to the ladies room. Once inside and sure she was alone she took out here communicator and pushed one button. "General, it's Alex. The Infinity storage room has been burglarized. We need to find a Brian Marino who worked for the production company's inventory team before anyone else does." There was a short pause. "Yes sir, I will stay with Mr. Chen and keep you fully informed."

CHAPTER
33

Michael's evening with Lacy and her family was very pleasant, even enjoyable. They were a warm family who clearly doted over their only daughter. Importantly, they were true supporters of the Hippocratin movement and Andy was very open about the issues that the police had to deal with as a result of the protests and counter protests.

"You have to understand Michael, the first reaction for most in the police force is to side with the establishment. That of course is Med-Met. Many on the force have jumped to the conclusion that those who protest against Med-Met are causing all the trouble. There are however a group of officers and some of the brass who get their health care at the Hippocratin clinics. We have seen patterns that suggest that things remain fairly peaceful until the counter demonstrators, the pro-Med-Met crowd, come in and stir things up. They seem to bait the opposition and then fall down quickly to make it appear that the violence is being perpetrated on them."

"Well, why not do something about it? I have heard that many of the counter demonstrators are being paid to heat things up."

"We can't because we do not have any proof as of yet. Usually by time the police arrive the whole thing has escalated and you can't tell who started and who finished. Things clearly worsened after the computer virus. It has become easier for Med–Met and the CHA to paint the supporters of Hippocratin medicine as the dangerous element."

Lacy jumped in, "But Dad, the people who did the virus weren't Hippocratins and they weren't the same people who protest peacefully. A lot of my friends are out there and they would never do anything that malicious."

"I know angel, but people have a hard time sorting it out. There have been some who were in both groups." Michael wasn't sure, but he thought Andy might have glanced his way, and he thought of Sara.

"Yes Dad, but just as many had ties to Med–Met. You don't hear much about that."

Just as the conversation was winding down Michael heard a familiar whirring sound coming from the kitchen. He excused himself from the table and walked in to see Rachel taking fresh coffee grounds and placing them in a coffee maker. "Wow, this is fantastic. I haven't had freshly brewed coffee in months. My equipment was confiscated when the police took the stuff from my, er, friend's apartment. This will be a real treat."

"The police took it, and haven't returned it after all this time?" Rachel had a stern look on her face. "We'll see about fixing that, as soon as we have our coffee and some fresh baked apple pie. All of us that is except my husband if he doesn't agree to get you your stuff back."

★   ★   ★

While Michael finished up dessert in southeastern Louisiana, Sara sat with Richard Dietrich, the man she had known as Plato, near the northeast border of Texas. Life at the ranch had settled into a routine, new members still trickled in and the total number had now risen to near forty. Sara ran a small medical clinic dealing with the routine injuries and infirmities of the group.

Sara had grown close to Richard. Although a little older than her, he was educated, gentle and he shared common interests with her. They would usually sit on the porch each evening and talk. The topics varied including politics, philosophy, and what their lives had been like, and what the future might hold for them. It surprised how much more she knew about Richard, and shared with him about herself, compared to her relationship with Michael. It wasn't that she hadn't felt close to Michael, but they always had studies, and medicine and never got around to sharing personal information and thoughts.

Richard was divorced and had two children, one just a few years younger than Sara. He hoped that they hadn't had to suffer too much when it had been discovered that he was with the Weps and had fled. They would get occasional reports from Spiderman about what was happening back in New Orleans. They knew of Michael's arrest and subsequent release. They followed the national news reports and Sara would feel the greatest longing for her former life when Jacob was featured. She hoped that he wasn't angry with her for what she did, and for not finishing her training. "Richard, do you think we will ever be able to go back?"

"I hope so, but right now it doesn't look good. I think we are going to need to stay away for a long time. Maybe the political climate will change but it will take something major for it to be anytime soon."

"Do you think we're safe here?"

"I think we are for now. I think the greatest risk comes from the inside. We have a handful of members who are not happy with laying low. If they do anything that draws attention to us, we may not be so secure.

"Sara, have you given my offer some thought?"

"If you mean about moving in with you, I have, and I will. I enjoy being with you, and besides the women's bunkhouse is not a barrel of laughs."

"Any regrets, or guilt about Michael?"

"I gave it a good deal of thought and the answer is no. I love Michael but I may never see him again. We never had an exclusive relationship, although once he moved in with me it became that by circumstance. I hope that he is able to move on and find someone. He's the kind of person who needs someone to share with. The right kind of person will help him to become a better physician. I think that he has all the tools to be one of the best. I think someday when they write the history of modern medicine Michael Guidry will be right there alongside Jacob Rokoff."

"Where will Sara Anson be in that history?"

"Perhaps a footnote. Perhaps nothing."

CHAPTER
34

Brian Marino presented to the Med–Met facility. It had been a little over three weeks since he had stolen artifacts from the Infinity room at the Chen Warehouse. For the past two weeks he had been feeling worse by the day.

After going through the materials he had stolen he distributed those that appeared to have value to a series of fences he had been referred to by a friend who was in the black market. He did not distribute too many items to any one source, in order to keep the questions of origin minimal. He had been able to get a reasonable return for the items, but was disappointed that the gems turned out to be industrial quality and had not that valuable. He hadn't gone back to his apartment after the break in, but instead took an efficiency in the Garbage District, which was more convenient to the individuals that he would sell the goods to.

His last hope for a bigger payday had been the locked box with the flashing lights that he had disconnected from the power source. He hadn't bothered to reconnect the device, and had worked on it with his tools to try and get it opened. Finally using a tool akin to a small jaws of life the lid popped open. In the process it flew out of his hands and the contents crashed to the tile floor of his kitchen area. What he saw again was not what he had hoped or expected.

A variety of tubes and vials lay on the floor. The vials had labels on them with letters and numbers, nothing that made sense. Several had broken and liquid seeped out. There were no gems, no precious metals, just broken glass and liquid.

The stuff was beginning to smell so he quickly moved to clean it up. In the process cut himself on one of the broken vials. Cursing he wrapped his finger and finished cleaning up. He took all the trash, including the now useless lock box and put them in the dumpster behind the unit. It was nearly empty which meant that waste removal had recently been there. Knowing how infrequently that occurred he figured it could be weeks before it was picked up again.

Now he sat at the Med-Met terminal answering question put to him by the computer generated voice.

"Please describe your symptoms."

"Well, I'm aching all over and get hot and cold all the time. My head is splitting, my throat hurts and I can't stop coughing."

"Any fevers?"

"I haven't taken my temperature, but when I'm not shaking with chills I do feel hot."

"Have you taken any prescription or over the counter medications?"

"Just some anti-inflammatory but it hasn't helped much"

"Thank you, the Technician will now escort you to the diagnostic scans."

★   ★   ★

Alexandra and her boss, Justin Riser, sat in his office, reviewing the current situation. "General, it has been over three weeks since the theft. Our people were at Marino's apartment before the police. It appears that he hasn't been there since the break-in. There was no trace of any of the missing materials in the place. We have however located some of the missing pieces for sale through black market sources. We traced them back to several fences all who describe an individual fitting Marino's description as the source. One gave us a name he used and we have just found a rental under that name off Jackson Avenue. Our people are staking it out."

"Have you recovered any of the materials?"

"Yes sir, any pieces that we've found for sale we've purchased. Any pieces that were sold that we could track down we either purchased, or acquired."

"Anything else of note?"

"Well sir, one curious thing. Several of the fences that we interviewed were not feeling well. Seems to be something going around in the underworld community."

"Thank you Captain, and how is our friend Mr. Chen doing?"

"He was obviously upset by the theft, he fired the security company that had messed up the card codes. He is forging forward with the movie project. It seems to have given him some direction. He has a much more positive attitude toward everything than before."

"And what about your relationship with him?"

"Going along very well sir. He trusts me, and I believe he is falling in love with me."

"Interesting, but understandable. What about your feelings for him?"

Alexandra hesitated and then answered, "It's a job sir, nothing more."

★   ★   ★

Michael found it hard to believe that he was already entering his third year as Jacob's student. Third year meant a regular clinic and patients of his own. It was what he had wanted but still it frightened him, the responsibility that came with it. He would be working directly with Patricia Murphy who had graduated a year earlier and had stayed on with Jacob as a staff physician and teaching faculty member. Patricia would supervise his activities and he would continue to attend the evening sessions that all students attended and additionally meet one to one with Jacob weekly. That evening a new student would be joining them and Jacob would be giving the opening lecture, a history of medicine including how things had occurred that led to the current state of affairs. Jacob gave the same lecture each year, but all students showed up each time to hear it and seemingly never tired of it. Michael had only heard it his second year, as he had joined late his first, so he was eager to hear it again.

★   ★   ★

"There was a time before the automobile when medicine was a horse and buggy profession. The doctor would drive miles in all kinds of weather to deliver a baby, and if the poor farmer couldn't afford to pay, he might accept a sack of flour or a chicken as payment. He was far from infallible, his tools were limited but he toiled long hours and added a human touch that had to suffice when no other treatment existed. He, most physicians were men in those days, was loved and respected.

"As the twentieth century began the pace of the world picked up, transportation, communications, and technology grew at an ever increasing pace. Medicine grew as well. Breakthroughs in basic science brought antibiotics, transplantation, genetic engineering and wonderful new machines. Machines were developed to detect, diagnose, and treat disease. More and more diseases once considered fatal fell by the wayside. More and more knowledge had to be consumed by the student of medicine. At the same time the economic situation in the world was reaching a crisis. The costs of medical school rose dramatically and students had to go into considerable debt to finance their medical education. Through the 1960's there was the availability of government guaranteed loans. The relatively high income of physicians made it possible for the best and the brightest regardless of economic background to seek a medical career." Jacob paused and looked around the room, all eyes were on him.

"In the 1970's and 80's the loans became more difficult to obtain and other, more lucrative and attractive professions began to drain off those who previously would have chosen to become physicians. Those who went to medical school accrued significant debt and when they graduated they needed to earn money rapidly to pay-off their debts, this led to a shift from the less financially rewarding primary care specialties to the more lucrative procedure oriented specialties. Invasive cardiology, cosmetic surgery, radiology, these became the sought after residencies while the physician who had the time to sit and talk began to go the way of the horse and buggy.

"The combination of these things the advancement of technology, the vast amounts to be learned, and the change in motivation of the medical students served to create an atmosphere that lead to change. At first the changes were subltle, but as time went on became more dramatic.

"Many mistakes were made, by the governments, by the medical profession, and by the individual physicians themselves." Rokoff held up his long index finger for emphasis. "If but one factor had been changed things might have been different, but they weren't.

"Several events and crises occurred during the late twentieth and early twenty-first centuries that created an atmosphere that was conducive to the development of Med–Met and the marginalization of the practice of medicine as we know it.

"Technology evolved rapidly, first with diagnostic tools and then treatment modalities. The CT and the MRI allowed one to look inside the body without making a cut. The PET scan allowed metabolic correlation of masses seen by CT and MRI and the Molecular Electron Tag Scan allowed detection of tumor gene defects without even taking a biopsy. This along with sophisticated molecular lab analysis including gene arrays and complete sequencing on small samples initiated a climate change that began to minimize the value of the history and physical examination." He stopped and quickly drained the bottle of water he had been sipping.

"As the twentieth century was ending and the twenty-first began, another dimension of the evolving crisis was the growing number of individuals without insurance coverage and therefore with limited access to care." He was now pacing around the room, circling the students. They craned their necks to follow him. "This was not only a problem for those people, but for the broader population as well. Those without coverage generally tended not to get preventive care, and to ignore illness until it became major. By that stage it became significantly more expensive to treat. When they reached the point where they could no longer ignore their condition they would go to hospital emergency rooms, which were obligated, by law, to provide treatment. As there was no compensation for that treatment the hospital absorbed the cost, and then passed that on to the insurance companies by raising charges for the insured. The insurance companies passed that on to the insured. When the individual could no longer afford coverage they dropped it and joined the growing ranks of the uninsured. I am sure you can see where that was heading."

The new student raised his hand to ask a question and the others waved him off. From experience they knew that Jacob was on a roll and he wouldn't be distracted.

"It became apparent that there needed to be reform in the health care system. In the early 1990's the Clinton administration attempted to address the problem. There was significant concern that part of reform would include rationing of health care. The Clintons didn't have enough support to pass their package. It took almost twenty years until the end of the first decade of the twenty-first century that reform was finally passed. The plan itself had excellent intentions, and certainly increased the number of covered individuals, leaving only a few without health care benefits. Unfortunately," he paused, "The plan had a key flaw, and left a lot to be interpreted and manipulated over the next twenty years. That as well as the rise of two medical industry giants paved the way to our current situation.

"Next week I will discuss the rise of Med-Met, and how the Health Care Reform of 2010 was manipulated to change medicine drastically." As Jacob finished he signaled Michael to wait.

After the other students drifted out, Michael made his way over to Jacob who was straightening up his books. "Hey Jacob, what's up?"

"Nothing much. Now that you are a third year, and working with Patricia, I don't see you as often. I just wanted to find out how you're doing. How do you like your clinic?"

"Come on Jacob. You know I'm thrilled. It's what I have been waiting for these past two years. Although, I was a little disappointed that I didn't get assigned to your clinic."

"That was my doing. I thought that being exposed to Patricia's style would be good for you. You have seen my way of doing things in fairly large doses. Patricia is compassionate, analytical and free of some of my bias from the old days. Don't worry you're still going to see plenty of me. How are things going for you otherwise?"

"By otherwise you mean . . . ?"

"I mean outside of medicine, socially, real life. You mentioned the young woman, the granddaughter of Mrs. Rubin. If it isn't inappropriate, can I ask how that's going?"

"Jacob, I don't think that anything that you could ask me would be inappropriate. Lacy and I have developed a really close friendship. We spend time together, talk a lot. I'm comfortable with her."

"That's it, comfortable? Sounds like an old sweatshirt. Are there no sparks?"

"OK, I may take back that 'nothings inappropriate' comment. To be honest there have been sparks, she has certainly hinted about wanting more, but I've been holding back. I mean it hasn't been that long . . ."

"Sara has been gone almost a year. You don't owe her anything. She left you and the rest of us holding a rather large bag. We may never see her again. Besides that, knowing Sara she would give you hell for sitting around and moping. I'm sure whatever guilt she feels for what she left us with would be magnified tenfold if she knew you had withdrawn into a hole after she left. If you like this girl you owe it to yourself to see where it can go."

"What you're saying makes sense but it isn't easy."

"It never is Michael, nothing worthwhile is ever easy. You know, with the beginning of the new term I will be having the students and faculty over to my place Saturday evening. I will serve my famous Gumbo Rokofsky, a blend of New Orleans and mother Russia. Amazing what a little vodka can do for a roux. Why not invite Lacy, she believes in our cause, and should get along well with the group."

"Thanks Jacob, I just may do that."

CHAPTER
35

Riser and Alexandra watched the latest news vid. The announcer commented that with the elections two months away, Technocrats in several key elections had built comfortable leads in the polls over their opponents. With the campaign theme of "Elect our candidate, Your life may just depend on it," they ran a basic one issue campaign. Med-Met candidates easily won Technocrat primaries with major backing from Med-Met and the companies that relied on Med-Met for their financial existence. Demo-Republican opponents tried to address a broad spectrum of issues, but it was Armbrister's strategy that their candidates not be diverted from his message. The message being that there were subversive forces that included the Weps, the Hippocratins, and anyone else who supported them that were out to deny the public the best possible health care. That was the care provided by Med-Met. Healthcare was the most essential right of all citizens and that one could not talk about other issues like education, labor reform, or space travel unless healthcare was secure.

He turned down the sound and addressed Alexandra, "So, what more have we learned about Marino?"

"As I mentioned the other day, we staked out the Jackson Avenue location. Our people went through the dumpster behind the building, several weeks of trash had built up, but they did find something that appears to be from the break in. In the list that Georgi gave the police was a heavy steel lock box that had been connected to a power source and maintained at extremely cold temperatures."

Riser stiffened, "What did Mr. Chen say was in it?"

"He didn't Sir, he never got around to trying to open it. With the apathy he had toward the whole lunar cache, it isn't surprising."

"Is it still intact?"

"No sir, it had been broken open. Inside the box, and in the immediate vicinity were several glass tubes and vials, some broken some intact. All had alpha-numeric labels but no guide to the code was found."

The General paused, "I see, and where is that material now."

"We have it in a secure location, awaiting your instructions."

"For now, make sure that as few people come into direct contact with the material as possible. Have it placed in a -80° C freezer, and if any of those individuals who have been in contact with it aren't feeling well, let me know about it immediately."

Alex raised a well shaped eyebrow, "Sir, is there more that I should know?"

"Not right now Captain, but I need to have the information that was on those labels. The materials should only be handled under isolation conditions, is that clear?"

She responded with a crisp nod, "Perfectly, Sir."

"What about Marino, has he returned?"

"No, he may have moved to another location. We do however know from our computer intercepts that he has been to a Med-Met facility several times in the past few weeks. We have added surveillance at that location in case he returns."

"Very good. You're dismissed, I have some calls to make."

★   ★   ★

Lacy was ecstatic after she received the call from Michael. Her mother noticed her reaction and smiled.

"Was that Michael?"

"Yes, and he invited me to a party at Jacob Rokoff's. I'm finally going to meet Rokoff. Mom, Michael's classmates will all be there also, this is the first time that he has let me into his world. Do you think it means anything?"

"It seems like it could be a step. How have things been between the two of you?"

"Well, it has been nice. We have a good time together, we talk a lot, he is very considerate, but seems to hold back."

"What about you, where do you want this to go?"

"I think I would like to see where it could go. He's smart, funny, good looking, and really cares about people. I feel really good when I'm with him. And mom …," Lacy paused.

"Yes."

"I'm not sure if I can tell you this."

"Lacy, you can tell me anything, you know that."

"Well, ok." Another pause. "He gets me really horny, and I'm getting very frustrated.

Rachel hesitated, took a deep breath and did her best to suppress a laugh, but the smile on her face was evident. "Lacy, I think you need to strike a balance between patience and initiative. It's obvious that he still carries some feelings for Sara Anson that he hasn't resolved, but this invitation is a big step. Remember, not only is he introducing you to his friends, he is introducing you to her friends as well."

"Thanks mom, you're great. What you've said really backs up what I've been thinking. It was just that I've never been out with a guy before who didn't try to jump my bones after the second date."

"Lacy, one more thing."

"Yes mom."

"Don't share with your father what you just shared with me."

★   ★   ★

On Saturday Michael picked Lacy up at her home. "You look great." He said and really meant it. On the way to Rokoff's he told her who was going to be there and a little bio on each of them. She was excited about meeting Rokoff, he was a larger than life figure to her. The news portrayed him as everything from Saint to Satan, but her sentiments went more toward the former.

Jacob opened the door when they arrived. Lacy thrust her diminutive hand upward to the very tall man in front of her. Jacob engulfed her hand in his and smiled down at her. "I see a lot of your grandmother in you, it is a pleasure to have you here."

"Thank you Dr. Rokoff, I have heard so much about you first from my grandmother and then from Michael. Although, I do have to tell you, Bubbie referred to you as Michael's helper."

Jacob laughed, "your Bubbie may be a prophet. The way he is progressing someday I may be Michael's assistant. Please, call me Jacob."

Michael stood listening to the exchange blushing slightly.

"Michael," Jacob addressed him. "Please take Lacy in and introduce her around. Lacy, I hope we have a chance to sit and talk later. I'd like to hear about your studies."

"Thank you Jacob, I would enjoy that."

Michael and Lacy grabbed drinks and worked their way through the room making introductions and small talk. At the other side of the room Earl was holding court with his date, the new student and her date.

"Michael, come on over here brother. Who is this lovely thing? It is about time you got over your funk about that radical traitor bitch."

Michael opened his mouth to lambast Earl, but before he could say anything Lacy jumped in. "Hi, I'm Lacy Livingston. I am not a thing, I am a woman, and you are?"

"Earl, Earl Carter, and if I offended you I beg your pardon. I am just a little old southern boy. Sometimes I am a little old fashioned."

"Well, I am a little ol' southern woman, and we are almost in the twenty-second century so don't confuse old fashioned with being a jerk. If you were referring to Sara Anson with that last comment I don't care what she has or hasn't done. She was Michael's friend so there must be plenty of good in her."

With that she spun and headed across the room, leaving Michael behind with Earl and his party. "Well," Earl offered, "You sure can pick them."

Michael ignored the sarcasm in Earl's comment, "Wow, I sure can. Have a good evening Earl." And to Earl's date, "Good luck," as he walked away.

Lacy found Jacob across the room who signaled her to have a seat next to him. "Michael tells me you are working on your Masters at Tulane."

"Yes, I am in the Disasterology program, I have finished my course work and now I am working on my dissertation."

"What are you writing your dissertation on?"

"Well, a lot of people have studied the lunar disaster and almost every aspect of that has been examined. I have decided to focus on the impact of the recent Chen space ship tragedy and how it has had a recall effect on the psychic impact of the original lunar tragedy. In a sense making us relive the disaster and reinforcing the isolation mind-set that prevailed after 2050."

"Is it going well?"

"Alright, I guess. I have read about everything that is available, but I wish I could get some kind of angle, some kind of insight."

"Do you think an interview with Georgi Chen might be useful?"

"Are you kidding, that would be unbelievable, but I wouldn't know how to approach him."

"I think I can help you there. Georgi's father was my closest friend, and I think that Georgi might do me a favor. Let me check with him and I'll let you know."

Lacy jumped out of her seat and gave Jacob a big hug. "Michael's right you are the best."

Later, Lacy and Michael stood at the front door of her parent's house. "Michael, I want to thank you for inviting me tonight. I really enjoyed meeting Jacob, and the opportunity he has given me to meet Georgi Chen will really help me with my thesis. I liked your friends, at least most of them."

"Earl can be a real jerk, I'm concerned about what kind of physician he'll be. He speaks without thinking, or at least without a filter on what comes out. You really handled him well. Did you see the look his date was giving him after you finished roasting him?"

"Well, daddy used to take me on those 'bring your daughter to work days'. I would sit on the other side of the two way mirror and watch the cops handle the scumbags, I guess I picked up some pointers."

"I'm glad you enjoyed yourself." He leaned in to give her a polite kiss on the check. Lacy turned into the kiss and pulled him close, not letting him pull away. She kept the kiss going and slowly ran her tongue over his lips causing them to part and soon he was fully engaged.

Slowly she eased away and looked up at him. "Would you like to come in for awhile?"

"It's kind of late, I wouldn't want to disturb your parents."

"You won't, they're not here. They went to visit my mom's sister in Baltimore. Won't be back until tomorrow night."

"Well, still it is late and I have a lot of studying to do tomorrow."

"I'll tell you what, I will make sure you're awake and out of here early enough tomorrow, and with a good breakfast in you so that you can study at top efficiency." With that she took his hand led him through the door and closed it behind them.

CHAPTER
36

Alexandra gave her report to Riser. "Marino was found this morning."

"Have you had a chance to question him?"

"No Sir, he was found dead. Our people tracked him to a house on Prytania, about two blocks from the Jackson Avenue apartment. There was evidence that several people were living there, but none were present. Estimate is that he had been dead for at least two days, so we assume the others have been gone at least that long."

"Were any Infinity materials found with him?"

"No Sir, and the lack of any cash on him seems to suggest that his housemates may have taken anything valuable before they left. We made a thorough search of the premises and surroundings, removed any traces of our presence and then made an anonymous call to the police. Our caller claimed to be a neighbor worried that the occupant of the house in question had been ill, and now wasn't answering his door."

"Do you have any idea who the other occupants of the house are?"

"We know who the house is leased to and we found some papers indicating a few other names. We are in the process of tracking them down."

"Thank you Captain, keep me informed."

"Yes Sir. Sir, there is one more thing. Rokoff has asked Georgi to meet with a young woman from Tulane who is doing a Master's thesis on the Chen ship explosion."

"Did Chen agree?"

"He said he would, as long as the information would be used for academic purposes only. Also pending approval by the production company's lawyers, due to the exclusivity agreement."

"Captain, if the lawyers give their approval, I want you to be with him when he talks to her. If you see the conversation going in any direction that could be dangerous for us, find an excuse to end it."

★   ★   ★

After the police completed their examination of the house, and canvassing of the neighbors, they released the body to the coroner's office. The coroner's office entered the information, regarding the name and estimated time of death and assessment that it was from "natural causes", into the Universal Healthcare Databank (UHD). The information in the UHD was automatically entered into the Med-Met database and linked to Marino's file. The central computers then incorporated the earlier presentation, treatments provided, follow-up visits, and death into its vast amount of data, compared it with known illness and stored it for comparison to future events. A non-urgent flag was placed on the record as there had been several cases in the past few weeks presenting with similar symptoms.

★   ★   ★

Michael finished with the last of his patients for the day and met with Patricia for his sign-out and review. "How did it go today Michael, anything we need to go over, anything unusual?"

"Nothing specific, but it has seemed busier than usual this past week. A good deal of upper respiratory symptoms, headache, myalgia and fever. Isn't it early for the seasonal flu? We've barely begun the vaccine distribution."

"I agree it is early, I've been seeing the same thing. I'll mention it to Jacob and find out if others here have been seeing it, and what's happening at the clinics in other cities.

"By the way, I enjoyed meeting your friend Lacy. She seems really bright, and definitely full of life. You should bring her around more often."

"Thanks, I think I will."

★   ★   ★

At the Med–Met clinic two men sat waiting to be seen. They recognized each other, both being engaged in the business of buying and reselling goods of questionable origin. Both operated in the Garden District and Uptown. They nodded to each other and the older of the two asked, "What's up man?"

"Ida know, feel like crap. Been goin' on the past couple of weeks. Figured I'd get checked out and get somethin' to take for it."

"Yeah same here, must be something going around."

CHAPTER
37

Two weeks after the evening at Rokoff's, Lacy got her chance to meet Georgi. Georgi suggested that Lacy and Michael meet him and his girlfriend for dinner. Georgi knew Michael casually through Jacob, and Jacob had mentioned that Michael was seeing Lacy. Alexandra had been anxious to meet them and encouraged Georgi to make it a foursome. Georgi's limo picked them up at Lacy's house and whisked them across Lake Pontchartrain to a lovely French country inn. It reportedly had been there for over a hundred years. The atmosphere was quiet and warm and they had a private corner table that gave them the opportunity to talk. In the relative darkness of the limo Lacy noticed that Georgi's girlfriend Alexandra was very attractive. It wasn't until they got out at the restaurant and she got out in the light that she saw how totally stunning Alex was. As Alex unfurled to her full five foot eleven Lacy compared that with her own petite stature. Her ego wasn't helped by the way Michael stared. Any resentment that Lacy might have felt, was quickly washed away by Alex' gracious manner.

"Lacy, I am so exciting about meeting you. Jacob told us about the dissertation work you're doing. I insisted that Georgi let me come along and hear more about it. Being from New Orleans I have always been fascinated by the impact that Katrina had on our city and its reinvention. I think it is so exciting that you have a chance to analyze and break down the immediate and long term implications."

"Thank you. That's probably the best description of Disaterology that I have ever heard. Is it ok if I share it with my professors?"

"It's all yours, glad to help."

As the hostess led them to their table Georgi asked Michael how he was doing at the clinic.

"First, let me express my appreciation for the support you have provided to the clinic. It's obvious from some of the things Jacob says that you have been extremely generous and that it has meant a lot to our ability to provide care to more people."

"Come on Michael, that can't be me. Don't you watch the vids, I'm just a spoiled playboy."

Alex interrupted, "Don't listen to him, he is a caring and giving individual. I don't know why he perpetrates that image."

"Hey, it got me a hot girlfriend."

After the waiter took their orders Georgi again asked Michael how things were at the clinic.

"It's been incredibly busy lately, a lot of upper respiratory illness. Some of the people have really been sick. Something is definitely going around. It seems relatively contagious because one person in a family or an office gets it and then quickly those around them show up with the symptoms. Jacob has sent inquiries to the other Hippocratin clinics to see if it is local or broader. I hope its self-limited."

"I second that," Georgi said, raising his glass of the wine that just been poured. "I would like to make a toast, in honor of Lacy's chosen field of study. May all our disasters be history and when our futures are studied they will be hailed as golden days of accomplishment."

Over dinner Georgi shared with Lacy his recollections of the moon, and the devastation of the dome collapse. He only mentioned Infinity in passing, saying that the full impact of the disaster could only be elucidated by further exploration, considering that there were facilities that were not even mentioned in existing records. Alex was able to relax once it was clear that the secrets of Infinity were not going to be discussed further.

The foursome enjoyed excellent food and wine, and when the evening was through made plans to get together again. Lacy and Michael were dropped off at her parent's home and Georgi and Alex drove off silently in the hover limo.

"Michael, they're really nice. From what the media portrays, you would think that Georgi is a shallow self-centered boor. He's nothing like that."

"I know, Jacob says that he has really changed lately, and attributes a lot of it to Alex's influence. What do you think of her?"

"Really nice, and intelligent. I hate to say it but I figured that anyone that good looking would be an air-head. What did you think?"

"I agree, nice and intelligent."

"How about her looks?"

"Not bad."

"Not bad, I thought I was going to have to catch your eyeballs when they popped out of your head. You were like one of those cartoon characters. I expected a caption over your head that said "BOING", and it wouldn't just be referring to your eyes."

"Whoa, Little Bit, so I looked. The eyeballs may have been for her, but the rest was for you. After all you were digging your nails into my thigh at the time."

★   ★   ★

In East Texas Sara sat with Dietrich sipping on a Shiner Bock and said. "I haven't seen much of Alpha lately. He seems to be avoiding us."

"I've noticed that the meetings have been quieter, but I'm not sure I want to complain", was his initial response. "Without his faction around things move much smoother. Their interruptions get annoying."

"I know, but wasn't it the ancient Chinese general, Sun–Tzu who said, "Keep your friends close and your enemies closer."

"Funny, I always thought it was Don Corleone who said that. Sara, do you really think that Alpha is our enemy? Aren't we all on the same side?"

"I'm not sure Richard. I'm no longer sure he is looking at the ends, but instead he is solely interested in the means. He seems to look at violence as both a means and an end. I have heard that he has frequently left the ranch for several days at a time. He could jeopardize all of us."

"Well, keep your eyes and ears open. I'll invite him over for a casual chat soon. Hey, if you're getting up could you grab me another Shiner?"

On another part of the ranch, Jeremy Jeffers, aka Alpha, met with one of his followers. "I am getting sick and tired of just sitting here in East Butt-fuck waiting for something to change. Nothing is going to change without action."

"Do you think that creating a martyr is the way to go? I mean why don't we just go for that Walters creep."

"As I've explained before, Med-Met is like a multi–headed snake, you cut off one head and it will grow another. If we take out Rokoff and make it look like it was the Med-Met crowd, we turn the public against them and make recruitment to our side a whole lot easier."

"When and how are we going to do it?"

"I need a little more time to figure that out. I need to make a trip down to New Orleans and see what is going on there, check out the doc's schedule, and look for locations. Get a sense of the climate in town. Go get some sleep, we'll head out tomorrow."

CHAPTER
38

The following week Michael learned that he was going back to the Northshore. Jacob announced that the students were going to take a field trip in lieu of their weekly group session. More surprising to Michael was that Jacob extended an invitation to Lacy. He told Michael that she would find it relevant to her studies.

They arrived at an elegant raised home on Mandeville's lake shore. The waters of Lake Pontchartrain glittered in the late afternoon sunlight. An assortment of well kept homes and inviting restaurants with balconies and patios stretched up and down the street across from a linear park rich with old live oaks. The students looked at each other expectantly having no idea why they were here.

As usual Michael spoke for the group, asking Jacob why they were here.

"Well Michael, I figured that the next installment in our history lesson would be better served if you heard it from someone with a unique perspective. As I have not been able to get him to cross the lake for the last twenty years of so, I figured I would bring you all to him. Miss Livingston, as a student of history, I thought you would find this most enlightening."

As they climbed the curved staircase to the front door which was on the second level, they were as confused as they had been before

Jacob's answer. The door was answered by a middle aged women who greeted Rokoff and said, "Please come in, he's expecting you, he's in the sitting room, and is quite excited that you are all here." They followed her through a doorway on the right into a large airy room with windowed doors across the front looking out at the lake. Despite it being February the doors were open allowing a gentle but cool breeze to enter. The well decorated room had comfortable looking sofas and chairs placed strategically and they had been supplemented with folding chairs to accommodate the group. At first Michael thought the room was empty. Then what had initially looked like a pile of blankets on a chair in the corner, moved and a frail figure emerged and headed to Jacob. The two men embraced while the group stood and watched.

The elderly man looked somewhat familiar to Michael, but he couldn't quite place him. He was somewhat stooped but appeared to have been tall at one time. He was thin but not malnourished. He walked without a cane or other assistance. Michael guessed that he must be somewhere in his eighties.

Jacob turned to the group, "Students and friends, it is my great pleasure to introduce to you your teacher for this evening, Dr. Marshall Ellis." There was a simultaneous sucking in of air by the students. "Twenty years ago Marshall and I founded the Hippocratins in an effort to protect and preserve the practice of medicine as we knew and loved it. I thought that he better than anyone could tell you about health care reform and the rise of Med–Met, being that he lived and practiced medicine while it occurred. Why don't you all take a few minutes to introduce yourselves while I check and make sure that the dinner that I ordered for us is on the way.

Michael quickly remembered that the man he was staring at was not in his eighties, but had celebrated his one hundred and second birthday the previous year. It had received quite a bit of media coverage and had raised the question with many about the relative merits of Hippocratin medicine versus that of Med–Met. "Sir, it is a pleasure to meet you, I am Michael Guidry."

"Well, Michael, the pleasure is mine. Jacob has told me a lot about you, and of course I have seen the infamous vid clip where you figuratively flip off Darren Walters in front of the whole world. That alone made it worth passing the century mark."

Michael stood blushing as Lacy pushed forward and introduced herself, as did the other members of the group. Jacob returned and the group took up their seats around Ellis.

His voice was clear and strong with barely a tremor. "In 2010 we were at a point in healthcare where most agreed that a change was needed, but none could agree on the direction of that change. The result of course, after a long and contentious battle, was a compromise. This compromise, like many others, did not satisfy the desires of any the factions but rather dissatisfied them equally and thus was judged to be fair. The essence of the plan was to provide access to healthcare to all. The problem was how to fund it without costs and taxes spiraling out of control. The answer was to eliminate waste and inefficiency and to not provide futile care, or more expensive care where a lower cost alternative existed. The term used was comparative effectiveness. Taken in its purest form it made sense and initially it seemed to work. Initially health care organizations partnered with physicians and other providers along with the insurers to form Accountable Care Organizations (ACOs) to meet the goals of the reform plans. Competition became fierce with each group looking to be more efficient and economic than the others. Over the following fifteen years groups merged forming larger and larger ACOs and the smaller players got squeezed out. In 2023 two giants Med Standard and Metmedico joined together to form Med–Met. By 2051 all other companies had either been consumed by Med–Met or gone out of business.

His eyes were clear and expressive and he used his hands and thin fingers to emphasize his points. "Med–Met succeeded through a combination of automation of medical care and a formulaic method for determining futility and eventually adopting euthanasia as a method of dealing with it. Initially, physicians were involved in the

Med-Met system performing the traditional history and physical, interpreting all the diagnostic tests and scans and recommending a treatment plan. Slowly, piece by piece, procedure by procedure, the physician was replaced by automation and technicians." He narrowed his eyes and raised himself out of his chair. "The patient history went from being entered by physicians into electronic medical records to a direct interview between the patient and computer. The physical exam was replaced by a diagnostic scan, and the data interpretation was entirely computerized. For a time physicians remained to review the results and plan with the patient, but that too eventually was abandoned."

"Patients were just given their prescribed treatment by a technician, they accepted it and followed it. If the algorithm determined that the cost of treatment would exceed the expected economic output of the individual over the remainder of their life, they would be given a prescription to return at a predetermined time for their appointment with the cheerful, canary clad, euthanasia attendants. That was the ultimate comparative effectiveness." He shook his head slowly and he had a look of sadness and disappointment on his face.

Lacy raised her hand and asked, "That is the way it is now, and most people are content with that, and believe it is the way of the world. Didn't people resist the change?"

"It was a slow and insidious process. It took place over decades and before we knew it, it was our culture. As you all know there were those that didn't fully accept the change and tried to maintain an alternative, but the economics were not in their favor. With the decreasing demand for physicians the medical schools closed one by one, the last, Georgetown, graduated its last class in 2060. That was Jacob's class."

Earl jumped in, "Dr. Ellis how does Med-Met introduce new treatments or technology into its system, and algorithm?"

"That young man is an interesting question. With the decline of the medical profession there has been a decline in innovation. In general if something can be acquired for a lower price the savings are entered into the algorithm. For the most part treatments have remained unchanged for the past 50 years. The system is dependent on the knowledge programmed into it many years ago. That includes both treatments and diagnoses, essentially it was assumed that everything that can be seen, already had been seen."

"Isn't that a dangerous assumption?" Earl persisted.

"Yes, quite dangerous. It seems the food has arrived, let's eat and continue the discussion."

CHAPTER
39

Activity at the clinic continued to grow. More and more people seemed to be coming down with what initially seemed like a flu, but did not run the usual course. It appeared to be resistant to the common multivalent vaccine. At the weekly meeting, that included all staff physicians and students, Jacob reviewed the situation.

"It has been approximately four months since the first cases presented. The numbers that we are seeing increase every day. From what we can estimate there is a high contagious risk with about half the routine contacts of our patients also contracting the illness. Most of those infected show upper respiratory symptoms and those not seen early are presenting with secondary bacterial pneumonias. Gastrointestinal symptoms are also present. About one quarter of the patients are manifesting severe symptoms, including extremely high fevers and hemorrhage from mucous membranes, especially the nose and GI tract. Those that are presenting at this stage have a very high mortality."

One of the younger physicians raised her hand and asked, "Jacob, is this a local phenomena or is it being seen elsewhere?"

"I've been in touch with our clinics throughout the region and also some farther away. It seems that by far the largest concentration of cases is in the New Orleans area, but it is rapidly spreading throughout the South and Southeast. There are cases beginning to appear as far away as Portland both Portlands for that matter, in Oregon and in Maine. Efforts to track the appearance of cases and the time line clearly lead back to New Orleans. The first case apperared sometime in September or October. It is rare that such a precise documentation of the origins of an epidemic can be made."

"What about Med–Met?" Michael asked. "Are they seeing the same thing?"

"Med–Met has been very quiet on the subject. In response to a question from the media they issued a statement that essentially said, *Med-Met is confident that the increased reports of flu-like illness represents the usual seasonal fluctuations that occur. If you experience symptoms please report to your nearest Med-Met facility where you will receive all the benefits of the world's most advanced healthcare system.* They have not reported any statistics on incidence or mortality.

"The Public Health Department is taking a more active role. They are working on tracking the origins of the epidemic and identifying the agent. They have issued the usual public health advisories on hand washing, and on staying at home if you are feeling ill. We are working with them and sharing our data, hopefully Med–Met is as well."

"Boss," Patricia Murphy, Jacob's clinic director interrupted, "it's getting pretty hairy in the clinic, the staff is having a hard time keeping up."

"I have noticed the same thing Patricia that is why we are going to make some changes. Starting next week the second year students will begin having regular clinic hours. The fourth years are going to need to work independently so that the faculty can see their own patients as well as supervise the second and third years. We will increase the hours that we are open. Some reinforcements are going to come in from the areas that are not currently seeing a lot of cases." He paused and looked around, "Are there any other questions? If not thank you, get some sleep and make sure that you take care of yourselves."

★ ★ ★

The next day Jacob took a long walk to clear his thoughts. He always found that he could focus better amidst the hustle and bustle of the French Quarter. The puzzle of the current epidemic required that he focus absolutely. He stopped at Café Du Monde for a coffee turning down the server's offer of beignet. He shook his head slightly as he observed the tourists and locals downing the balls of fried dough covered in powdered sugar. He wondered if any of them realized how bad the things were for them. If they did, did they really care?

Lost in his thoughts he crossed the street to Jackson Square and unconsciously dropped change into the hat of one of the ubiquitous human statues that performed in the square. He nodded to the silver painted figure. Jacob didn't notice another man who had been following him since the time that he had left his home. The man following him was clearly experienced in this type of activity, and was careful not to be spotted by Rokoff. The stalker paid little attention to the silver street performer. He regarded him as no more than a lamp post or stop sign. The statue however clearly observed the predator and was aware of his identity and that of his prey. The painted man at other times had worn the uniform of a superhero, or dressed in homeless rags. For now he watched them for as long as he could without abandoning his stony stance. He would definitely share this information with others as soon as he could get away from his post.

CHAPTER
40

At CHA headquarters the word of the moment was "contain". The election was drawing closer and the death toll from the epidemic was mounting. Armbrister ran the meetings and planned the strategy. Darren had become increasingly distracted.

Armbrister asked the assembled team, "What is the latest on the situation? Does there appear to be any decrease in the case rate?"

Angela Davis gave the report on behalf of the current Med-Met administration. "There has been no decrease in the number of cases. They seem to be continuing to accelerate, and now are being seen with increasing frequency in other regions. The number of terminal diagnoses is at an all time high. Frankly, I don't know how much longer we can keep the lid on this."

Wil did not look pleased. "We need to remain firm." He turned to Darren's assistant, "Suzanne, what do the polls show? What is the public opinion of Med-Met and of the Hippocratins? How are our candidates doing?"

"All are still in our favor but there is some slippage. Some are beginning to question whether Med-Met is being totally open in providing information. The opposition is gaining traction by asking for an investigation of Med-Met. They want the records opened and a complete disclosure of terminal diagnosis numbers."

"What about our insinuations that the Hippocratins created the virus?"

"There is a segment of the population that firmly believes it. Others however find Rokoff's openness reassuring."

"Then we need to turn the heat up on the Hippocratins. Let them keep reporting gloom and we will hold steady that it's business as usual."

Darren who had been sitting quietly finally spoke, "Angela, what have we learned about the epidemic, and what are we doing about it?"

"The systems show no recognition of the disease. Patients with the signature symptoms are classified as 'Diagnosis Unknown'. If the symptoms reach a critical point the patient is assigned to euthanasia.

"We have tried to cross reference all known health databases with no results. We also tried to recreate the data that had been wiped out in the terrorist event but again nothing worthwhile."

The head of the CHA looked tired and unhappy. He seemed to have missed a day of shaving and in need of a haircut, "Then what do we do?"

"We just continue to provide service, and hope that it runs its course."

Darren turned to Wil, "If this thing continues I may need to leave the CHA and resume my duties as Med-Met director."

"Whoa, hang on," Wil said shaking his head. "We can't put out signs that this is more than a routine flu. Besides, Angela is doing a great job."

"I have no complaints about how Angela has handled things. My point is that if we truly have a medical crisis, my places is at the helm of Med-Met. I don't think we are at that point yet, but if we get there I expect you," pointing at Wil, "to put a positive spin on it."

★   ★   ★

Michael felt as if he had not had a break in weeks. He finally was able to take a full day and evening off. After sleeping most of the day, he picked Lacy up and they headed into the French Quarter. Food remained an important cultural element in New Orleans and they ate a great meal at their favorite café. They enjoyed the strolling opera singers almost as much as their dinner.

As they walked down Bourbon Street, Lacy pointed out the relative lack of people. It was Saturday night, and the heart of the Quarter would normally be packed with tourists and locals. Michael nodded agreement and told her that it was likely due to fear of the epidemic. More and more people were staying home.

They decided to stop in Pat O'Brien's. The sign out front proclaimed, *"The Original Hurricane served since 1933"* Michael turned to Lacy. "I hope you don't mind a little tourist experience?"

"No, it's been awhile, and it should be fun."

They found a table and ordered. The waitress asked if they wanted Hurricanes, but both ordered beer from a local brewery. Michael scanned the large room and noticed a table occupied by his former Med–Met colleagues. Staring at him was Marsha Walsh. As Michael's eyes met Marsha's she narrowed her gaze and purposefully turned away. Next to her was Michael's old friend, Sil Campano. Sil turned to see what Marsha had been looking at, saw Michael and waved. Marsha punched Sil in the shoulder and pulled his arm down.

Michael watched as Sil spoke with Marsha, shook his head and then picked up his beer and headed toward Michael's table. Sil had a big smile on his face as he approached. "Hey old buddy, we miss you down at Med–Met." He looked back at Marsha, "Well, at least some of us do."

Before responding to Sil's statement Michael introduced Lacy.

"A pleasure," Sil said taking her hand. "When we worked together Michael and I were good friends. We lived in the same building, worked the same shift. Contrary to what you may hear in the media all of us do not want to see him drawn and quartered."

Lacy returned Sil's handshake. "It doesn't look like your friend over there agrees with you."

Sil laughed, "Marsha? Don't worry about her. She used to have a thing for Michael. She's more annoyed that he dumped her than that he left Med-Met. I think she was ready to kill him the time he brought his Hippocratin friend ..."

Michael interrupted before Sil could add any more details about Sara's work-up. "So, how is it going these days?"

Sil paused before speaking. "It's really crazy. The number of flu patients increases every day. We just keep processing them through. Thank goodness I have some vacation time coming up. I am totally exhausted."

"They're letting you take vacation? I would have thought they would want all hands on deck." Michael asked.

"Ah, you forget the benefits of a union shop. I am overdue for time off. So it is off for two weeks on an island that has not seen this damn flu yet."

Michael steered the conversation back to the patients. "What's being done for them?"

Sil shrugged, "You remember how it goes. I'm diagnostics. I work 'em up and send 'em on. They either get better or they get an appointment with the canaries. With the constant flow of patients we don't have time to do any follow-up. Even if we did have the time things have gotten a lot tighter."

"What do you mean?" Michael asked.

"Well," Sil took a sip of his beer. "You remember how it was. We all hung around together. Diagnostics, treatment, A.O.D., we would have lunch together go out after work. It's not like that now." He leaned in, speaking softly, "We are discouraged from socializing outside of our own group. Look at our table, all diagnostics. Speaking of our table, I'd better get back. Mike it's great to see you. Lacy, I hope we get a chance to get to know each other, take good care of this guy." Sil walked back to his table where he was met by a barrage of questions from Marsha and the others.

Their beers arrived and Michael asked the waitress to bring some char-grilled oysters. Lacy asked Michael about Sil. After taking a pull on his beer, Michael shrugged. "Not much to tell. He's a good guy. We covered for each other at work, hung out. Our apartments were on the same floor in the company complex."

"And what about Marsha?" Lacy asked.

Michael shrugged again. "Another of the diagnostic technicians. We had a few dates. I think she thought it was more serious than I did."

"What did he mean about her wanting to kill you? It had something to do with a Hippocratin friend." Lacy looked at Michael as she picked up her glass with one hand and covered his hand with her other.

"It was nothing. One time Sara came to the Med–Met clinic to see what I did. Marsha saw us together and got all pissed." With his mention of Sara's name Lacy took her hand off Michael's.

Michael noticed her change. "Lacy, what is it? Every time she's mentioned you react. She's gone, she's the past. Why does it seem to bother you so much?"

Closing her eyes, Lacy spoke softly. "She's not here now, but what if she comes back? I love you, and I don't want to lose you."

"Lacy," Michael took her hand. "She's gone more than physically. What she and I had is over. You are the one I care about and that won't change."

Lacy remained silent. Before either of them could say anything further their food arrived and the conversation ended.

★ ★ ★

Richard Dietrich asked Alpha to meet with him. On the ranch the members of the Weps had taken to using their real names, but Alpha preferred to be called by his pseudonym. Alpha sat stiffly as Richard began. "I thought we all had agreed that it was in our collective interest to stay close to the ranch. If any of us are recognized we could be followed back here, jeopardizing everyone."

"So, what's your point?"

"My point," Richard replied, pointing for emphasis, "Is that you have been off-site quite a bit lately."

"I feel cooped up. I go out into the country, ride, shoot. I need to keep my skills up, never know when I'm going to need them."

"Cut the crap, Jeffers." Richard used Alpha's real name to make his point. "You were seen in New Orleans two days ago. What the hell were you doing following Rokoff around?"

Alpha was silent for several seconds before speaking. "Where did you hear that?"

"It doesn't matter where I heard it. I can assure you the information is reliable. You may think you are some type of experienced operative but the fact is you're sloppy. You're putting all of us in jeopardy. Now, why are you following Rokoff?"

Although visibly shaken by being discovered, Alpha did not back down. "You!" he said, as he stood and pointed down at Richard, "Do not tell me what I can and can't do. As far as I'm concerned you have given up the rights of leadership by sitting here and doing absolutely nothing. Some of us aren't content to stay on the side-line. We plan to shake things up."

"If you are to remain on this ranch, I will tell you what you can and can't do. My top priority is protecting our people." Richard was now on his feet facing Alpha. "How does this involve Rokoff?"

"I will not share any of our plans with you. You have made it abundantly clear that you are no longer one of us. As for your precious ranch, you can set four fewer places for dinner."

That night Richard filled Sara in on the details of what had occurred over the past two days. First the report he received from Spiderman, who was currently working as a human statue in Jackson Square, and the subsequent confrontation with Alpha. They had two problems to deal with. With Alpha taking chances the ranch was no longer safe. They would have to find another location, one that Alpha and his followers did not know. The other problem was figuring out what Alpha was planning. They both remembered the previous discussions of creating a martyr and that seemed the most likely scenario. Sara wanted to go right in and warn Rokoff. Richard argued for using their resources, including Spiderman, to monitor the situation. When they had more accurate information that something was going to happen they would do whatever was necessary to stop it. First they needed to move. They wouldn't be able to do anything if they were caught.

CHAPTER
41

The work load at the clinic continued non-stop. There was no way that any of them could take any time off. The pace was exhausting and the students began to notice that even the usually tireless Jacob was showing signs of wear. Michael was on a shift with Jacob and found him sitting with his head hanging down. "Are you okay?"

Jacob slowly looked up. "Just tired I guess. I'm not as young as I used to be. It's tough keeping up with you youngsters."

Although still a student, Michael's clinical skills were growing and he noticed that Jacob looked flushed and his breathing seemed rapid and shallow. "Would you mind if I listened to your lungs?"

Jacob tried to wave him off. "There really is no need for that. I just need to sit here and get my second wind."

"Jacob, you've taught me to trust my observation skills. Right now they are telling me to listen to your lungs."

Jacob slowly moved to the exam table, sat on the edge and allowed Michael to exam him. "Jacob, it sounds like you have fluid on your lungs. In addition your heart rate is accelerated and you feel feverish. Let's get an x-ray and I will discuss the findings with Patricia."

"There is no need to bother Patricia, you can discuss this with me."

"With all respect sir, you can't be your own physician. Let's get the tests, and you get some rest. Doctor's orders."

Jacob raised his prodigious eyebrows and tried to smile, "What have I created?"

Later that day Michael reviewed the findings with Patricia. Clearly Jacob was experiencing the signs and symptoms of the epidemic. The chest x-ray displayed edema, or fluid in the tissues of the lung. They would need to take him off the clinical rotation, even though they needed every possible team member. Convincing him wouldn't be easy but it needed to be done.

Patricia and Michael met with Jacob and explained that it was not in the best interests of the patients for him to continue being clinically active. He agreed and promised to rest and follow their instructions of care as long as he could remain involved in planning and oversight.

That evening at the group meeting Jacob sat off to the side and wore a respiratory mask to prevent infecting others. Patricia reported to the group on Jacob's status and a general discussion of the epidemic ensued.

Jacob spoke more softly than was normal for him, and clearly with effort. "There's a major discrepancy between what we're seeing and what Med–Met is reporting to the public. I have heard from a reliable source that Med–Met is hiding the true statistics. I fear that this is only serving to worsen the situation. With Med–Met's proclamations that all is well, people are not taking the precautions that they should." He pointed to his mask, "And that is accelerating the infection. We need to get a better handle on what they're really seeing and what is happening to the infected patients.

"Michael," he continued after pausing to cough, "You mentioned a recent conversation with one of your former co-workers."

"That's right," Michael answered and proceeded to share the conversation he had with Sil at Pat O'Brien's. "Basically it sounds like they have it just as bad as we do. I'm concerned about their treatment plans."

"Why?" Patricia interrupted.

"Sil mentioned that Med-Met is isolating the different technician groups from each other," Michael explained. "That's a big change. They always encouraged us to interact with the other groups, one big happy family. Now it appears as if they don't want one hand to know what the other's doing. It makes me wonder," Michael trailed off not completing his sentence.

"What do you wonder?" Jacob asked as he struggled to sit up in his chair.

Michael took his time in answering, "I am just wondering if they are trying to isolate the groups to limit the information regarding the disposition of the patients. Someone needs to get inside Med-Met and look at the records."

Earl who had been quiet up to that point jumped in. "Sure, no problem. We'll just waltz up to the front door. Excuse me, do you mind if we examine your records and expose you to the world? They'll provide comfy chairs, fix tea and cakes, and open up data ports."

Jacob held up his hand "Earl may be a little over the top, but he is right. No one can get in there and access the data."

Michael leaned forward in his seat, "It may be possible. I know someone who might be able to help."

★ ★ ★

Alpha and his team had relocated to New Orleans. They could now operate relatively safely. The search for the Weps was no longer a priority. The epidemic was growing and law enforcement was spread thin, as were all professions. They proceeded with their plans to assassinate Rokoff and make it look like a Med-Met operation. The plan was fairly straight forward. They would pose as Med-Met representatives and pay people to protest at a Hippocratin press conference. They would provide signs some of them bland but others with phrases like "Stone the Heretics", "Burn the Witches", and "Terminate Rokoff". When the protestors were later questioned by police they would fully believe that they were paid by Med-Met. While the attention was on the protestors, Alpha would be positioned at a strategic location and use a high-powered rifle to eliminate Rokoff. There was no debate in the group, these were Alpha's people. They patiently followed the vids and the public announcements looking for the right opportunity.

★   ★   ★

Michael needed to talk to Alex about how to get into Med-Met. He couldn't tell Lacy about it. He figured that she would try to stop him from doing it. She would be concerned about the danger plus being a cops daughter she might feel compelled to tell her father. He knew that Alex had a background in security so he arranged to meet with her and Georgi.

"I need to get into Med-Met and get to one of the computer terminals. If I can tap in to the system, I can at least get the statistics on the incidence of the illness. What will be more difficult is disposition and outcomes," Michael explained.

Alex quickly responded, "If you can get inside and log on to a computer, I think that my company can help get access to all the data. The challenge will be to get inside. Do you know of any way to do that?"

"I've given it some thought. Here's what I am thinking," he told them. "Feel free to shoot holes in it. Better that than having someone shooting holes in me.

"My friend Silvano is going out of town on vacation. His apartment is next to the one I used to live in, he has never locked his door. Few in the complex do, because the building is felt to be secure. Only fellow Med-Met workers live there.

"When I left Med-Met one of my uniforms was being cleaned and I didn't realize that I still had it until I picked up my laundry. I can put on the uniform and hang out near the building until shift change. When a group goes into the building I just join in and slip inside."

Alex interrupted, "Don't they have security cameras? Won't you be recorded? What about someone recognizing you?"

"I know where the cameras are," Michael continued. "I'll make sure that I am looking away when I pass them. As for being recognized I'll go in when a shift different than the one I was on is returning. On top of that, from what I hear, the workers are so exhausted these days that they'll only see the path to their beds.

"Once inside I go straight to Sil's apartment and 'borrow' his ID card. That will get me into Med–Met and access to the computer."

Georgi, who had been listening, quietly spoke up, "But that will only get you access to part of the information that you need?"

"Right," Michael replied. "Sil's access is limited to what he needs to do his job. I am going to need help getting beyond the firewalls that segment the data."

"That's where I may be able to help," Alex said. "Let me talk to the head of my security company and see what he suggests. Let's meet again tomorrow."

★ ★ ★

When they met the next day she explained. "My boss is more than happy to help. Seems he is not a Med–Met fan. They gave a big contract to his competitor. He is excited about the chance to crack their systems."

She removed a small pouch from her pocket and laid the contents on the table. "There are three things here that should help you get what you need." First she handed him a small ear bud and what looked like a band-aid. "The ear bud is obviously a receiver. The band-aid is a transmitter. Just place it anywhere on your neck or chin, like you nicked yourself shaving. It will pick up your voice, even if you whisper."

The third item appeared to be a normal data stick. "This," Alex explained, "is a data transceiver. Log in as your friend, plug this in and our computers will do the rest. An extra bonus is that it will wipe out all traces of the session. That way no questions will be raised as to why your friend was logged in while on vacation."

"Will it also be able to remove record of my, or his, entry into the building?" Michael asked. "I wouldn't want him to get in trouble."

"As long as all the systems are tied together it shouldn't be a problem," she answered. "In addition we will be prepared to create a diversion in the event that you're discovered. If at any time you feel that you need an escape just say the word 'lunar' and all hell will break loose. Pull out the transceiver and find the nearest exit."

"Alex," Georgi said, "You and Riser have got some serious technology here. I knew that you were in security, but this is more like espionage."

"Well dear," she answered, "To guarantee security you have to be adept at all the ways of broaching it. We figure that if we have access to the anti-security technology we can devise ways to protect against it. I assure you, none of these toys would work against one of our clients."

CHAPTER
42

Darren studied the reports. He was becoming more and more concerned with the shear numbers of patients being seen. "Wil, I can't sit here at CHA while this epidemic continues to get worse. The stats Angela provided show a dramatic increase in patients assigned to euthanasia." He shook his head as Wil seemed about to interrupt. "It's going to be difficult to contain the information much longer."

Wil waited until Darren took a breath and spoke rapidly. "Darren, we can spin this. Leave it to me and my people."

"No, Wil spinning isn't enough. Personnel morale is at an all time low. The staff are have an incredible work-load and its obvious to them what is going on. One of the A.O.D.s self-terminated for God's sake. I've made my decision, I need to return as Regional Director of Med-Met and provide a morale boost." He continued pacing around the large office. "I'm going to do more than just occupy the office. I'll visit the facility regularly, stop in on different days and shifts to interact with as many employees as possible."

"Come on Darren, what good will that do. You think a visit from the 'suit' is going to make a difference? What they really need is to be reminded about how good they've got it."

Darren stopped pacing and stood looking down at Wil who sat in a comfortable chair. "You're wrong. They need to see that the company supports them and I want to get a feel for how they're holding up under the strain."

Wil craned his neck, he couldn't get up from the chair with Darren standing over him, "Why don't we leave things as they are and just make some well-produced Vids to pump up the troops. Not only will this be a waste of your time but think of the potential of being exposed to the bug."

Darren just shook his head, "My mind is made up, prepare a statement."

★   ★   ★

All reports suggested the strategy was working as complaints went down and productivity increased after Darren's visits. Initially the media raised questions about the timing of his return to Med-Met and what it signaled. It didn't last long as Wil spun his media magic and was fairly convincing that this had been their plan all along.

★   ★   ★

Michael entered the facility with the eleven P.M. shift. He easily blended into the crowd in his diagnostic techs uniform. He had never worked the late shift and didn't recognize anyone. He hoped that no one recognized him.

Sil's I.D. card was accepted without incident. Michael made sure that his head was down or that he was facing away whenever he passed a camera. He checked the work schedule to determine which stations were operating that night and would be manned. He picked a location remote from the active sites got settled and logged-in with Sil's credentials. The log-in went smoothly plugging in the transceiver he whispered, testing his band-aid voice transmitter. "I am in, acknowledge. I am in."

"We've got you Michael." Alex's voice sounded gently in his ear. "Just move through the first few steps and we'll take it from there. I'll let you know when we have what we need."

Michael sat back in his chair and watched as data flew across the screen. He thought to himself, *"this is going well."* He was thankful that he would be out of there before long.

Darren had been making his rounds talking to the staff as they went about their work. Normally the center was relatively quiet on the late shift. With the epidemic in full swing the activity was substantial. Darren referred to his hand held device to see which locations were active and on-line and systematically visited each one.

It seemed odd that there was one active location separated from the others by several that were inactive. He made a note to have someone review that as it seemed quite inefficient. He made the trek down the long corridor to the remote work station. A technician sat back in his chair looking at his monitor. No patients were in sight. Darren surmised that he was probably doing some type of maintenance check which would explain why he wasn't closer to the active stations.

From the back Darren could see that it was a young man and chuckled thinking how surprised the tech would be to see him. As he approached he cleared his throat. "Hey son, how's everything going?"

Michael jumped, he hadn't heard anyone approaching. The voice seemed familiar, but he wasn't sure. Maybe he could bluff his way into getting this guy to leave. Trying to keep his voice calm he answered. "Going fine. Listen I'm really busy doing a systems check. Can't talk right now. How about coming back in about a half hour, I'd love some company then."

Darren continued forward. "I'll probably be gone by then. I just wanted to stop by say hello and thank you for your dedication."

Michael froze recognizing the voice. Darren walked to Michael's side. The smile on his face rapidly dissolved when he could see the young man's face and recognized who it was. "What the fuck are you doing here?" he shouted.

Michael jumped out of the chair fumbling unsuccessfully to grab the transceiver. "Lunar, lunar, lunar," Michael yelled. Darren grabbed at Michael's uniform pulling him back away from the transceiver. In his ear he heard Alex.

"Try to leave the transceiver in place for fifteen seconds. When the alarms go off grab it and go."

Darren screamed into his transmitter. "Security, to terminal 185. We have an intruder. Notify the police. Move!" He held Michael's uniform tightly. Michael pushed at Darren and twisted his body. Darren tightened his grip on the cloth, pulling Michael toward him. Michael swung his free left arm striking Darren in the side of the head. At that moment alarms went off and the sprinkler systems engaged. Darren was caught off guard by the combination of the blow to the head, the alarms and sprinklers. Michael twisted free and grabbed the transceiver from the terminal and ran.

As Michael broke away, Darren lunged for him, slipping on the wet floor. He shouted into his hand-held. "Shut those damn things off. Secure all exits. It's Michael Guidry. Call the police. Send his image to all security personnel. Secure all the exits."

Michael ran blindly and found himself in an unfamiliar sector. Alarms and sprinklers persisted as he searched for an exit. In his ear he heard Alex. "Get out of there as fast as you can. The police have been notified and are on the way. They think they've locked all the doors. We've overridden the door to the service drive at the south end of the building. We'll have someone meet you there."

Michael's cool was gone. "I have no idea where I am or how to get to that door. Should I ditch the transceiver?"

"No, take it easy. Hold on to the transceiver. We're using it to track you. Head down to the end of the corridor you are in and turn right. After that take the second left and it will lead you to the exit."

Michael headed down the hallway toward the exit. He was soaked from the sprinklers but saw the exit light and started to jog. He looked over his shoulder and saw Darren turn the last corner behind him. He ran as fast as he could despite the wet floor. As he hit the crash bar on the door the voice in his ear shouted, "Abort, police are on the service drive!"

It was too late. With his momentum and the wet floor Michael plunged out of the door and into the service drive. The only exit was blocked by a police vehicle. He tried to go back through the door he had just exited. Better to try and elude Darren Walters than the police. Before he could get through the door he was grabbed from behind and two strong arms locked around his chest. A deep voice said, "No you don't, you're coming with me."

Michael was partially dragged, partially carried and deposited in the back seat of the cruiser. The doors locked and an electrostatic barrier separated him from the front seat. The vehicle lifted and quickly backed out of the drive. Michael was surprised that there were no sirens or flashing lights as they headed away from Med-Met. Two men, one white, one black, sat silently in the front seat, neither turned to look at Michael. Michael stared at the back of their heads and finally spoke for the benefit of those listening to his transmitter. "Where are you taking me in this police vehicle headed uptown on St. Charles?"

There was a chuckle from the front seat and the driver spoke. "Forget it kid, this vehicle is shielded. No transmissions get in or out."

The man in the passenger seat added, "We knew sooner or later we'd have you in our custody again. You just can't keep out of trouble can you?" He turned to face the back seat and Michael recognized Detective Beatty and guessed that the driver must be Sergeant Jackson. "You really did it this time."

Michael was sweating, he figured that Beatty still resented the time that Lt. Livingston had him released from Beatty's custody. "Where are you taking me?"

"Not so fast." Beatty answered. "I have some questions first."

"Did anyone other than Darren Walters recognize you at Med-Met?"

"I don't think so." Michael answered tentatively.

"Do you think you were picked up on any of the security cameras, or did you touch anything without gloves on?"

Michael didn't like the tone of the questions. "Look, I'm not answering any more questions until we get to the police station and my lawyer is present."

Beatty had turned to look straight at him and had a big grin on his face. "But we aren't going to the police station. You won't need any lawyers where we're going."

Now Michael was really frightened. "You won't get away with this. There are others who knew where I was tonight."

"I am sure there were, but we are counting on them to remain quiet and not implicate themselves." As Beatty finished the vehicle pulled into a driveway. "Well, here we are. End of the line."

Sweating, Michael looked out the window and was shocked to see they were at Lacy's house. "What're we doing here?"

Jackson turned and spoke for the first time in a while. "Nothing, we're not here, and you've been here all evening with your girlfriend."

"I don't understand did Lt. Livingston send you?" Michael asked, confused.

"No, Andy's out of town. The princess called us herself. She was in her dad's office, heard the scanner and the report of your name. She called and asked us to get you out of there."

"And you would do that for me?" Michael was incredulous.

"For you? No way." Beatty answered. "We would do it for the princess though. If we didn't she'd make our lives hell. Princess is unhappy, daddy is unhappy. Daddy is unhappy, Beatty and Jackson are miserable."

"So, here's how it goes." Jackson added. "As long as no one but Walters saw you, and you weren't on camera and left no fingerprints, than it's your word against his. Your girlfriend says you were with her all night."

"But what Walters says is going to carry a lot of weight. Why would he make it up?"

"Who knows?" Jackson said, shrugging his shoulders. "The man's under a lot of pressure lately, and everyone knows that he hates you. He needed someone to blame for his problems. Listen, when they locate you, they are going to question you. Stick to the story. There'll be plenty of heat but they'll have to produce corroborating evidence."

Alex' voice was in Michael's ear again. "Michael, they turned off the shielding and we were able to hear the last exchange. Don't turn down a gift. Get out of the car. Georgi and I will meet you at Lacy's. After all, we've all been there since the lovely dinner party she threw earlier this evening."

CHAPTER
43

Darren swore out a complaint alleging that Michael Guidry had trespassed in the Med–Met facility, and may have attempted to sabotage the computer system. As soon as the police were gone he convened his executive team.

"He obviously had help," Darren began. "He exited through the door without a problem. When I got there it was sealed. By time I got security to unseal the exits there was no sign of him."

"What was the little bastard up to?" Wil asked.

"I don't know. He was clearly logged in to the computer system, but I have no idea what he was looking at. He pulled some kind of device out of the jump drive as he ran. I have asked Biggs to do an analysis of what information was accessed."

Wil was pacing, "We've got that scumbag dead to rights this time. How the hell did he get in and how did he get access?"

"Both good questions," Darren answered. "Biggs is also pulling the video records to see where and when he got in, and how he logged on.

★   ★   ★

When Michael returned to his apartment that night there were uniformed New Orleans police waiting for him. He took some slow deep breaths and prepared himself for the questions he knew were coming.

One of the officers approached and asked, "Are you Michael Guidry?"

Michael answered that he was.

The officer continued, "Where were you tonight between 10:30 PM and midnight?"

Michael feigned ignorance, "Why, is something wrong?"

The officer smiled, "I'm asking the questions. Please answer."

"I was at my girlfriend's house," he answered seeming perplexed. "She had a dinner party."

"A dinner party," the officer said. "I suppose she can back that up."

"Sure why not?" Michael answered, hoping that he seemed convincing.

The officer still pressed his questions, "Was there anyone else there, or just the two of you?"

"No," Michael quickly answered. "There was another couple there as well."

The officer had been told that Guidry might have a convenient alibi. Most likely his fellow Hippocratin conspirators. "We need to question all those who were at this dinner party," he said not hiding his sarcasm.

"OK," Michael replied, "The other couple was Georgi Chen and Alexandra Hemingway. And of course my girlfriend, Lacy Livingston."

The officer who had been recording furiously, stopped with his digi-pen in mid-air. "Lacy Livingston? Lt. Livingston's daughter?"

"Yeah, that's her," Michael answered looking the officer in the eye.

The officer was no longer so self-assured, "And she will verify that you were with her all evening."

"Of course," Michael answered.

The officer now took on a different and more respectful tone. "Mr. Guidry, do you know why Darren Walters, the regional

Med–Met director would claim that he saw you at the Med–Met facility tonight?"

Michael continued to act confused by the whole situation. "None what–so–ever. You may know that Mr. Walters and I have a, – er, history. But I don't know why he would make those type of accusations."

The officer excused himself, moved out of earshot and made a call on his communicator. Michael could see that the conversation was animated but couldn't tell what they were saying. He closed his communicator and chatted with his partner, keeping an eye on Michael at all times. His communicator then chirped, he listened nodded and approached Michael. "Mr. Guidry, I just spoke with my sergeant. Ms. Livingston backs up your story, so for the time being we are not going to bring you in. Please don't leave town. After we've spoken in more detail to Ms. Livingston and the others we may have more questions for you."

Michael shrugged, "No problem. Can I go catch some sleep now, it's really late and I need to work tomorrow." When the officers left he let himself into his apartment and collapsed on the sofa.

★   ★   ★

Early the next morning Darren's team reconvened at Med-Met headquarters. The large bulk of Biggs dominated the room as Darren, Wil, Suzanne and Angela arrived to hear his report. Wil began to sit, but quickly jumped back-up. "I can't believe they didn't arrest the little prick."

"What do you mean they didn't arrest him? How could they not after Darren's statement?" Angela was incredulous.

"Apparently," Wil answered sarcastically, "He has an alibi." Three credible witnesses according to the police. One of them a police Lieutenant's daughter. Guidry's probably fucking the lying bitch."

Darren turned to Biggs, "What do the tapes show? If we have him on camera he and his lying friends are dead."

Biggs hesitated before beginning. "Well Mr. Walters, the problem is we don't have any good images. I think we have tracked down when he entered, and his movements to where you say you saw him. Unfortunately, he's always facing away from the cameras. All we can say is that it's someone his approximate size and hair color wearing a technician's jumpsuit." Biggs pulled a pen like device from his pocket and projected a series of holo-images showing a figure mostly from the back."

Walters pointed at one image and asked, "From the entry photos it looks like he came in on an ID card. It should be registered in the system whose card it was"

"That's another problem sir. It seems that there's an eighteen minute gap in the log-in records. Before you ask, same thing with the terminal he logged onto. No record of the log-on, and no record of what he accessed."

"Angela," Darren said. "Get our security people to question everyone who worked last night. Someone has to have recognized him. Even if they hadn't worked with him directly, his face is pretty famous from the vids."

"We're already on it Darren," she answered. "Biggs has shared the entry film with security. They will start with the workers who entered around the time as our mystery visitor."

Darren managed to appear calm, "Let me make it perfectly clear to everyone. This is not a mystery visitor. This is Michael-fucking-Guidry, and he is not going to get away with this."

★ ★ ★

Alexandra stood straight in her usual place across from Justin Riser's desk. He spun in his chair to address her. "Captain, have you reviewed the material we down-loaded from Med-Met?"

"Yes sir," was her reply.

"Well, what's your interpretation?"

"My interpretation is that they are actively suppressing information as to the extent of the disease. Further, large numbers are being sent for terminal treatment," she answered crisply.

"That is how I read it as well," he paused. "I think it is time for us to have a talk with Michael Guidry and Jacob Rokoff."

★   ★   ★

Wil called the head of Med-Met security into his office. "Whatever you find out, I want you to report it to me before anyone else. Is that clear?"

"Mr. Armbrister," the chief replied. "I report to Ms. Stuart. It is my responsibility to report my findings to her."

Wil slowly shook his head, "I am not asking you not to report to her, just to report it to me first. For that courtesy I will do you a courtesy. A monetary courtesy. A generous monetary courtesy."

"I see sir. I suppose it would be alright. As long as I can brief Ms. Stuart right afterward."

"Absolutely," Wil assured him. "Now, what have you learned so far."

"Well," the chief said. "No one definitively saw Guidry. There are two people who think they might have seen someone who could have been him. They never worked with him but did see him on the vids."

"Names, give me names," Wil demanded. He quickly dismissed the man as soon as he got the information he needed.

★   ★   ★

Alex introduced Justin Riser to Jacob and Michael. Riser briefed them on the information from Med-Met. Jacob, wearing his isolation mask, sat at a distance from the others. His breathing appeared difficult and he coughed frequently. "Tell me Mr. Riser," he asked struggling with his words. "What percentage of the patients are being referred for terminal therapy?"

"Our estimate is approximately twenty percent." Riser said.

Michael jumped up, "That is more than twice the natural fatality rate of the disease. More than half of those people might live with supportive care."

Jacob struggled to speak, "Michael's right. These numbers are alarming. We need to let the public know the extent of the epidemic, and what Med-Met is doing. Suggestions on how we should go about this?"

"I think you need to be as public as possible," Riser said. "If you try any other, more subtle way, or give Med-Met any warning it will allow them room to cover-up some of the incriminating evidence."

"I agree," Jacob said between coughs. "The questions are timing and forum."

There was a knock at the door and Michael got up to answer it. An attractive woman stood on the other side. She seemed somewhat familiar to Michael. She tried to peer around him to see the others in the room.

"Mr. Guidry," the woman said, "I'm looking for Jacob Rokoff." She was able to see past Michael and got her first glimpse of Jacob. A look of shock passed across her face. "Oh my god!" she exclaimed. "Uncle Jacob, what's wrong?"

Jacob sat up trying to look stronger than he was. "Well my dear, it seems I have a touch of what is going around." He looked to the others, "Let me introduce you. This is my niece, Suzanne Hartstein. Suzanne this is Justin Riser, Alexandra Hemingway, and you obviously know Michael Guidry."

Michael recognized the name and now could place where he knew her from. She was with Darren that day at Med-Met when Michael was ambushed in front of the camera crew. "Jacob, this is your niece? She works for Darren Walters."

"Yes Michael, she is my niece and I believe she does work for Walters. The two facts are not necessarily mutually exclusive." Jacob replied.

"Uncle Jacob," Suzanne interrupted. "I need to speak to you and Mr. Guidry." She appeared obviously agitated.

Jacob asked Alex and Riser to excuse them. When they left he asked Suzanne what was wrong.

"I need to warn you," she told them. "Darren believes that he saw Mr. Guidry at Med–Met last night. I don't know if it's true. Darren has been under a tremendous amount of pressure lately.

"Anyway, they have no real proof that you were there," she said looking at Michael. "The reason I am here though is to warn you that Wil Armbrister is manufacturing evidence and is going to try and have you arrested."

"What type of evidence?" Jacob asked.

"He as much as told me that he is going to pay two employees to swear that they recognized Mr. Guidry last night. The slimy creep thought it would impress me to know how clever he is. Of course he has no idea that I am your niece."

Michael still shocked from the information that Jacob's niece was a Med-Met insider sat quietly.

Jacob spoke to his niece. "I appreciate you coming to see me. The information you shared with me last week was very valuable. The situation may even be worse than you thought. The number of people being diagnosed and terminated at Med-Met exceeds our fears."

Suzanne looked from Jacob to Michael and back, "And you know this, how?"

Jacob managed a faint smile, "The how is not important. What is important is the knowledge. Thank you for warning us about Armbrister, and be careful."

"I will Uncle Jacob, and please, take care of yourself." She nodded to Michael and let herself out.

Michael waited until the door was closed before speaking to Jacob. "Your niece works for Walters? Do the others know?"

"No Michael," Jacob said. "Until now no one else in the Hippocratins has known, and I would like to keep it that way. The fewer people that know the more likely it will be that Suzanne can continue to provide me information."

Michael recalled last week's conversation where Jacob had referred to information about the scope of the problem at Med-Met. "So she is your reliable source?"

"Yes. She came to me concerned that her bosses were hiding the true nature of the epidemic. I had suspected that but she gave me confirmation. With what she has told us the need to get the information out has a greater urgency. We need to strike before they try and have you arrested. Once it the public becomes aware of what they're doing they won't have time to worry about you." Jacob sat back in his chair, straining to continue, "Please call Patricia and let her know what's going on. Ask her to assemble the staff, and senior students in two hours. Also see if Alexandra and Riser can join us. We have a press conference to plan.

"If you don't mind I am going to get a little rest," Jacob said as he tried to rise.

Michael watched Jacob struggle to get out of his chair and head-off to find a place to lie down. He was deeply concerned. He had never before known Jacob to need rest.

CHAPTER
44

Dietrich had moved his remaining companions to a motel in Hattiesburg, MS. The search for his group had cooled off but he still didn't feel comfortable being any closer to New Orleans. He had gotten word to Spiderman of their new location. Dietrich was out when Spiderman arrived at the motel. He was in his derelict persona when he knocked on the door of Dietrich and Sara's room.

Sara having seen him in this particular garb before wasn't surprised, she quickly got him into the room before anyone else spotted him and reported a suspicious "bum" to the police.

"Where's Richard?" Spiderman was out of breath and obviously distressed.

Sara offered him some water and a chair before replying. "He's gone to Jackson to get supplies."

"When will he be back?" Spiderman asked anxiously.

"Maybe tonight, but possibly not until tomorrow. He has to be careful where he shops. He needs to avoid places where he might get recognized."

"Well, that's what he gets for not disguising himself. If you ever ran into me without a costume you wouldn't know it was me." Spiderman smiled as he spoke.

"I'm sure I would. There are things about you that I would be able to pick up."

"You think so." His smile broadened, "Did you enjoy your jog around the Southern Miss campus last weekend?"

"Yes," she said with a furrowed forehead. "How did you know?"

"Remember when you caught up to that small group of runners? You were very friendly, chatted with a few."

"We're you ...?" she stammered. "Which one?"

"I guess I made my point. Any way no time for guessing now, I need to talk to Richard."

"We'll have to wait until he gets back, I have no way of contacting him."

"Crap," Spiderman was visibly upset. "I think it's going to happen tomorrow. I think they are going to try and kill Rokoff."

Sara jumped to her feet. "What makes you think so?"

"I've been keeping track of Alpha, he and his friends have a small apartment in Fauberg-Marigny. They have coffee every morning at Café DuMonde. I can watch them from the corner where I do my human statue gig.

"This morning they're drinking their coffee as usual. Some guy is walking around handing out some type of flyer. He gives them a couple. They read it and get all excited. Start talking rapidly and a lot of hand waving. They grabbed the flyers and left before they finished their coffee, heading down Decatur towards Esplanade. They dropped one as they went.

"When they were out of sight I crossed the street and picked up the paper. It said that the physicians of the Hippocratin Society will be giving an update on the epidemic tomorrow morning at ten in front of the Hippocratin New Orleans Clinic. At the bottom it said, *Learn the truth. Don't be misled by the Med-Met cover-up.* I'm sure they are going to try and do it then."

Sara paced the room as Spiderman finished. "Shit," she said. "We can't wait for Richard. He might not be back until it's too late. You have to take me to New Orleans!"

★   ★   ★

Jacob planned the conference, it was important that the public knew the full extent of the epidemic. He planned on speaking but had rapidly gotten sicker. By that morning he was confined to bed. Patricia and Michael stood over him. "Help me up you two." He managed to get the words out in a whisper laced with coughs. "I need to tell the world what's really happening."

Patricia eased him back to his pillow. "You have a high fever and your respiratory status is deteriorating. You rest, Michael and I will handle this."

Jacob tried to rise to protest, but didn't have the strength.

Once again Michael was being thrust into the uncomfortable role as Hippocratin spokesman. He stood at the podium while the crowd gathered and the media set-up. He wondered if his mind was playing tricks on him. While scanning the crowd he thought he saw a furtive figure darting in and out. He hadn't gotten a good look but a few things registered on the edges of his consciousness, lithe, female and dark hair. The way she moved was imprinted in his memory. Could it possibly be her? He strained to see if it was, but she was gone.

Shaking his head to clear the image from his mind, he perched on the front stairs of the Hippocratin clinic. He and his colleagues were going to try and answer the public's questions about the epidemic. At least they would share what they knew. No information was coming from Med-Met. They had confined their public statements to accusations that the Hippocratins had somehow created the illness.

On a rooftop a short distance away a man sighted Michael through the scope of a high powered rifle. He preferred a weapon that dispensed solid ammo over laser or sonic based guns. His spotter on the ground relayed that it had been announced earlier that Rokoff was too ill to address the crowd. In his place Michael Guidry would lead off and Patricia Murphy and others would address the issues. Michael stood where Rokoff would have been. The gunman swore to himself. He had to make a decision. Rokoff was the primary target, but it was too late to turn back. The damn kid would have to do.

As Michael prepared to speak he looked around once more. He stepped up to the microphone. The gunman prepared to squeeze the trigger but had to wait as the street car glided by the front of the clinic on a curtain of air. From his vantage he couldn't hear the artificial clackity-clack sound that it made to simulate the original cars.

As it passed Michael began, "Good afternoon ..." He was interrupted by a blur to his left and when he turned he saw her. Sara was running toward him. He began to smile as she launched herself into the air, flying directly at him. Instinctively he put out his arms to catch and embrace her.

She hit him full in the chest and together they tumbled to the porch floor. Michael held her and called her name. He felt a warm wetness on his hands. Tears? She was limp in his arms. The warm liquid was thick and sticky, definitely not tears. Things happening around him slowly came into focus. People were running, screaming, some hid behind columns. Patricia was on her knees beside him, asking if he was okay. Others were taking Sara from him and gently setting her on her back. She wasn't moving.

Patricia was speaking to him again, "Michael were you hit?"

His head fuzzy he slowly responded, "Sure, Sara hit me, but I'm okay. What's wrong with Sara?"

"She was shot. She knocked you out of the way."

The police, who had been on the scene for crowd control, were herding the spectators to a safe area. Other officers fanned out looking for signs of the shooter.

Michael got to his knees and crawled to where Sara was being frantically worked on by his teachers and classmates. She was covered in blood. Someone was performing CPR, someone else was preparing to intubate. The wail of police sirens grew rapidly closer.

Michael wanted to help but he was still groggy and confused. Patricia was running the code while trying to keep Michael out of the way. They stabilized Sara as well as they could, placed her on a board and carried her into the clinic's trauma room.

Michael trailed behind. As he headed to the entrance, Lacy fought through the crowd to his side. She was in tears and yelled above the noise of the crowd and sirens. "Michael, are you all right?"

Michael looked at her blankly. "Yeah, but Sara. I gotta go. I gotta go." He headed in to the clinic leaving Lacy alone on the stairs. Lacy stood staring at him unsure of whether to follow or leave.

★ ★ ★

Alpha quickly packed his gear and proceeded with his escape plan. He could not believe that the Anson bitch had knocked the target down just as he had depressed the trigger. At that point he had no idea that she had taken the round. His weapon broke down nicely and fit neatly into a saxophone case. He exited the building quickly and proceeded to cross Canal Street and head to the French Quarter. Just another musician trying to make his way in the Big Easy.

★ ★ ★

Lacy was standing alone on the blood-stained porch when her father arrived. He was there to lead the investigation of the shooting. He quickly changed focus when he saw his daughter standing there in tears. He enfolded her in his arms and tried to comfort her. "It's okay baby. I know it must have been terrible, but you're alright and my reports tell me that Michael is fine. That woman, whoever she is, saved him."

"It was her Daddy. I know that she saved him, but he still loves her."

"Her? We don't have an I.D. yet. Who is she?"

"Sara. Sara Anson. Dad, I rushed to him to make sure he was okay. He looked right past me. He didn't even know who I was. All he wanted to do was get to her."

"Lacy, don't jump to any conclusions. Michael is probably in shock. He was shot at and the woman who saved him took a bullet that was intended for him." At that moment Sergeant Jackson arrived and addressed his boss.

"Andy, some of the witnesses gave us a pretty good idea where the shots came from. They want you over there."

"Thank you Sergeant. If you could would you please get Lacy settled. Take her statement yourself, she was pretty close and has identified the woman. Also, could you please call my wife to come down and be with her."

"Sure Andy. Anything for our girl." The burly Sergeant escorted Lacy to a nearby police vehicle, while her father got into another waiting car. It lifted off and took him to the roof-top a few blocks away where witnesses had reported seeing unusual activity.

CHAPTER
45

Michael stumbled into the trauma room. His colleagues were working feverishly on Sara. He found Patricia, he took at deep breath, appearing to be more in control of himself, and calmly asked. "Where was she hit?"

Patricia answered clinically and unemotionally. "As she leapt at you she took the bullet in her left side. It entered her spleen and then on into the thoracic cavity. Right now it appears that she is having profuse abdominal bleeding. I need to perform a splenectomy. She also has a hemothorax, we have a chest tube in place."

Patricia was the senior physician on site, and Michael respected her skills. Despite that he had to ask. "Does Jacob know? Is he going to perform the surgery?"

Patricia appeared not to be offended by what others might take as a slight on their skills. "No, Michael. Jacob's sedated and requiring high oxygen. He is not in any condition to help."

"Well, what can I do to help?" Michael asked. He brushed his hand across his face and his eyes pleaded with her.

"Right now, I need to concentrate on Sara. You may still be in shock. You would be a liability in the OR. I don't want to have to worry about you too. Please, go get some rest. With the epidemic I need all hands functioning at full capacity. The police are going to want a statement. I've told them you are being sedated and unavailable right now."

Michael didn't go rest; he went to Jacob's room in the in-patient section. Jacob was lying quietly, an IV line in his left arm and wearing an oxygen mask. Michael called his mentor's name but didn't get a response. He swallowed hard and reached out to touch Jacob, still nothing. Tears welling in his eyes he pulled up a chair and took Jacob's limp hand in his own. He looked at the man in the bed, so pale and frail. The signature red hair seemed to have more white in it. This was the icon who once could fill up a room, both physically and by his personality. Sara had invited Michael to that first Hippocratin class, but it was Jacob who had been responsible for his staying. Now Jacob was showing all the signs of progression of the atypical influenza, and Sara was undergoing emergency surgery. Michael leaned on Jacob's bed-rail and began to sob. The sobs progressed to shaking and unrelenting heaves which didn't stop until he fell asleep.

★   ★   ★

Hours later, Michael woke with a start. He had heard his name called. He looked at the bed, but Jacob remained as he had been. Michael's head ached from where it had been pressed on the bed rail. He heard his name again and turned to see Patricia in the doorway.

"I wondered where you went," she said. "How are you feeling?"

Shaking off the haziness in his head Michael asked, "How's Sara?"

"She is alive, but still critical. The bullet did a lot of damage and she lost a lot of blood. She was hypotensive for too long. We removed her spleen, repaired some vessels and drained her chest. She has a chest tube and remains intubated. She hasn't shown any signs of regaining consciousness." Michael noticed Patricia's fatigue.

Sara lay in a high-tech intensive care bed with monitors indicating her status and tubes draining or infusing fluids, going in all directions. Her skin was pale and gray in the artificial light. Her chest moved rhythmically up and down in synch with the respirator.

Michael brushed a stray hair off her face, wiped the tears from his own cheeks and took her hand. He stretched back and hooked the leg of a chair with his foot, pulling it toward him, never letting go of her hand. He continued to stroke her fingers until, for the second time that night, he fell asleep at the bedside of someone who had changed his life.

★ ★ ★

Lieutenant Andy Livingston reviewed the eyewitness interviews. Most had been paying attention to the activity on the stage and gave various versions of Sara running onto the stage and knocking Michael down. Many of the anti-Hippocratin protestors related they had been approached by people who had paid them to carry signs and to disrupt the press conference. They said the individuals who approached them were well dressed corporate types, and their vehicles had Med–Met logos. A few said they were warned not to get too close to the stage, and to "keep their head down".

On the surface, it seemed to point to a Med–Met involvement in the shooting. To Andy, that seemed too obvious. He would certainly pursue an investigation of Med–Met, but he was keeping other options open.

★ ★ ★

Wil argued that he had two perfectly good witnesses, "I am telling you, they'll swear that they had seen Michael at Med–Met that night. Just let them give their statements to the police and then we use political pressure to make sure that Guidry gets arrested.

Darren rubbed his temples his growing frustration with his PR man showing as he spoke. "First of all, Guidry was almost killed today. His girlfriend took a bullet for him and by all reports is near death. In addition to that we're suspected of having arranged the shooting." He pointed his finger at Wil for emphasis. "If we go after

Guidry now it will only feed the sentiment that we are out to get him and the Hippocratins."

Wil pushed on, not backing down. "We have to maintain the initiative. That was one of the areas where Nixon's team failed." He nodded, "Instead of pressing the issue that the hippies and protestors were criminals they allowed them to become the good guys. The media sentiment swung in favor of the miscreants. We've gotta go after them with everything we've got."

"No Wil," Darren pressed back. "I've done some of my own reading about your precious Nixon and his cronies. They created much of their own problems through dirty tricks and illegal activities." He paused staring at Wil, "They may have even bribed witnesses to stretch the truth."

Wil broke eye contact with Darren, but said nothing.

"For now," Darren resumed, "We leave Michael Guidry alone."

★   ★   ★

Michael again was awakened from a deep sleep; still in the chair at Sara's bedside. Her hand lay on the bed, not much different in color from the white sheet. He looked at the monitors, the signs were unchanged. His communicator chirped, he realized that was the sound that had woken him. The staccato chirps were in the ancient Morse code pattern of SOS, the international distress signal. Jacob had thought this a clever signal for medical emergencies. Michael looked at the read-out, room 17. Jacob's room, he jumped up knocking over the chair and ran down the hall.

The scene in the room was chaotic. Nurses scuttled about the bed adjusting fluids and changing settings. Monitor alarms were sounding. Jacob's chest moved in an erratic pattern. None of the physicians had arrived. Michael grabbed a nurse and asked for an assessment.

"Oxygen sats dropped. We've increased the O2 and pushed diuretics. He's tachy and his BP is dropping," she reported efficiently, with a nervous edge in her voice.

"Chest x-ray?" he asked.

"Yes, the auto-imager recorded an image as soon as the drop in saturation was detected," she replied. She pushed a button on a remote control and an holo-image floated above the bed.

Michael studied the image the lung fields in the rotating three dimensional image. Both sides were mostly white with very little normal black area. He moved the electro-stethescope across Jacob's chest, listening to the sounds and watching the wave pattern that appeared below chest x-ray. A read-out on the bottom flashed, "*Consistent with severe consolidation*", supporting Michael's clinical impression.

Noting the worsening vital signs, Michael called out in a clear voice, "We need to intubate. I need gloves and a 7.5 ET tube."

The senior nurse in the room came over and said softly, "Jacob has a do not resuscitate and do not intubate order. When he was admitted he reconfirmed his living will."

Michael looked at her, uncomprehending. "This is Jacob, we have to do everything possible. This isn't Med-Met. We give people every chance."

Patricia had come in and signaled the nurse with a tilt of her head. The nurse gathered the rest of the staff leaving Michael and Patricia alone with Jacob.

"You're right Michael," Patricia said. "We do give people a chance. We also know when it is time to let go. We're not Med-Met. We don't accelerate the process, but we don't provide futile care. You know this. Jacob taught you this."

"But Patricia," Michael said his voice cracking. "Maybe there is a chance. Jacob's a fighter he just needs some help until he recovers."

"You know better than that," she told him. "You've seen the course of this infection over and over. Jacob gave me explicit instructions not to treat him differently than any other patient. He was clear that we were not to ignore his wishes regarding resuscitation."

As she was speaking the indicators on the monitors continued to worsen. Jacob's breathing became more irregular with gaps between breaths. Patricia leaned over the bed and listened to the stethoscope.

She moved the stethoscope around his chest, her expression becoming grimmer with each new placement. She put her fingers on his neck to feel for his pulse. She then leaned further over and kissed him gently on the forehead. When she turned back to Michael there were tears streaming down her cheeks. "He's gone," she said. "Jacob is gone."

Michael stood, shoulders slumped, head down. He did not look at the bed where Jacob lay, nor did he look at Patricia. He muttered, "I need to get back to Sara."

Patricia, still crying, came to his side and tried to put an arm around his shoulder. He shrugged her off and pulled away. She backed off, visibly stiffened, and told him, "If you are going back into a patient's room, you need to clean yourself up. You're still wearing the clothes you wore yesterday. Sara's blood is still on them. Either shower and put on clean scrubs, or go home and take care of yourself."

Michael shuffled out of the room and headed down the hall to the locker room. He cleaned up as directed and returned to Sara's bedside. Over the next several days he rarely left her. Staff brought him patient food trays and he occasionally went to the locker room to shower and put on fresh scrubs. He spoke to Sara frequently. He would not leave her side to resume his clinic activities and refused to take part in planning Jacob's memorial service.

Patricia became increasingly irritated with Michael. On rounds one morning she vented her anger. "Have you seen the lines at the clinic lately?" she asked him. "Jacob is gone and two others are too sick to see patients. While you wallow in despair the rest of us are working round the clock.

"Do you think that you are the only one grieving over Jacob? Don't you think that the rest of us are concerned about Sara? Damn it, Michael, most of us have known them both a lot longer than you have. We all still have work that needs to be done, people who need to be cared for. You need to pull yourself together and help us."

He looked up at her with a blank expression, "Why? We aren't doing any good. With all our knowledge and skill we couldn't help Jacob. Despite everything you've done Sara isn't getting better.

"Maybe Med–Met has it right after all. At least they don't let patients hang-on and suffer, in the end the outcome is the same. If Jacob hadn't stayed up 24/7 taking care of the incurables he might not have gotten sick. He'd still be alive. Why do we even bother?"

Patricia glared at him, "You know, if the woman in that bed could hear you she would kick your ass so hard you would be back at Med–Met. I never thought that you would be a quitter. I guess Earl is right about you, no backbone."

Michael spoke in a monotone, not looking up at her, "Well fuck Earl and fuck you." He went back to stroking Sara's hand as Patricia stormed out of the room.

★   ★   ★

Lacy sat at the kitchen table with her mother. "I haven't heard from Michael in days. He hasn't returned to his apartment since the shooting. I've called and left messages, but he doesn't call back. Dad says I need to give him some time. That he's been through a huge shock with Jacob's death and Sara being shot. I don't know, shouldn't I try and help him?"

Rachel smiled at her daughter. "It's hard to know what's the right thing to do. Do you wait for him to work things out for himself, or do you try and help. If he isn't ready for help it could make things worse."

"How do I know?" Lacy asked.

"You won't know by sitting here," her mother told her.

★   ★   ★

Michael sat with the unconscious Sara. He spoke to her, filling her in on everything that had happened since she and the other Weps had gone into hiding. He was telling her of how he met Lacy and the connection between Lacy and Lettie Rubin. "I hope you don't mind," he told her. "After you left I didn't date for quite a while.

When Lacy came along I pushed her away at first. She was persistent, pushy. Reminded me of another woman I know," he said squeezing her hand.

"She's really smart, and funny. She's doing her Masters at Tulane. I feel good when I'm with her. What you and I had was special, but this is different. I know the two of you would really like each other. You have to get better so I can introduce you. There's so much going on. Jacob is gone. Med–Met is trying to have me arrested."

At that moment Lacy arrived at the door to Sara's room. She was about to let Michael know that she was there but he continued to talk to Sara.

"So you see," he told the woman in the bed, clutching her hand tightly, "You can't leave me now. I need you. I really need you."

Lacy quietly turned tears welling in her eyes. She dropped a plate of cookies, that she had brought, on the nurse's station counter and left, her fears confirmed.

CHAPTER
46

Alex was summoned to Riser's office. She was surprised that he wasn't in his usual high backed chair. Instead he sat in an upholstered chair in a small sitting group on the side of the room, he had a drink in his hand. He held out the glass and asked if she wanted anything. She shook her head. He motioned her to take the seat next to him.

"Alexandra, circumstances are such that I need to fill you in on certain information that very few people have access to. The progression of the epidemic, the death of Rokoff, and the information that Guidry brought out of Med-Met makes it no longer tenable to keep silent."

Alex looked at her boss, gave a slight nod, but didn't interrupt him.

Riser continued, "As a young man I worked for a firm that provided security in the lunar colony. I was only in my twenties, but I had risen rapidly in the ranks. At the time of the lunar disaster I was second in command of security for a secret laboratory called Infinity.

"I am alive today because I had been sent back to earth to acquire some biologic materials needed for the laboratory's work. Our ship was on its way to earth when the dome collapsed. Had I not been on that mission I would have died with the others."

When Riser paused, Alex sat and waited.

After a minute of silence he continued, "The presence of Infinity was known to very few. The space authority on earth was not aware of it. The scientists at Infinity were concerned that there was a great risk of a lethal epidemic within the confines of the lunar dome. Their mission was to prepare for such an event by identifying all potential pathogens, and creating vaccines against them."

Alex spoke for the first time, "Excuse me sir, but if they were creating vaccines, why the secrecy?"

Riser thought for a moment before answering, "At the time, tensions between the earth and its lunar colony were increasing. Some colonists were advocating independence. Authorities on earth said they would never allow this because of the economic implications. The fear on the moon was that a biologic weapon could easily be used against them. Infinity was established to provide defense against that possibility." He got up refilled his glass and continued.

"They created vaccines or treatments for known pathogens. They also made recombinant organisms, combining components from existing viruses. The thinking was, they could anticipate what "super-bugs" might be created to be used as biologic weapons."

"Sir," Alex interrupted, "Couldn't these same "super-bugs" be used offensively against the earth?"

Riser raised an eyebrow, "It seems, whether there was any intent or not, that is exactly what has happened. For that reason that we need to share this with those who might be able to do something with the information. I would have taken this to Rokoff, but now we need another alternative. I need you to get me a profile on Dr. Marshall Ellis."

★   ★   ★

When Michael returned from the locker room Sara's bed was empty. He rushed to the nursing station to find out where she was. The nurse saw him coming and began speaking, anticipating his question, "They've taken her back to surgery. Her pressure started dropping rapidly, and her crit is low. Patricia thinks that she is bleeding internally. They pushed fluids, started transfusion and rushed to the OR."

Michael turned to head to the OR. "Wait," the nurse put his hand on Michael's shoulder. "Patricia asked me to let you know that you are not welcome in the OR. I'm sorry."

Michael considered forcing his way into the operating room. He decided that the disruption he would cause would not be in Sara's best interest. Instead he went to the physician's lounge and called up the OR on the vid screen. He sunk into a chair and watched as they frantically worked to stop the bleeding.

Patricia's skill was evident as she worked to stem the bleeding. "The vessels are extremely friable, I can't get a good surface to attach a graft." Her voice came clearly through the speaker as Michael used the zoom feature to get a better view of the operative field. The suction had trouble keeping up with the bleeding. He watched as the suture entered the vessel and then tore the tissue as Patricia attempted to tie a knot.

Someone yelled, "Pressure dropping!"

Another voice responded, "Open all fluids wide, hang another two units synthetic RBC."

Michael zoomed out and viewed a wider field. The operative team was covered in blood. There was blood everywhere. The anesthesiologist was injecting something into an IV line. "Patricia, we're losing her. I can't hold her pressure." A moment later he spoke again, "V-fib!"

CHAPTER
47

The cemetery off of Elysian Fields was very active, as were all of the cemeteries in the New Orleans area with the epidemic in full swing. Michael stood by himself at the cemetery. The Hippocratins had decided to have a combined internment for Jacob's and Sara's ashes. They gathered outside the Rokoff family mausoleum. As Sara had no family to claim her, Jacob's family had offered her a place of rest near Jacob.

Lacy stood with her father amongst the mourners. He was there on official business, the murder of Sara still unsolved. She was there to offer Michael moral support, if he wanted it. If he had given her any sign or acknowledgement she would have gone to him. He had not seemed to notice her, or for that matter anyone.

The crowd was large. Hundreds of patients and supporters had turned out to honor Jacob. Jacob's sister was there with her daughter Suzanne. Suzanne wore a black veil to conceal her face and prevent recognition. Patricia and Georgi both spoke about Jacob's life and accomplishments. Patricia also added kind words about Sara and her compassion for the patients she had treated and how she had tragically died so young in an act of heroism.

Michael paid little attention to what was going on. He stared out over the crowd noticing little. Once or twice his line of site passed

Lacy but he only saw the trees in the distance. She tried to catch his attention but it appeared that he was looking right through her.

Andy Livingston stood with his daughter. He knew her heart was breaking. She had told him that she heard Michael profess his love for Sara, and now he was seemingly rejecting Lacy. Despite his need to support his daughter he also needed to do his job. Scanning the crowd he looked for any actions that might provide some clue regarding the shooter. It always amazed him as to how often murderers showed up at funerals to admire their own work. Studying faces in the crowd he hardly noticed the man who had moved to stand beside him. The man appeared to be in his fifties. He had light brown hair with graying temples. He wore an expensive business suit and was well groomed. He could have been a banker or a lawyer.

Andy took all this in as the man spoke to him. "Lieutenant Livingston?"

"Yes," Andy said.

"The person that you should be looking for is named Jeremy Jeffers."

"I'm sorry," Andy responded. "Looking for in regard to what?"

"In regard to the shooting of Sara Anson," the man responded. "You already knew that."

"How can I find this individual," Andy asked.

"His last known location was an apartment over the new jazz club on Frenchman. I doubt if he's there any longer. If you check you will find that you already have a file on him."

"How do you know all this, and why should I believe you?" Andy looked around to see if he could get the attention of any of his officers. He had come to the funeral without a weapon or even cuffs. If the man was armed it could endanger Lacy.

The man spoke as he turned to leave. "My name is Dietrich, you can look up my file as well. Then it's up to you to decide what to do with the information. Sara was not the target. She had learned of Jeffers plan and sacrificed herself to save her friend." With that he slid quietly between mourners until he was out of Andy's sight. Andy turned to go after him but the crowd shifted, reacting to something happening on the platform.

Marshall Ellis stepped forward to give the final eulogy. His words were strong despite his advanced years. "The two people that we honor today had a common goal. They both fought for the same thing, although their methods were very different." he paused, "Human dignity! They both fought for the right of self-determination. The fought for the right to choose for oneself. They fought for the freedom not to have to lie down and let machines make decisions for us.

"Earlier this week there was to have been a press conference. That conference was cut short by a cowardly act. A sniper hidden safely in a loft fired a shot that ended the life of Sara Anson. The purpose of that conference had been to share with you vital information. Vital information about a massive cover-up being perpetrated by Med-Met." There was a stirring in the crowd and the Vid reporters increased their attention.

Ellis took a drink of water and went on, "Med-Met has not told you the truth about the number of cases of this epidemic that they have treated. More importantly they have not told you how many individuals they have sent to their deaths who might have survived. So today I issue two challenges. I issue a challenge to Med-Met to open up their records to the press and the world. I issue a challenge to each of you to honor the memories of Jacob Rokoff and Sara Anson. Demand full disclosure of Med-Met and push forward to insure the dignity of man."

The crowd grew more disorganized following Ellis's remarks. Reporters streamed forward to try and ask Ellis questions. People turned to each other to verify what they had heard.

Lacy had planned on approaching Michael when the service was over. She turned to where he had been standing, but he was gone. She wanted to ask her father if he had seen where Michael went, but Andy was busy searching for Dietrich. A rabbi said a final prayer that no one heard and the crowd slowly dispersed.

★ ★ ★

Andy did not spot Dietrich again. After the crowd dispersed he dropped Lacy at home and went to his office. He quickly found the files on Jeremy Jeffers and Richard Dietrich. He now knew that they were both members of the Weps. Sara Anson had also belonged to that organization. If Dietrich's information was correct, then Med–Met was not behind the shooting. He knew the club on Frenchman that Dietrich had described. It had opened recently close to where some historic clubs had been fifty years before. A team was dispatched to the building. There were three apartments on the floor above the club. The residents of two were at home, but the third was empty. The neighbors related that four people, three men and a woman had been living in that apartment a short time. No one had been seen them coming or going for several days.

A warrant was obtained and the apartment searched. It had been cleaned leaving little trace of its former occupants. They did however find a flyer for a Hippocratin conference.

That night on the Vids were images of Jeffers and his suspected collaborators. The identities of the others were deduced from the descriptions given by the neighbors and the files on known Weps. The neighbors confirmed the suspicions when shown holographs of the four. It was announced that these four individuals were wanted for questioning in connection with the murder of Sara Anson. The image of Richard Dietrich was also shown but it was stated that he was not a suspect, but a person of interest. The public was warned not to approach these individuals, as they might be armed and dangerous. If spotted they were asked to contact the NOPD immediately.

At Med–Met Darren and Wil watched the reports. "Well that's a relief." Darren said as the announcer moved on to another story. "Hopefully now the police will stop harassing us over this shooting. I can't believe anyone would have actually believed we were behind it."

Wil was up and pacing. "Now that we're no longer the prime suspects can we get back to the issue of Guidry and the break-in?

We need to get the police to come back in here and interview our witnesses. Then they can go and arrest the little shit."

Darren was quiet before replying. "I'm not sure that's the best strategy right now. According to the people that you have following Guidry, he's a mess. Other than coming out today for the funeral he just stays in his apartment. He hasn't been to work since the shooting. I don't think he's the one we should focus on."

"Are you telling me that you don't want us to do anything?" Wil sputtered saliva as he spoke.

"No," Darren answered. "I think the one we should worry about and go after is Ellis. The speech he gave at the funeral really stirred things up. They media replays it incessantly. If he comes out of retirement and becomes the Hippocratin spokesperson he could incite the public even more. He seems to have information that could only have been obtained from inside Med-Met. We have to be careful of how much emphasis we put on that. It could back-fire and validate his information. We need another hook to use to catch him. Wil, I am sure you can come up with something."

Smiling now Wil headed for the door. "Give me a few days boss, I've got an idea."

CHAPTER
48

Michael stirred on the couch It had been weeks since the funeral. He had rarely gotten up, and had only been out of the apartment once. The background din from the vid box was his constant companion and the sole distraction from his thoughts. His pattern had been to lie on the couch, eat on the rare occasions that he felt hungry, and go to the bathroom when the urge was persistent. He hadn't answered any form of communication nor had he bathed or even changed clothes. He didn't notice the mess or the smell around him.

Something on the vid broadcast caught the edges of his attention. An elderly man was being led away in handcuffs by the police. He turned up the volume to hear the reporter. "St. Tammany Parish Sheriffs deputies today arrested Dr. Marshall Ellis at his home in Mandeville. The 102 year old co-founder of the Hippocratins is being held on suspicion of medical terrorism. Unnamed sources tipped authorities that Ellis, along with the late Jacob Rokoff, had secretly engineered a mutant virus that has caused the recent worldwide pandemic. Ironically, Rokoff's death last month is believed to be from that virus. A warrant was also issued for Georgi Chen, whose current whereabouts are unknown, and who is suspected of financing the lab where the virus was created."

Michael sat up and replayed the report. He grabbed his idents, and headed for the door stumbling over debris along the way. He expended more energy in the first few feet than he had cumulatively since that day at the news conference. Without realizing how he got there he found himself pounding on Lacy's door.

Her initial smile quickly faded as she took him in with her eyes, and her nose. "Michael, what's wrong? You look terrible. I've been calling, and I've been to your apartment. I've been so worried."

"I'm sorry, and I have a lot to explain, but right now I need to see your father."

Her initial surprise at seeing him faded and she snapped, "Why do you need to see Daddy?"

"Please, is he here? Just get him."

Lacy spun and headed off to get her father. Michael paced nervously, trying to understand what was happening.

As Lacy and her father entered the room Michael launched himself toward them. "Lieutenant, er, Andy I need your help."

"My god Michael, what happened to you?"

"It's not me, it's Ellis. They've arrested him. You have to get him out."

Andy took a step backward. "I know about the arrest, but I don't think I can help get him out. First of all it was St. Tammany police that arrested him, and secondly the feds are involved. There is no way an Orleans Parish lieutenant can intervene."

"There has got to be something we can do?" Michael pleaded.

"Let me make a call. A friend of mine is chief of detectives up there. In the meantime, go clean yourself up, you reek. Lacy will get you some of my older clothes, from when I didn't carry so much authority around" he said patting his stomach as he walked away.

Andy went off to make the call leaving Lacy alone with Michael. She stood back from him both because she was emotionally conflicted, and because of his odor. Michael stepped toward her and she retreated. "Listen," he said. "I know that I've a lot to explain."

She interrupted him, "First get cleaned up and then we'll talk, you're kinda making me gag right now." She showed him where the bathroom was, gave him some soap, shampoo and a large plastic trash bag for his clothes. I'll leave some daddy's old things on the chair in the bedroom. Find me when you're human again."

While Michael cleaned up, Lacy looked for her mother. Rachel was in the kitchen. Andy had given her a quick version of what was going on and he was now off in another room making calls. Lacy stood in the kitchen doorway until Rachel noticed her.

"Dad tells me that Michael is here." Rachel said nonchalantly.

"Yeah, he's here," Lacy said, and then added, "To see Dad."

"Do you think that is the only reason he came here first, after he has been living like a recluse these past months?" her mother asked.

"As far as I can tell. He stormed in didn't even say hello and demanded to see Daddy."

Her mother studied her, "Nothing else? No explanation, nothing?"

Lacy thought about it, "Well he did say something about explaining later, but he was awfully agitated."

Again Rachel waited before speaking, "Are you going to give him a chance to explain?"

"I'll think about it," was Lacy's answer. "It had better be a damn good explanation."

Andy came back just as Michael emerged having showered and changed. Here's the deal, I talked with my friend and he has arranged for you to visit with Ellis at the prison. I'll drive you up there." He turned to his daughter, "Lacy, why don't you come along and keep us company.

On the trip across the Causeway Lacy sat in the front with her father. Michael sat alone in the back. It was an uncomfortably silent ride. Andy tried to make conversation, but neither Michael nor Lacy was talkative.

When they arrived at the St. Tammany Parish Sheriff's Department Alexandra Hemingway jumped up from the bench that she had been sitting on and rushed toward Michael, Lacy and Andy.

"Oh Michael, I'm so glad you came. Dr. Ellis asked for you before he was taken away."

"Alex, this is crazy. They said they are looking for Georgi also. What the hell is going on?"

"I don't know where to start, Riser is working on getting the best representation and working on bail. I'm here in case anything changes." Just then Andy came from across the room from where he'd been talking to an older man in a suit.

"O.K. Michael, you have fifteen minutes and that's it. My friend is going out on a limb. The fewer people that know about this the better. Lacy and I will wait here with Alex."

As Michael was about to follow a guard Alex ran over a slipped something on his shirt. Here, wear this, I think Marshall will appreciate it." It was a small pin with the Hippocratin cadeus.

Michael shrugged, "Sure."

★   ★   ★

Dr. Ellis appeared older and frailer than Michael remembered. He was brought into the small interview room and cuffed to the metal table. As the deputy left the room he turned to Michael, "Fifteen minutes bro, then I'll be back."

"Dr. Ellis, what in the world is going on? They said you created the virus."

"Yes, well we know who was behind that lie, don't we? We don't have a lot of time, and I have a lot to tell you." He looked around him and up at the ceiling. "By any chance Did Alexandra give you anything before you came in?"

Michael looked down at his shirt, "Just this little pin."

The old man smiled. "I love that girl and her bag of tricks, If I was just fifty years younger, and she wasn't already in love with Georgi, who knows. I'm sure the pin is a jammer. I am pretty certain that these walls have eyes and ears, she told me to be careful and not say anything unless it was to someone who had a gift from her.

"Riser has provided us with information about the origins of the virus. With that knowledge we've made much progress in elucidating the viral structure. Earl has been working with me and a team of researchers. We've developed a treatment that blunts the symptoms, and we were getting close on a vaccine."

Michael jumped out of his chair, "Earl? Are you kidding? Earl is a lazy worthless jerk. He doesn't care for his patients and is just plain stupid."

"No Michael, you are wrong. Earl may be a jerk and an ass, but he is not stupid. We all knew that he had terrible interpersonal skills, and a worse bedside manner, but it turns out he is a whiz in the lab. He has made some great progress."

"Where is he? And what about Georgi?"

"They're working in a lab at the old primate center. Georgi, Alexandra and Riser have helped pull together a team and they're working day and night. Most people think that the Primate Center has closed down, bought by some Foundation and turned into a preserve for the primates and their descendants. In part that's true. It is a haven for several species of monkeys. It's also true that I and my colleagues in the Foundation have maintained a medical research lab there, just in case. Well, now is just in case."

"We have to get you out of here."

"Riser's working on that, but you have more important work to do."

"Me? I have no lab experience. Aside from that, I am not good for anything. Everything I touch turns to shit and everyone I love winds up dead."

"Spare me the self-pity, Michael. Jacob believed in you, Sara believed in you, and Lacy believes in you, and loves you. If we're going to beat this thing you have to believe in yourself again. Believe in yourself like you did when you walked away from Med-Met. Our fifteen minutes is almost up, so you need to listen to me.

"Go to Covington and get caught up on where the team is. It is up to you to organize the clinical application of the anti-cytokine treatment and when it's ready the vaccine."

"Why me? Why not Patricia? She's been running the clinic, and has far more experience than I do."

"Patricia will play an important role, but she can't play the role that you can. She is not Rokoff's heir, you are. She is not the one who publically thumbed their nose at Med-Met, you are. She is not the one that the public saw crying in anguish while trying to save a bloody Sara Anson, you are. Michael, I'm old and I'm tired but I'm not giving up, we all have a part to play. The question for you is what is your part and are you willing to rise to it? Do you walk away now and crawl back into whatever hole you were hiding in, or do you go to Covington and answer the question for yourself? I think I already know your answer, Jacob always chose well." At that moment the deputy entered the room and removed the cuffs from the table and led the old physician scientist away.

Michael walked back to the reception area. As he entered Lacy, Alex and Andrew all rose together. Lacy approached him slowly and waited for him to say something. After taking a deep breath he smiled at her, a smile she had not seen for too long. "If you can put up with me a while longer, I need you to take me somewhere."

"Sure," she said, "but how about a clue as to where?"

"Well, how do you feel about monkeys?"

Andy left them with Alexandra and he headed home. Alexandra drove them a short distance north on Causeway Boulevard to the facility that once was the Tulane National Primate Research Center. This time Michael was in the front seat and Lacy in the back. Alexandra's presence prevented Michael and Lacy from opening up about what they were each feeling. Alex briefed Michael on what she knew of the research that his colleagues were currently undertaking in the laboratory hidden by the heavy foliage of the 500 acre site. She gave him as much information as she had grasped about the recombinant viruses that had been engineered on the moon. Alex quickly got them through security. "Once the research began at the facility Riser took over the security. He sent his team in to upgrade the systems with the latest equipment, and is providing twenty-four hour on site guards."

They had not been aware that their hover car was being trailed by a surveillance device. As soon as they entered the perimeter of the facility Riser's systems detected it and eliminated it.

At Med–Met Wil had been monitoring the transmission from the device. He was surprised when he saw them turn in to what was supposedly a monkey retirement home. He was focused on the screen as Michael's group entered the grounds when the picture went blank. He turned to Biggs, Med-Mets chief of I.T., "What the hell happened to the picture? I need to know where the fuck they're going."

Biggs was inputting commands and staring at the screen with a perplexed look on his face. "I'm not sure Mr. A, it was performing beautifully and then poof, image gone. I'm playing the last few minutes back now. Here's where the transmission ends. Look at the way it cuts off. No static, no warning, just gone. That tracker was one of the newest and most secure. It isn't supposed to be able to be blocked by jammers."

"Well then what happened?"

"I can't say for sure, but either a complete system failure, which I doubt without some warning signs, or the thing was vaporized.

"Vaporized? How?"

"I am not sure, but I know there are some security systems that can pick up the presence of these trackers and zap 'em. Then poof, no more bug."

"This is an animal retirement facility for crissake," Wil spat, "Why would they have that kind of system?"

"I don't have any idea, I'm just giving you my opinion."

Wil snatched up the phone. "Suz, be a good girl and get me a few minutes with Darren?" After a pause, "Great I'll be right over."

Wil stormed into Darren's office. "Darren, there's something strange going on. I've had people and tracker drones keeping tabs on Guidry for weeks. He hadn't left his place since the hippie girl's funeral. Then all of a sudden he zooms out the door and goes to the new girlfriend's place." Wil paced around the room with his hands clasped behind his back. "After about an hour there, he, the girl and her cop father head across the Lake to the St. Tammany Parish jail. That makes sense because that's where they are holding the old guy, Ellis.

"At that point I pull my men off him because I didn't want them having to explain themselves to the police. The tracker drones picked them up when they left the police station, and Chen's hot girlfriend has joined them." Wil licked his upper lip, "Now it starts to get really interesting. They drive to the old site of the monkey research center in Covington. The tracker picks up the guard clearing them through and then poof, "Wil snapped his fingers, "The tracker quits working. Biggs thinks the tracker got zapped."

Darren had been having trouble sleeping and had eaten little. He looked drawn and had bags under his eyes. His usual perfectly pressed clothing showed wrinkles. His tie was loose, his top button undone, and he needed a shave. Slowly Darren shifted his attention from the window to Wil. "I guess if you use snooping devices you take the risk of losing them. What's the big deal? We can afford it can't we?"

Wil spoke slowly, as if to a child. "Of course we can afford it. That isn't the issue. The first question is why are they going to a facility that is supposed to be a sanctuary for non-human primates? More importantly why all the sophisticated security if it's only what the signs say it is?"

"Interesting questions," Darren paused. "I assume you've given some thought to the answers."

"I have. I am not sure what they're doing in there, but I know they are using it as a hide-out. Chen must be in there maybe even Rokoff."

"You do know that Rokoff is dead?"

"I'm not so sure," Wil replied. "We never saw the body, just an urn. I want to send someone inside to find out who is in there and what they are doing."

"Who exactly do you want to send in?"

"Don't worry about it, I know some people we can use."

★   ★   ★

"Michael, Alex and Lacy drove slowly down the main entrance road of the former Tulane National Primate Research facility. The foliage was extremely heavy and encroached on the road. They had to adjust the hover, moving up and down, left and right to avoid branches.

Under the tree cover sat a concrete-and-steel building. The only visible windows flanked the entrance. A sign hung over the portal, 'Lackner Bioenvironmental Laboratory'.

Alex placed a card in a reader. A pleasant voice spoke requesting voice and DNA identification. She stated her name and placed her palm on a metal pad, which triggered a rapid DNA sequence analysis. The door slide open. She led them into a small lobby where they were greeted by a guard in a uniform similar to those at the gate.

The guard stood and saluted Alex. "Good evening Captain."

Michael and Lacy exchanged puzzled looks. They knew Alex worked for a security firm, but this was very military.

"Good evening corporal," Alex replied. This is Michael Guidry, and Lacy Livingston. Please provide them with key cards and establish their biometrics."

"Yes sir," said snapping off another salute. "If you two will come over here with me we will get you all set-up."

After completing their registration Alex led Michael and Lacy through several doors, each time re-establishing her credentials. When they reached another door Alex gave them instructions. "This door leads into the lab. We each need to enter our own creds to be admitted. Only one person will be allowed in at a time. The first door will admit you to a small chamber. that door will then close and the second will open into the lab. This helps prevent any large forces storming the lab. I'll go first. Just use your card, hand and voice as I've done. I'll see you inside."

After Alex had passed through the doorway Lacy turned to Michael and said, "Do you believe this? It's like something out of the old spy Vids. You would think they were worried about an invasion."

Michael again gave Lacy a smile. "I'm not sure what to think anymore. I would have never thought anyone would take a shot at me. I guess Alex and Riser are being super careful." You go ahead. I'll be right behind."

When they were both through to the other side they found themselves in a modern lab. Michael wasn't sure what the equipment was but it all looked new. Several people were working at the benches. Earl was moving between the researchers, looking over their results and making comments. Alex was off to one side chatting with Georgi. She noticed them and waved them over.

Georgi greeted them. "Hi guys, welcome to our little viral research lab. We've scheduled a briefing for you in thirty minutes. I'd show you around, but I'm still trying to figure out what everything does."

Michael and Lacy waited in a small conference room. Several researchers walked in, then Earl moved to the front of the room and waved his hand a the vid wall lit up. "First, I will do my best to get you up to speed on where we are. Dr. Ellis should be telling you this, but unfortunately he's been detained." Earl looked over at Michael. "Nice to see you, brother. Welcome back to the land of the living."

"Listen Earl," Michael said as he stood to face Earl. "I am not in the mood for any of your crap."

Earl took a step back and held up both hands, palms out. "Not to worry, this is the new Earl. Now let me show you what we have learned."

The screen displayed a three-dimensional electron micrograph that looked like a ball with a variety of spikes poking out of its surface. "This," Earl began in his soothing southern drawl, "Is our culprit, the virus causing the current flu epidemic. It looks like a typical influenza virus, but it is far from that.

"Our friend Mr. Riser provided information to Dr. Ellis and Georgi that has allowed us to make significant progress." Earl turned to Riser who was sitting with Alex in the rear of the conference room. "Mr. Riser if you would please."

Justin Riser moved to the front of the room and took the small controller from Earl. The image on the screen changed to show a low-roofed functional-looking structure. Behind the building stood the intact dome of Sheppard City and the lunar landscape beyond that. "The structure that you are looking at is the Infinity Research Laboratories on the outskirts of Sheppard City prior to the Great Disaster. Scientists in this laboratory were carrying out infectious disease research. At that time there was concern that an infectious organism, either acquired naturally or otherwise, was a serious risk for the inhabitants of the moon.

"A major focus was development of vaccines to all known pathogens, and also to some not yet known to exist. To accomplish the latter a variety of recombinant micro-organisms were created in the lab. One approach was to take segments from different epidemic viruses and combine the worst elements of each."

Riser looked at Georgi as he continued. "We believe that among the items brought back from the moon by the Chen expedition was a temperature-controlled containment box that held one of these viruses. Our investigation indicated that a worker at the Chen warehouse, Brian Marino, stole the box along with other goods. Marino apparently exposed himself to the virus and became the index case for this epidemic."

Michael interrupted, "Sir, do you know what this particular virus is composed of?"

Riser answered, "Not specifically. There was a code on the vial that Marino exposed himself to, but we do not have a key to that code. I do have some direct knowledge of some of the viruses that were being studied. I have shared that information with Dr. Ellis and Earl and I believe that has helped them with their progress."

Earl thanked Riser and resumed talking, "With this information, Dr. Ellis formulated a plan to determine the composition of our virus. It contains elements of at least three of the major flu epidemics of the last two centuries. A large portion is based on the 1918 virus. That virus was highly lethal with a death rate between ten and twenty percent of those infected," he pointed at the screen and a gene sequence appeared, a large portion changing color to indicate the 1918 segments.

Earl continued speaking, "Another major component of the virus is derived from another H1N1 strain, this from around 2009 which was highly infectious. Finally there were elements from the 2031 flu which caused severe pulmonary reactions and again was highly lethal." As he described each portion corresponding segments of the genome took on new colors.

Michael raised his hand "So the components of these three viruses yielded a virus with high infectivity and lethality?"

"That and more," Earl said. "The designers of this bugger also added a kicker. They inserted a stealth gene. It makes the virus virtually invisible to the immune system. Thankfully, we had Marshall Ellis on our side. He systematically figured out the composition and then designed a strategy to combat it."

Following the briefing Michael and Lacy were invited to stay overnight at the facility. Patricia was going to join them the next morning, and treatment and vaccination strategies would be discussed. They were advised to stay within the fenced in compound, which included a fence over the top as well as the sides. It was explained to them that they lived in the cage and the rest of the five hundred acres belonged to the monkeys. They were warned that the animals looked cute, but were far from friendly.

CHAPTER
49

The small camouflaged paramilitary force slipped silently through the dark waters of the Bogue Falaya. The river was swollen from recent rains making passage easier. Wil Armbrister sat in the rear of the last of the three pirogues. He wanted to be there personally when they uncovered whatever illegal activities were going on at the primate center. He felt pumped up in his fatigues and face paint, a real adventurer. The commander of the group of contract soldiers that he hired hadn't wanted him along, but the pay was good. Wil had made it even better on the condition that he could be on the team. Wil had to agree to follow all orders and stay out of the way. The commander assigned one of the team to babysit Wil and keep him from interfering.

They moved into the Abita River and reached a spot, to the southwest of the center, where they planned to enter. A high chain-link fence enclosed the property to protect the non-human primates from the human ones and vice versa. About six feet from the fence the commander silently signaled them to hold. One member of the team took out a small hand-held device that seemed to be a detector of some sort. He pointed it at the fence and looked at the read-out on the screen. He then came over to where the commander stood. Wil pushed in to hear what they were saying.

"Well," the soldier began. "There is motion detection directed externally. It extends to about two feet out from the fence. It's unidirectional. That makes sense. If it went internally the animals would be triggering it all the time. Also, there is a mild electric charge that's triggered by contact with the inside of the fence. Not enough to injure but probably good enough to discourage the monkeys from trying to climb. If you notice the tree line is pretty far back from the fence, and the canopy is trimmed to keep a large distance from the fence. It's probably to prevent the animals from jumping over it."

"Thank you Sergeant, can you get us through it?"

"No problem, sir. We will set up an electronic corridor to pass through, and peel back a section of the fence. We'll reattach it when we get through and activate it remotely for egress."

Beyond the clear cut area between the fence and the tree line the forest grew naturally. The small troop fought through the underbrush trying to remain as quiet as possible. Wil sweated heavily and swatted at mosquitoes. He began to wonder if this was going to be as much fun as he originally thought it would. Branches cracked beneath his clumsy footfall. The leader called a halt and walked back to Wil. He spoke quietly through clenched teeth, "Listen fat boy, I know you are paying the bills but I'm the one responsible for carrying out this mission. If you can't be quieter we'll either leave you behind or abort the whole fucking mission." Wil huffed and thought to himself, *this is my damn expedition,* but decided to keep his mouth shut.

They made slow progress and were able to see some light coming through the trees ahead. They stopped, and one of the soldiers silently eased ahead to scout the area. He returned and reported that there was a large building inside another fence. The building was well lit and heavily guarded by well-armed military-types.

Before they could start again, there was a heavy rustling in the branches above them followed by screeching, hooting and grunting. Wil felt something wet and soft hit him on the side of the head. He reached down and picked it up. It mushed between his fingers and the odor hit him. "Shit!" he yelled.

The team leader spun on him aiming his weapon. He spoke in a harsh whisper, "I told you to keep your damn mouth shut. I am not going to have you put me and my men at any further risk, no matter how much you're paying us."

"But," Wil responded, holding out his soiled hand "The fuckers are throwing shit at me."

One of the shoulders elbowed another and whispered, loud enough for Wil to hear, "One good turd deserves another." Other soldiers in hearing range chuckled.

Wil, now angry, was about to go over and rub the feces in the obnoxious soldier's face when he heard the commander call his name.

The leader looked at Wil and then spoke softly. "Turn around slowly. Don't make any sudden moves."

Wil turned and five feet away on the trampled brush they had just passed over stood a large male rhesus macaque. He stared at Wil, his eyes wide, ears flat against his head and mouth open. Wil looked at the animal who stood a little over two feet tall and weighed no more than 40 pounds. He thought it looked cute. "Hey little buddy, let's be friends." Wil reached into his fatigues and drew out a banana. He looked the animal in the eyes and gave him a great big grin showing his pearly white teeth. Wil's back was to the leader who couldn't see that his employer had just made every mistake possible in dealing with a wild monkey.

The rhesus gave a loud grunt and leapt at Wil. Wil shielded his face with the hand holding the banana and the animal went for it. Wil didn't let go of the banana and the monkey clawed at him and bit his arm. Wil screamed and rolled around on the ground.

One of the soldiers shot the animal with a distance taser. The charge hit the animal between the shoulder blades. he monkey was fully engaged with Wil and they both absorbed the charge. They stop struggling and lay together on the ground, stunned.

The sight of their downed comrade caused the other monkeys to become more agitated and aggressive. They darted in and out of the woods attacking and retreating. Animals overhead shook the branches violently. The soldiers tried to immobilize the animals with their tasers but the targets were too elusive.

One rhesus sprung forward and grabbed a taser from the hand of a soldier who was focused on another of the animals. The soldier drew his hand gun, spun and shot in the direction of the retreating monkey. The monkey eluded the shot but the sound of gunfire triggered the sensitive security system. The system was set to filter out animal noises, but an artificial sound such as gunfire triggered an alert. The sector was registered and night vision cameras in the trees sending images back showing the intruders.

With Wil down, and the monkeys continuing their aggressive behavior the leader signaled a retreat. Two men dragged Wil back down the path they had created coming in while the others did their best to keep the animals at bay. Suddenly music began to play in the trees and the animals disappeared into the woods. The invaders had no idea what had happened to cause their attackers to leave, unaware that this was a signal that food was available at routine drop points.

The soldiers, relieved, that they could now retreat in peace, were slow to recognize the approach of the armed security force. A stun grenade exploded near the back of the team causing the two in the rear to go down. Others returned fire, but were unsure of where the attack was coming from.

★   ★   ★

At six in the morning Darren was awakened by the chirping of his communication system. From his bed he ordered, "Audio on. Who is this, and you'd better have a good reason for calling at this hour."

After a hesitation a voice said, "Sorry to disturb you sir, I'm calling from the Med–Met inpatient facility."

Darren sat up and hit a switch and soft light filled the room, "Is there a problem at the facility?"

"Well sir, do you know Mr. Willis Armbrister?"

"Of course I know him, he works for me. Did he tell you to call me?"

"Er, no sir, someone dropped him in the emergency department, earlier this morning. He's unconscious and appears to have been in some kind of fight or accident."

An hour later he stood next to Wil's bed in a VIP suite. Wil had been sedated most of the night. He had scratches and what looked like bite marks on his face, neck and hands. According to the staff he had said little. Whenever the sedation was wearing off he would flail his arms and mumble something that sounded like, "Get them off, get them off." Beyond that they had no idea what had happened to him. According to the scans and lab tests he had not suffered any major injuries, and had only required suturing of a few of the larger wounds.

Darren recalled that Wil had left his office a little early the evening before. The last thing that he remembered was Wil telling him, "Don't worry boss, by tomorrow morning we will know exactly what those Hippies are up to." When Darren had asked him what that meant, Wil had winked and told him, "Not to worry, better that you don't know," and then Wil had walked out the door.

Darren found the senior technician on the unit and asked, "What do the diagnostics say about the scratches and bite marks?"

"I'd rather not say until we have a chance to review and reconfirm the studies."

"Why?" Darren asked. "Is there something wrong with them?"

"Well sir, the report doesn't make any sense. I want to repeat them."

"You can go ahead and repeat them, but I would just as soon hear what you do have." Darren said in a tone that made it clear he expected to be told.

The technician cleared his throat a few time before beginning, "The reports state that the injuries are from animal bites and scratches. Specifically, non-human primates. Something called Macaca Mulatta."

Darren, started to tell him that it sounded ridiculous, but caught himself remembering Wil's reports on Guidry and the primate center. He sighed and ran his hand down his face. "Don't bother repeating the tests. They're accurate." He thanked the technician and returned to Wil's bedside.

CHAPTER
50

Michael awoke well-rested. Over the past several weeks he had slept mainly on his sofa. Now he was in a strange bed. It took him several minutes to remember where he was. He was startled by the stirring next to him and turned and looked into Lacy's soft, brown eyes. The irises were flecked with green and gold. She smiled and said, "Hi.".

After the briefing was over last night he and Lacy had gone to a small lounge with Riser, Georgi and Alex. Riser brought out a bottle of Scotch whisky. Michael mainly a beer drinker didn't know one Scotch from another. Lacy seemed to immediately recognize the label and asked Michael, "Have you ever had Lagavulin?"

Michael knitted his brow, "Have I had what?"

Riser answered Michael's question. "Lagavulin is a whisky distilled on the Island of Islay, off the west coast of Scotland. The malts from Islay have a unique taste and texture." He poured a dram and handed it to Michael. "Before you drink it enjoy the aroma."

Michael sniffed. The smell was not what he expected. The best description he could think of was smoke over a wet swamp. He recoiled at the first taste, then relaxed as it slowly eased down his throat. Lacy slowly sipped her glass and laughed at the face he made.

Over the next several hours the five of them worked through the bottle. Michael's enjoyment increased with each succeeding glass. As they drank they discussed the epidemic, the progress that had been made and what still needed to be done.

They were each assigned a dorm-like room in the lab complex. Michael, a little unsteady on his feet, had walked Lacy to her quarters where they spent the next several hours talking. They began with small talk, but eventually spoke about their feelings. Michael said, "I need to explain. I've been really stupid."

Lacy interrupted, "You don't need to apologize. I can only imagine how I would've behaved if I'd gone through what you did. I should apologize for being mad at you, for not being more understanding."

She stopped and took a deep breath. Her voice was shaking and tears began to well up in her eyes. "I guess I made too many assumptions about our relationship. Maybe I read too much into it. I want you to know that I care a lot for you, but if you just want to be friends I can handle that."

Michael felt confused. "Why do you think I only want to be friends? Is it because I shut you out? I know it was a really lousy thing to do. I was so consumed with self-pity I forgot about the great things in my life, like you."

Lacy looked down and appeared to be suppressing the welling tears that threatened to overflow like water over a levee. "I know I can never replace her. I don't want to just inherit you now that she's gone."

Michael was quick to reply, "No, that's not true. Sara was an important part of my life, but it's you I'm in love with. I just have been too self-absorbed to tell you. You don't take second place to anyone. You're beautiful, brilliant and you have a sense of self and family that I have always wished I could have."

"Don't make it worse by lying to me. I heard what you said to her in the hospital. You told her you needed her and that she shouldn't leave you."

"When? How?" again, he was confused.

"In the hospital," she said. "I came to see if you were alright. I baked cookies for you. You were holding her hand and talking to her. When I heard what you were saying I knew that I had been right all along. It was her that you loved and I was just a substitute. I got away as fast as I could."

"You didn't hear the whole thing," he said. "I spoke to her a lot. I told her about all the things that happened since she left. I told her all about you. I told her that I wanted her to get well so that she could meet you, and see how happy I was. I told her we needed her to come back and help us fight this epidemic."

Swallowing hard he continued "I've been through a lot of pain, and I haven't handled it as well as I should. All that has happened so far, all that I have lost would be insignificant compared to what it would mean if I were to lose you."

They embraced, exhaustion and the Scotch catching up with Michael. At some point, he couldn't remember exactly when, he had fallen asleep. He didn't recall undressing. Lacy slid over toward him under the sheet. She rolled and placed one leg over his. He could feel her wet warmth and the softness of her pubic hair against his thigh. His eyes widened realizing she was naked, and he said, "Did we...?"

She shook her head, cutting him off. Before he could speak again she wiggled her eyebrows at him and smiled. He leaned in to kiss her, feeling her breasts press against his chest. Their lips parted, as they began to melt together there was a sharp knock. Earl's lazy drawl penetrated the door and the mood. "Let's go y'all. Patricia's here and we've got work to do, an epidemic to stop. Breakfast awaits."

Michael looked at Lacy pleading with his eyes. "Later, she whispered," as she slid out of bed and headed to the shower.

★ ★ ★

Michael was surprised by how many people were at breakfast. When he had first arrived, the previous afternoon, only a portion of the lab and security personnel were present. All were now assembled to eat and to discuss the next steps. Michael saw Patricia standing off to the side. He was unsure how she was going to react to seeing him, considering how things had gone between them after Jacob's and Sara's deaths. The suspense only lasted a few minutes. Patricia turned and seemed to notice Michael. She strode across the room directly toward him. He braced himself fearing that she was going to give him the chewing out he deserved. Instead she threw her arms around him and gave him a huge hug. "Michael, how are you?" she asked.

Michael didn't remember Patricia as much of a hugger. He didn't remember her ever having physical contact with him beyond a hand shake. Surprised and relieved he said, "Better. I'm a lot better. Thanks for asking."

Patricia broke the hug, aware that everyone in the room was watching, backed off looking embarrassed. "Well, let's get some breakfast and get to work," she said too loudly, and headed to the food line.

★   ★   ★

It was almost noon when Wil woke up. His eyes darted around the room until they fixed on Darren, sitting in a chair by the bed. Still somewhat sedated Wil asked, "Where am I? What happened?"

Darren put down his work and leaned over. "You are in a hospital room. I was hoping you could tell me what happened. Our diagnostics say that you were attacked by monkeys."

"Oh shit," Wil tried to sit up. He grabbed his head and eased back onto the pillow. "Feels like I got hit with a bag of quarters."

"Well, that could be because you were tased. Do you want to tell me what happened?" It was a command not a request.

Over the next half-hour Wil filled Darren in on the incursion of the primate center, up to the point just before he was tased. He had no memory from then until a little while ago, when he woke up in the hospital.

Darren looked worried and said, "So you don't know what happened to your mercenaries?"

"No, I guess they brought me here," he stopped, recalling something. "I do remember the advance scout coming back and reporting seeing a building. He said it was large, modern-looking, with a lot of security."

"What did you make of that?" Darren asked.

"Don't know, but it supports my theory that the place is more than they say it is." Wil placed his hand on his forehead shielding his eyes. "Can we talk later? My head is pounding and I need something for pain."

Darren headed for the door. "I'll let a tech know that you need some meds, and then I'm heading to the office. When you're head feels better find those mercenaries and make damn sure they keep their mouths shut."

★   ★   ★

Michael heard clapping coming from the other side of the room. He looked up to see Riser enter, with him was Marshall Ellis. The applause began to sweep through the crowd. They approached the table where Michael, Lacy, Patricia and Earl had been working. Marshall appeared tired, but had a smile on his face.

Earl was the first to jump up. He grabbed Marshall's right hand and shook it gently. "I am so glad to have you back sir. I did my best to keep things moving, but it isn't the same without you."

Marshall smiled at Earl, "Don't underestimate yourself, young man. You have been an adept student. While in prison, I was confident things were in good hands."

Patricia stood and hugged Marshall. Michael was amazed. Over the weeks during which he had been a self-exiled hermit, Patricia had become a hugger and Earl a respected researcher.

Patricia said, "It's wonderful to see you Dr. Ellis. How did you get out of prison?"

Riser answered, "Our attorney arranged bail. They didn't have any real evidence, and the judge could not justify incarcerating a 102-year-old. Think of how that would have gone over in the daily vid-news." Ellis acknowledged Michael with a soft smile and slight nod of the head.

Alex and Georgi joined the group, she approached Riser and said. "Sir, we have a match on the DNA from two of the blood samples we found in the woods."

Riser nodded at her and said, "Let's go somewhere a little quieter and you can give us your report."

The group moved to the lounge where five of them had been drinking scotch the night before. As Alex was about to start her report she was interrupted by Riser, "I consider this group our inner-circle. We have done an in-depth background check on each of you." Without smiling he said, "You all passed. I trust that you will keep everything you hear confidential. Ms. Livingston, that means you will not be able to divulge some of this to your father. Can you handle that?"

Lacy nodded and Riser told Alex to begin. "The results are very interesting. Last night, after our troops repelled the invaders, we searched the woods. We found several fresh spots of blood, and one distance-taser. We had rapid DNA sequencing performed on the blood, and found two distinct human patterns. One of the individuals is someone that we have encountered before. He is somewhat of a soldier-for-hire, who has a little military experience. He has a substantial criminal record, that's where we found the DNA match. He's been known to do just about anything if the money is right." She paused and looked to Riser. When he nodded she resumed speaking, "The results on the second sample caught us by surprise. The blood belongs to Willis Armbrister. He goes by Wil, and is the Director of Public and Media Relations for Med-Met and the CHA. Many refer to him as Darren Walter's hatchet man."

Patricia asked, "How did you match his DNA? Does he have a criminal record?"

Alex once again looked to Riser, who again nodded. "No, he doesn't," Alex said. "We had access to another source of DNA records, perhaps the world's largest." She took a breath. "When Michael broke-in at Med-Met we were able to download the DNA sequencing on all patients who visited the facility in the last fifty years," she smiled. "Now we have it."

"Conclusion?" Riser asked.

"It would seem," Alex said, "That Med-Met was behind the invasion."

Michael said, "I know that Armbrister guy. He's a fat little prick with slicked back hair who wears old-fashioned suits. I would never have expected him to be part of a military operation."

"Well, it seems that he was. Our sources tell us that early this morning he was hospitalized at Med-Met," Alex said, ending her report.

★　★　★

On the third morning, following the primate center incident, Wil went back to work. He seemed energized. The first thing he did was ask Suzanne Hartstein, Darren's executive assistant, to call a meeting of the Med-Met leadership. At ten he looked at the small group, Darren, Angela Stuart, Joel Rogers, and Suzanne, who was there to record and fetch as needed.

Darren watched his PR man pace, preparing. When all had settled in Wil began. "I am sure that by now you have all heard about my little adventure the other night. I admit it did not go as smoothly as I had hoped."

Angela Stuart stopped Wil and said, "I would say that is an understatement. It was a disaster." She narrowed her eyes and stared at him. "You go off and play toy soldier, without discussing it with us. You were injured, nearly captured, and to top it off the whole thing was a total waste of time, and money. How much did this fiasco cost us?"

Wil, still standing, shifted uneasily and said, "I've already admitted that it didn't go well. I'm sorry I didn't discuss it first, but thought that if you knew you wouldn't let me do it."

"That's damn sure," Darren said.

Wil took a breath and said, "Despite that I think we did come away with something that we can use." He looked at the others to see if there were any more interruptions, before continuing. "That place is supposed to be some sort of refuge for the monkeys. A protected habitat, where they can exist undisturbed. So tell me this, if that's all it is, why is there a building in there that is defended like a fortress?" He looked at the others for reaction.

Darren leaned in and asked, "Did you see this building?"

"No," Wil said, "The scout saw it and he reported that it was large, surrounded by a chain-link fence and patrolled by armed guards. The uniforms and weapons were very military."

"That is curious," Darren said, "But how does that help us?"

"Think about it," Wil said, now pacing more vigorously, pointing to his temple, and then ticking off his points on his fingers. "Secret building; high security; monkey facility that used to be an infectious disease lab; lots of monkeys; and Hippie scientists sneaking in and out." He looked to see if any of them had reached the conclusion that he saw as obvious. When no one said anything he resumed. "It's not too big a leap to figure out that they created the virus in there."

Joel Rogers the company CFO asked, "Do you have any proof?"

Wil chuckled, "Always the pragmatist. Who needs proof when one has circumstance, innuendo, and the right media connections.

"It's time we went back on the offensive." Wil said leaning over the table, hands resting on the edge. "The Hippocratins have been accusing us of covering up the epidemic, of needlessly sending people to terminal treatment. Are we going to back down and get defensive? Or," he said looking at each of his colleagues successively, "Are we going to punch them in the gonads?" He reached down and threw an uppercut for effect, only to wind-up wincing from his injuries.

For the next hour he laid out a plan to convince the public that the Hippocratins had created the virus. That they had allowed it to reach a crisis and then would miraculously announce they had found a cure, and become the heroes. They debated the pros and cons, the wording and method of disseminating the story.

By the end of the session all in the room seemed quite pleased, except one. Suzanne recorded all that was said, but appeared ill-at-ease. Wil noticed this, as it detracted from what he thought was a brilliant display of strategy. He always wanted to impress Suzanne, hoping it might lead her to appreciating him more.

Wil asked, "Suzanne, you okay?"

"Not really," she said. "It's my stomach. It may have been something I ate." Looking at Darren she said, "If we're all done, can I leave?"

Darren looked at the others, "I think we all need to get back to work. Wil, excellent plan, put it into action. Suzanne, why don't you take the rest of the day off? Get some rest, take care of yourself. We are going to need all hands once this plan of Wil's gets moving."

CHAPTER
51

That afternoon the Hippocratins returned to New Orleans. They quickly planned a party for the evening. They would share the news of their laboratory success with their colleagues, lay out the strategy for rolling out the treatment and vaccine. Then they would celebrate New Orleans style. Georgi made the arrangements, reserved a club and used his show business connections to line-up a few name acts. The atmosphere in the clinic was upbeat as the workers became the first to receive the vaccine.

Marshall and Earl remained in Covington supervising the continued medication production. They would drive in for the party, and the next morning's planned press conference.

Patricia was in command at the clinic arranging schedules so they could remain open twenty-four hours a day to try and meet the demand.

Michael was now revived and eager to work. With the help of the nurses and some students he began administration of the anti-cytokine cocktail to the sickest patients on the in-patient unit. "The idea is that this medication will blunt the cytokine storm which is responsible for the most severe symptoms," he explained.

Later in the day he was catching a brief rest in the lounge and one of the nurses came in with a big smile. "Michael, can you come with me? I need to show you something."

They walked through the ward and at each bed Michael called up the patients data. "This is amazing, several of the patients that we treated this morning have decreased fever, and improved breathing." He swallowed hard, "There is a long way to go, but this is encouraging. It's just sad that we didn't have it earlier, to help Jacob and so many others."

Nodding the nurse said, "Sure, but think of all those that we can help now."

Early that evening, Michael finished-up at the hospital and headed home to clean up and get dressed for the evening. He hadn't been back to his apartment since he had abruptly left the day of Marshall Ellis arrest. When he opened his door the first thing that he was aware of was the smell. It was a combination of wet sweat socks, sour milk, and the body odor of an overweight long haul driver who hadn't seen a shower in weeks. This was followed by the visual assault of the mess that had accumulated over several weeks. Empty and half-empty food containers, all types of clothing, and a small dumpster from the ally that he had brought up to collect garbage, but never returned.

Not having time to deal with it he suppressed his gag, and headed to the shower. After showering, shaving, trimming his nails and nose hair he headed for his closet. He hoped that he would have enough clean clothes left to dress for the evening. Fortunately, he had plenty of clean clothes, because he hadn't changed often during his hermit-hood. Shaking his head as he walked back through his living room, he headed out the door and off to pick-up Lacy.

★   ★   ★

Lacy greeted Michael at her front door wearing a broad smile, a tight pink sweater top and a white skirt. Michael nearly melted at the sight. He opened his mouth twice but no words came out. Finally on the third attempt he said, "Oh my."

"Oh my," Lacy repeated eyes wide. "A girl waits all her life to hear words like that." With a playful smile she added, "I feel so sorry for the women who date uneducated men."

"No, what I meant," Michael said as his face turned crimson, "What I meant to say is, Wow."

"Well, that's much better," she giggled, taking his hand and leading him into the den. Her parents were there and got up to greet him.

"I must say," Lacy's mother Rachel said, "You look totally different from the person who stormed in here a few days ago."

Michael smiled at her, "I am, and I don't think you will ever see that other me again. I want to thank the two of you for helping me that night. Has Lacy told you the good news about the progress that has been made toward ending the epidemic?"

Andy got up from his chair and walked over to Michael, "She has. We can't wait until you make the announcement tomorrow so that we can tell others. What do you think the chances are that these medications will be effective enough?"

"Theoretically, it seems that it will, but theory alone has never cured anything. I did have a chance to give it to some of our sicker patients today, and saw some objective improvements."

Andy clasped Michael's shoulder, "that's good to hear. You two go out and enjoy yourselves tonight. I know you have some long, hard days ahead of you. Have fun while you have the chance."

★　★　★

Michael and Lacy arrived at the club that Georgi had rented, a converted warehouse on Tchoupatoulis. As they walked in the door they were greeted by servers of both sexes wearing outrageously scant costumes. Drinks with smoke billowing from the tops were thrust into their hands as they approached an arched entry. The archway was decorated with alternating fleur-de-lis and caduceus. A trumpet blared the familiar four-note opening of the second-line march. All the people who had been drinking, talking and dancing stopped and turned toward the door. The quartet of notes sounded again, followed by Earl's voice. He was standing on a table with a microphone in hand.

"Ladies and Gentleman of the Hippocratin Society," Earl announced, "I give you the very lovely Ms. Lacy Livingston. Accompanying Ms. Livingston is the recently reincarnated Michael Guidry. Michael has returned to the land of the living following a sojourn in his own private hell."

Michael, feeling angry and embarrassed, tried to head in Earl's direction. Lacy held his hand tightly as he continued to pull forward. A slender, but firm hand clasped Michael's shoulder from behind. Alex leaned in and spoke in his ear. "Relax, he's giving all of us 'special' introductions. My new name is 'Amazon Jungle Princess'. Just go with it and have some fun."

Michael's tension eased slightly and he stopped pulling Lacy's arm.

Earl held up a necklace, set with small bones and skulls, and he also produced a black top hat. He said, "Such journeys are not unheard of in New Orleans. Tonight we crown you Michael Guidry, Voodoo Prince." A beautiful young woman, with little concealed by clothing, took the necklace and hat from Earl. She brought them to Michael, placed them on him and gave him a big kiss pressing herself against him. Michael broke off the kiss when he felt Lacy's small fingers tightening around his. He thanked the girl, and then turned and bowed deeply to Earl. He thought, *This guy may have helped save the world, but he is still one giant asshole.*

The crowd cheered, and then resumed their previous activities. Michael and Lacy waded through the crowd stopping to greet friends and chat. It seemed as if it had been years since he had seen so many happy people. Everyone said how excited they were to see Michael. One of the nurses from the hospital thanked Lacy for the cookies and gave her a little wink.

Again the trumpet roared its herald call. Michael looked to the door to see a litter carried by four muscular and well-oiled men in loin clothes. On the chair set a frail old man in regal robes, a long wig, and a crown. He had a huge smile on his face. Earl stood on the table again. "Mesdames et Messieurs. I present to you his majesty, Rex, King of Mardi Gras."

Marshall Ellis raised a scepter in one hand and waved royally to the guests with the other, as he was carried up and down the aisles. When Michael realized that the venerable and brilliant scientist could let down his hair, or at least his wig, he finally relaxed.

After two full tours of the room, Marshall was brought to an elevated throne where he could sit and view the whole proceeding. On each side of him stood a beautiful woman who fanned him with ostrich feathers, and would bring him food and drinks whenever he asked.

Michael and Lacy headed toward the platform where Marshall held court. Patricia was already speaking with him and appeared to be introducing him to an elegant Asian woman with silky black hair that extended to her waist and shimmered in the lights when she moved her head.

Patricia stepped down from the platform as Michael approached. She took the other woman's hand in hers and said, Michael Guidry, I'd like you to meet Valerie Liang," and after a pause, "My girlfriend."

Valerie smiled at Patricia and held out her hand to shake Michael's. "Mr. Guidry, it is a pleasure. I have heard a lot about you."

Michael returned her firm handshake, "All good I hope."

Valerie pursed her lips and said, "Let's just say it is now."

Michael joined Lacy on the stage, where she was talking to Marshall, "Sir, you look…," he paused searching for the right word. The first one that came to mind was 'ridiculous', but he ruled that out.

Before he could commit to a choice of words, Marshall came up with one for him, "I believe the word you are looking for is regal. Am I right?"

Michael laughed and said, "That is the perfect word. How in the world did they talk you into this?"

"It was easy. I've lived and worked in New Orleans for over half my life. More than fifty years, and I never was asked to be King of Carnival. Now I was given my chance and no way was I going to turn it down."

Lacy leaned in and kissed him on the check. "Well Doctor I think you are an absolutely perfect king, and a much better sport than the voodoo man over here." They all laughed and then Patricia and Valerie excused themselves and walked away hand in hand.

"So that's it," Michael said.

"That's what?" Lacy asked.

"That explains the changes in Patricia. Lately she's been smiling, whistling, hugging, touching. Now I know why."

"Why?" Lacy and Marshall asked simultaneously.

"Because," Michael answered, "She's in love."

Lacy narrowed her eyes and looked at Michael, "And what do you know about love?"

Michael blushed, and turned to Marshall, "Sir, would you excuse us?"

Looking amused, Marshall said, "Certainly. You two run along. I will discuss the life cycle of viruses with my two colleagues." He indicated the two nubile young women who remained at his side.

Michael led Lacy by her elbow to relatively quiet corner. He hesitated before speaking and Lacy spoke first, "Well, I am waiting. How are you an expert on love?"

"Simple," he said. "I know about love, because I'm in love. When you're in love you want to hug everyone. You're so happy you want to share the feeling. There is one thing that you absolutely have to do."

"What is that?" she asked teasingly.

"It is very important, very, very important, to be sure to let the person that you love know that you love them." He looked in her eyes and took a deep breath, "So, Lacy Livingston, if I didn't make it clear last night I want you to know that I am totally in love with you."

"Well, now that I know the rule," she said, stopping to get up on her toes and give him a gentle kiss on his lips, "I am forced to tell you that I too am in love with you."

Just then the band kicked off another second-line and a serpentine line of dancers swept Michael and Lacy into their rhythmic procession as it weaved through the crowd. They both now carried small umbrellas that had magically appeared in their hands. They bounced and danced to the beat, waving umbrellas in the air. Everyone was laughing and letting go of the tension that had been their companion for months. Michael looked at Lacy who looked beautiful and carefree. He thought, *Everything is going to be alright from now on.*

★ ★ ★

Wil had remained in his Med-Met office well after most others had gone home. The first of two important calls came around nine. "Wil, it's Joe at Metro Vid-News."

Wil leaned back in his chair recalling the photogenic dull witted reporter, "Oh yeah, listen Joe, I don't have anything for you right now, but I should have something good by tomorrow afternoon."

"Well, I just called to warn you, something big is coming down tomorrow morning. The Hippocratins are holding a press conference at ten. I don't have a lot of details, its supposed to be some kind of major announcement about the epidemic."

"Thanks Joe, let me know if you hear more."

"Sure thing, and don't you forget who's your buddy when you've got something good, okay?"

Wil mumbled, "Sure," and disconnected, sitting back, swirling his drink. Ice cubes tinkled against the glass as he contemplated what the Hippies were up to.

The second call came about an hour later. It was from one of the spotters, who was still following Guidry. "You ain't gonna believe this boss. Those Hippies I'm following, they're holding some kind of big party on Tchoupitoulous. Guidry showed up with the Livingston girl, and then they carried the old guy in on some type of big chair. They got live music and a bunch of near naked women."

"Get me some images, damn it," he shouted at the man on the other end of the line. "I don't care how you do it. Get in there and record what is going on."

After listening to the man's reply, Wil, in an even louder voice said, "Just do it. If you don't, forget about getting paid, and forget about any future work from us." With that he cut off the communication.

Following the second call, Wil contacted Darren. Wil could tell that Darren was not happy about being called so late. He seemed equally annoyed that that Wil wouldn't give him details about the crisis until Darren came to the Med-Met.

Darren arrived about forty-five minutes later. He walked into Wil's office and slammed the door behind him. "This better be good," he said pointing at Wil. "I'm still trying to catch up on my sleep, after my early morning trip to the hospital the other day."

Wil ignored Darren's mood, and offered him a drink. Darren took the glass, sat down, looked at Wil and said, "Well?"

"Alright," Wil began. "The Hippies are up to something. They've called a press conference for tomorrow morning at ten. In addition to that they are having one huge celebration tonight." He took a sip from his own drink, "The press conference is supposed to be some big announcement concerning the epidemic."

Darren, glass in hand leaned forward and said, "Is that all we know?"

Wil walked around the office as he spoke, "That's all we've been able to find out so far. I think it's clear what they're going to say." He looked to see if Darren was going to ask a question, and when there was none, he continued. "Ellis is out of prison. I think they are going to pick up on his accusations that we have been covering up the extent of the epidemic, and the numbers sent for terminal treatment."

Darren nodded and said, "Why the party?"

Wil quickly replied, "The little snots are so confident that they are going to embarrass us, or worse, they're already having a victory bash."

"That's one possibility, there must be others."

"Wil shrugged, "I can't think of anything." He chuckled, "Maybe they found a cure."

"Alright," Darren said. "If their plan is to attack us, how are we going to respond? After all, we really can't refute their claims."

"We don't," Wil now sat on the edge of his desk facing Darren. He rocked back and forth as he spoke. "We never give them the chance to attack us. We attack first."

Darren raised a questioning eyebrow.

Wil resumed, "We call a press conference for nine. We reveal the existence of the secret lab. Infer that they created the virus and that the public shouldn't be surprised one day when they announce they have the cure. We call for a full investigation of the Hippocratins, and their secret lab." Wil was on a roll, and Darren didn't interrupt. "We get the DA to give us a warrant to search the place. We need to call our political friends and get them behind the investigation. By ten o'clock tomorrow morning the Hippies will be running for cover. Any accusations that they make against us will look like feeble attempts to cover up their own crimes."

Darren slowly clapped his hands three times. "I like it. Instead of making whatever announcements they were planning, they will have to go on the defensive. I don't know if I buy your theory that they created the virus, but I sure would like to know what's in that lab." Darren put down his drink and said, "Okay, let's make some coffee. We've got a lot to do, and only eight hours to get it done."

CHAPTER
52

The last partiers left around three in the morning. Marshall had stayed until just after midnight. Around one-thirty, Lacy asked Michael if they could go back to his place.

Michael was about to say yes when he remembered the condition of his apartment. "I don't think that's a good idea," he told her. "I really need to straighten up a bit."

"I promise not to look," she said smiling. "We'll be fine as long as the sheets are clean."

Michael shook his head, "You wouldn't have to look, the smell would get you first. As far as the sheets go, we would have to find the bed."

"You're exaggerating, it can't be that bad."

"Worse," he said. "I haven't been much of a housekeeper the past few weeks."

"Well," she said, "We can't go to my place, Mommy and Daddy are home."

Michael pulled out his PDA and after a few keystrokes, said, "How's the Roosevelt Hotel sound?"

★ ★ ★

Michael and Lacy woke the next morning at seven-thirty. They had slept well in the downy comfort of the Roosevelt's bed. The plan was to meet at the Hippocratin Clinic around nine-thirty to make final preparations for the press conference. Michael was relieved that this time he wasn't going to be center stage. Marshall and Earl would be making the announcements.

After a playful shower they dressed and went down to the hotel dining room for breakfast. They returned to their room at nine to collect their things, check-out and head over to the clinic. They had left the vid-box on when they had gone for breakfast. Michael was about to turn it off when he heard an announcer's voice, "We now take you to Med-Met Headquarters, for a special report."

The image changed to a podium, with the Med-Met logo on it. Darren Walters stepped behind the microphones and began. "Good morning. I am here today to share with you some very troubling information we have learned. It involves the Hippocratin Society, and the current epidemic."

Lacy and Michael looked at each other, and then back at the picture as Darren continued. "It's not a secret that we have opposed the Hippocratin practice of so called 'traditional medicine'. We have made it clear that we believe that this alternative practice gives patients false hope, and keeps them from receiving the best in modern healthcare. The care that Med-Met delivers."

Darren looked at his notes and shook his head slowly, "Until yesterday, we believed that they were at worst a well intentioned, but poorly informed organization. We now have information that suggests they are far worse."

Michael quickly sent a text to the Hippocratin leaders, *Turn on the news.*

Darren's eyes narrowed slightly and his lips tightened in a slim line. "It has come to our attention that the Hippocratins are running a secret laboratory in Covington, Louisiana. This lab is cleverly hidden in the deep woods of the former National Primate Research lab. We have tried to find out what is going on inside that building but it is highly fortified, and defended by armed troops." Darren paused for effect and the screen showed the entrance to the Primate Sanctuary, and the heavy woods beyond the gates.

"I ask you," Darren resumed. "What is going on in there that is so secret and so sensitive as to require that type of security?" Darren now stared directly into the camera. "The current epidemic that we are suffering has been devastating. One of the main beneficiaries of all this sickness has been the Hippocratins. Their volumes have grown rapidly since the start of this medical crisis. People have left Med-Met looking for a miracle cure. Isn't it ironic that the Hippocratins were there, ready to take them in. I wouldn't be surprised if any day now they announced that they had found a cure for this disease. Think about it, who would have a better chance of curing something, than those that created it?"

Darren's voice grew stronger and louder as he worked toward his conclusion. "Hopefully we're wrong. Maybe there's an innocent explanation for the secret lab. You, the public, have a right to know. I call for a full investigation of the Covington facility, and the Hippocratin Society. As I speak, the St. Tammany Parish District Attorney is seeking a warrant to search the facility."

Questions were shouted at Darren from all directions. He put up his hands and when the crowd quieted he said, "That will be all for now. You can direct your questions to the authorities." With that he left the podium.

★   ★   ★

Anticipating the madness that he would face at the clinic Michael suggested that Lacy take a cab home. She agreed and he told her he would call as soon as things settled down. Michael had to fight his way through crowds of media, patients and protestors in order to get inside. He was quickly recognized by the press who swarmed around him, shouting questions and shoving microphones in his face.

"Michael, how do you respond to Darren Walter's accusations?"

"Michael, is it true? Did the Hippocratins create the virus?"

"Is it true that Jacob Rokoff is alive and hiding at the Covington laboratory?"

The protestors cursed at him, and wished that he suffer a long and painful death. Some threw rocks and trash in his direction.

When he finally pushed his way to the front door it opened quickly, he was pulled in and the door locked. Members of Alex's security team guarded the doors. Michael was directed to the conference room. The majority of the core team was already there along with Barry Mandel, the Hippocratin's attorney. Marshall asked whether Lacy was alright and Michael explained he thought it best that she go home. The clock indicated that it was nine-forty-five.

Patricia quickly filled Michael in on where they were. "We've had to cancel the ten o'clock press conference to allow us time to come up with a strategy." She handed him a copy of a statement they were releasing, "*The Hippocratin Society emphatically and without reservation denies the outrageous accusations made this morning by Darren Walters. We have never and will never do anything to endanger human life. As always our sole purpose is to provide personal and compassionate care to all individuals, promote health and ease suffering. In the immediate future we will release a more comprehensive statement that will clearly put these absurd claims to rest.*"

"That is not going to do anything to reassure the public or the authorities," Patricia said.

Mandel got out of his seat, "We debated whether to go ahead and reveal the progress on the treatment, but decided that if we make our announcement it will seem to validate Walter's claim. We need to be able to offer verifiable evidence that the Hippocratins didn't create the virus, and then show how you have systematically developed the treatment and vaccine."

Riser sat, fingers tented below his mouth, "Although I would rather not divulge the existence of Infinity, I am prepared to do so in order to allow us to move forward with attacking this disease. We have the transport box, and the vial that held the virus. Georgi can verify that it was part of the material recovered from the moon."

"That's a start," Mandel said, "But I don't think it's enough. You and your organization are already identified with the Hippocratins. You provide the security at Covington, and Georgi was Jacob's god son. Med–Met will just say that you invented a convenient cover-up. After all, Infinity doesn't exist in any official records, and no one is going to the moon to confirm your story."

The room became quiet as they all tried to think of other options. The door opened and one of the security team handed Riser a note. Riser read it shaking his head.

He shared the contents of the note with his usual military precision. "St. Tammany police are at the gate of the Covington facility. Our troops have denied them entry. They displayed their weapons, and we displayed ours. No shots have been fired, but it is a stand-off."

Michael asked, "How long can it stay like that?"

Riser answered, "Not long, my people won't fire on legitimate law enforcement. Sooner or later we'll have to back down." He looked to the attorney, "Barry, can you get us relief from the warrant?"

Barry looked up over his glasses, "I'll do what I can. I'll need to go to court to get it quashed. I'm sure the D.A. is in their pocket. They have no grounds for issuing a search warrant based on hearsay and supposition. Besides, the primate sanctuary is a federal facility, when it was turned into a preserve, the land was turned over to the government. That is all except the small parcel where the lab sits. The Parish court doesn't have jurisdiction."

Michael's communicator vibrated, checking the screen he saw it was from Lacy. He moved off to the side and whispered into it, "Hi baby, miss me already?" He stiffened when instead of Lacy's voice he heard that of police Lieutenant Andy Livingston, her father.

"No baby," Andy said laughing. "I do however have some info for you."

Flustered Michael straightened and said, "Yes sir, I'm sorry, I thought ..."

Andy cut him off and shared the information that he had called about.

Michael moved back to the group. "I just heard from Lacy's dad. He says the word is that the police will wait until five PM. Until then they will try and achieve a peaceful entry into the lab. After that they will use force as needed."

Riser nodded, "I need to inform my people at the center. I am also arranging for a security team to help keep the media and protestors at bay, and to assure that the patients can get through."

★ ★ ★

Darren was pleased with the way things were going. The media was all over the story, and for the first time in months the coverage was favorable to Med-Met. The armed stand-off at the Primate facility reinforced his accusation that it was more that an animal sanctuary. Visits to Med-Met were up dramatically since his press conference earlier in the day.

At three PM, Darren convened his executive team. Once Darren had greeted everyone he turned the floor over to Wil for an update.

Wil appeared to be in a great mood. His hair was slicked back, he was freshly shaven, and he was wearing another of his trademark wide-lapel suits. This one was some sort of green iridescent material. His shoulders were back and he seemed to suck in his gut as he summed up the day's events for his colleagues.

When he finished Joel Rogers, the CFO, asked, "Why haven't the police moved in yet?"

Wil nodded, "As I was saying, the guards inside are heavily armed. The police want to try and avoid a violent situation. They are trying to negotiate a peaceful entry. I have been told that one way or the other they will go in at five."

Darren then asked, "What's the status of the Hippocratins attempts to get legal relief?"

"Actually," Wil said, "It isn't the Hippies, but rather the Foundation that runs that animal facility that is trying to get the warrant set aside. If they're successful, we have a higher court ready to step in."

Angela Stuart, the Med–Met CEO, shifted in her chair, "Darren, what is it exactly that the Hippocratins are guilty of? Did they really start this epidemic?"

Wil started to answer, but Darren held up a hand and responded. "As far as we know they aren't guilty of anything, except of course being royal pains in our asses. The problem is…" He paused, put his hand to his chin, and took a deep breath, "The problem is our guilt, and what the Hippocratins know about it. We have hidden from the public the magnitude of this epidemic, and the huge numbers of people who have been sent for final treatment. If that information had gotten out many would have either taken their chances with the disease, or gone over to the Hippocratins."

Darren got out of his chair and got a glass of water from a credenza. "Our techies tell us the night I encountered Guidry at Med–Met a lot of information was accessed. They still haven't been able to figure out exactly what. Based on some of Marshall Ellis's statements it seems that they have a good idea about the numbers treated, and terminated."

"So you see," he continued as he sat down again, "The problem isn't what they have done, but what we've done. The best way for Med–Met to protect itself, is too destroy the credibility of the Hippocratins. We have to go after them and use every judge, every politician, and every media-source that we own. We will use innuendo, and when necessary, outright lies." He checked to be sure that all were listening. "When we're done we will have taken away their credibility, their clinics, and their freedom." All of his well polished restraint seemed to disappear as he finished, "I will personally castrate that little shit, Michael Guidry, and hang his balls on the wall over my desk."

Suzanne Hartstein, Darren's personal assistant, sat, her mouth in a tight line, as she dutifully, and accurately recorded all that was said.

★   ★   ★

The day seemed to drag on forever. The number of patients seeking care dropped off dramatically. It was unclear how much of that was due to the difficulty of getting past the crowds, and how much due to the impact of Darren's broadcast.

Michael spent most of the day caring for the in-patients. He followed-up on those who had been receiving the treatment regimen. Most continued to show progress, with a few more improving enough to come off the ventilator and breathe on their own. Unfortunately they were limited in how many patients could be treated, since the flow of drug from Covington was halted.

At four forty-five Michael joined the others in the conference room. He noticed smiling faces as he entered, and understood when he heard that they had just gotten word from their attorney that the warrant had been quashed, and the police left the area around the primate center. Drug shipments would resume later that evening after the crowds, particularly the protestors, had dispersed.

At five they watched the nightly news vids. The reversal of the warrant led the broadcast. Med-Mets attorney was being interviewed, "We aren't too concerned. We are certain that this is just a temporary reversal based on a technicality. The U.S. Attorney is preparing a warrant that will prevail."

Next, up was a state senator from Tangipahoa Parish, "I am calling on the President of the State Senate, the Speaker of the State House, and the Governor of Louisiana, to call a special session of the legislature to pass a law prohibiting the practice of Hippocratin medicine." The U.S. Congressman from Baton Rouge called for a Congressional investigation into the Hippocratin's role in creating the epidemic.

A live feed from outside the clinic showed angry protestors carrying signs and harassing people who tried to get in or out of the center. A large red-faced man carried a placard that said, "My mom is dead, my wife is dead, you're next." He vowed to extract revenge on the Hippocratins. Many in the crowd were chanting, "Die Hippies die, die Hippies die"

The commentator went on to say that the Hippocratin's had declined an interview, and had merely re-issued their statement from earlier in the day. He then looked directly into the camera and said, "We still don't know what is going on in the secret laboratory in Covington. What is it the Hippocratins have to hide? If you have done nothing wrong, then let us in. Channel Five is prepared to send a vid crew and veteran reporter to show the world your side of the story. As always, we promise fair, accurate and unbiased reporting."

They sat in silence. The relief they had felt over the court decision was short lived. It appeared that the media, the courts, the politicians and the public were aligning against them.

For safety reasons the medical team decided to spend the night at the clinic. The evening shift was advised to stay home, and the day shift agreed to pull a double. At seven a vid-link conference was arranged. Michael and the rest of the medical team participated from the clinic and Riser, Alex and Barry Mandel from Riser's office.

Barry opened the meeting, "As you know we were able to get the warrant quashed. This takes the pressure off for the moment, but the Med-Met lawyers have already approached the U.S. Attorney. I have filed a motion with the Eastern District Court for Louisiana to enjoin them from seeking another search warrant. Because of the volatility of the issue the court has called for a hearing tomorrow morning. Med-Met will get to make their case and try to show cause for a search. We will get to make ours as to why it should not be allowed. We need to decide on a strategy. We have talked among ourselves at this end and General Riser has a proposal."

Justin Riser's face came into the center of the image, "Thank you Barry, and there is no need to use the military title with this group. Briefly, I think that we need to be direct and honest. Lay it all out and make Med-Met show proof that there is anything sinister or illegal." He made a fist, covered it with his other hand and rested his chin on top. "We need to tell the whole story of the epidemic. Present all the facts, Infinity, the transport of the virus to earth by the Chen expedition, the theft, and subsequent infection. We disclose our efforts to create a treatment and vaccine. We answer all questions and then try and withstand their attacks on our credibility."

Earl spoke from the clinic conference room. "Why don't we turn the tables? We can accuse Med-Met of covering up the scope of the epidemic and sending millions to termination."

"The problem with that," Barry answered, "Is the source of your information." He looked toward Riser, "I don't know the details, but if it was obtained by illegal means, it can't be used. It would be great if there was another source of that info."

CHAPTER
53

The hearing was scheduled for ten the next morning in Federal District Court. Michael and Patricia remained at the clinic to care for the patients. Police escorted Earl Carter and Marshall Ellis the few blocks to the court to protect them from the crowds.

Darren Walters testified on behalf of Med-Met, arguing for reinstatement of the warrant. His testimony was essentially a restatement of his press conference the previous morning.

Barry Mandel tried to cross examine him. "Mr Walters, what evidence do you have that anything illegal is going on at the Covington facility."

Darren shrugged, "I think it is obvious to everyone that they are hiding something in there. If not why not open the facility to the authorities and the press?"

Mandel looked at the judge and pursed his lips and turned back to Walters, "Mr. Walters, I ask you again, what proof do you have of illegal activity that would warrant a search?"

Darren shook his head, "I believe I already answered that."

Mandel turned to the judge, "Your honor, would you please instruct the witness to answer the question."

The judge peered down, "Mr. Mandel, I believe that he has responded to the satisfaction of the court. Unless you have a different line of questions, the witness is dismissed."

Mandel stood with a look of disbelief as Darren stepped down from the witness stand, a smile on his face.

Justin Riser was the first to be called on behalf of the Foundation. After establishing his credentials he told the story of the Infinity Research Laboratory on the lunar colony. He described the work that was going on at the lab. The transport box and vial were produced and entered as evidence.

When Mandel was finished the Med–Met attorney began the cross examination.

"Mr. Riser, if we were to examine documents, official or unofficial, would we find any record of this Infinity Research Laboratory?'

"No, I don't believe you would."

"Aside from yourself, is there anyone alive who can verify your claims as to the work that was done there?

"To the best of my knowledge, I am the only survivor of the lunar disaster who has direct knowledge of Infinity."

"So you are telling us," the attorney looked directly at Riser, "That we should take your word about something that happened over forty years ago, and which cannot be substantiated by anyone else. Let me ask you something else Mr. Riser. Do you consider yourself a supporter of the Hippocratins?"

"If you mean do I admire the work that they do, the answer is yes." Riser answered directly and without hesitation.

The Med–Met attorney smiled, "Have you in fact provided financial support in the form of free security services to the Hippocratins."

Riser did not show any discomfort as he answered, "My company has provided some services free of charge, and others at a discount."

"Thank you Mr. Riser that will be all."

Mandel called Georgi Chen. Georgi testified that the box that Riser had produced was part of the inventory brought back from the moon by the Chen salvage expedition. He described the burglary the missing items, including the box.

"Mr. Chen," the opposing counsel began, "You have testified that you personally saw this Infinity Research Laboratory. Is that correct?"

"Yes it is."

"Did you enter the facility."

"No, I stayed at the base camp the day the team went in." A tinge of resentment was evident in Georgi's answer.

"So, is it not also correct, that you have no direct personal knowledge that this fancy box with the flashy lights actually came from Infinity?"

Georgi started to answer, "My father and brother…"

He was cut off by the attorney, "Unfortunately sir, your father and brother are dead, and cannot testify. Please answer the question. Do you have any direct personal knowledge of where this box came from."

Georgi hesitated and said, "No."

The attorney then established Georgi's ties to the Hippocratin Society, his father's long friendship with Jacob Rokoff, and Georgi's extensive financial support of the clinic. Having established his point he thanked Georgi and dismissed him.

Alex's testimony was similar. She described the investigation of the robbery, the focus on Brian Marino, and the discovery of the transport box, and broken vial in the trash behind his apartment. The state epidemiologists report identifying Marino as the probable index case for the epidemic was submitted into evidence.

On cross examination the Med-Met attorney once again focused on establishing ties between the witness and the Hippocratins. He asked Alex about her work for Riser, and her romantic involvement with Georgi. Finally he asked her if she considered herself a personal friend of Michael Guidry, which she confirmed.

The judge called a recess for lunch and asked that everyone return by two.

★ ★ ★

Michael was able to get away from the clinic and joined the rest of the group for lunch and to catch-up on the morning's courtroom activities. They met at a restaurant, around the corner from the courthouse, on St. Charles Avenue.

Barry gave his assessment, "I think we did as well as possible. You all did a great job with your testimonies. You were direct and showed no hesitation. As expected, Med-Met's approach is to cast doubt about your credibility, because of your ties to the Hippocratins. They still have not demonstrated cause for a warrant."

Marshall, using a fork with a shrimp on the tip for emphasis said, "So the plan for this afternoon is to tell them what's in the lab. Do we still go with that?"

"I think it's the best strategy," Barry said. "We're now playing to public opinion, as much as to the judge. We have to hope that they believe the explanation that the virus came from Infinity and was not created by us." There were nods of agreement around the table.

"Marshall will describe the background of the research lab, and how it was maintained as a safety net in case of an event just like the one we are currently facing. He will go through the process used to elucidate the structure of the virus, and design the treatment and vaccine. We will show images to support his words, including pictures from inside the lab. He will emphasize that a search of the facility could contaminate the production and delay delivery of treatment to those who need it."

Barry who had yet to touch his food, continued to describe the plan, "Earl, you will report the clinical results. We will show vid-clips of the patients who received the anti-cytokine and how they were able to begin breathing on their own again."

Earl looked over at Michael and then said, "Wouldn't it be more convincing to have Michael give the results. He's the one who has been treating the patients and can relate the improvement first-hand."

Barry, who was now chewing his first bite of food, swallowed and answered. "That may be, but I don't want Michael anywhere near the courtroom. We don't need to have him asked under oath whether he has made any recent nocturnal visits to Med–Met."

They turned at the sound of hearty laughter as two men walked out of an adjoining room, sharing a joke. The taller of the two slapped the other on the back as they headed out of the restaurant.

Barry put his hand to his forehead and said, "We're fucked."

Michael said, "I recognize the short guy. It's that Congressman from Baton Rouge, who called for the House investigation. Who's the guy he's with?"

"That," said Barry, pushing away his mostly uneaten food, "Is our judge."

★   ★   ★

The afternoon session went much like the morning. Marshall Ellis responding to Barry Mandel's questions explained the lab and its background. He gave a detailed technical explanation of the work they were doing, and the progress. At Barry's request he restated everything in layman's terms.

After several soft questions, that reestablished information already in evidence, the Med–Met lawyer then began to probe more aggressively. "Dr. Ellis, the laboratory that you've described for us is quite sophisticated, is it not?"

"Yes, one of the best I've ever worked in."

"It has everything that you needed to figure out the structure of the virus, and to determine how to combat it?"

"Yes, I have already explained that?"

The Med–Met lawyer paused and appeared to be thinking. He turned back to Marshall, "I was wondering, wouldn't this same lab have all the capabilities of creating a pathogenic virus?"

Marshall held up his hands in front of him, "that is not…"

He was cut-off, "Dr. Ellis, please answer the question. Is this lab capable of producing an infectious virus."

Marshall looked to Barry for help, and then answered, "Yes, I guess that it has the capability, but that isn't what it was used for."

The attorney went to his table and picked up an old medical journal. "Doctor do you recognize this?"

"Yes, it appears to be a copy of the journal Nature. They stopped printing a paper version about fifty years ago."

The attorney picked up his pace, "This particular edition is from 2035. You wrote an editorial for this issue." He passed the journal to Marshall. "Would you please read the title of that editorial to the court."

Marshall looked at the table of contents and seemed to deflate as he read. "The 2031 H1N1 Virus, A Flawed Killing Machine."

"That is a very intriguing title Doctor. The next lines are even better, I quote *The world narrowly escaped its worst infectious epidemic in over a century. The 2031 H1N1 had all the makings of a super-killer, except for minor flaws in its structure. These flaws were to our benefit as the epidemic was short lived. With a few alterations in the genome this could have been the worst epidemic in recorded history.* Your honor I submit this journal in evidence."

★　★　★

Michael and Patricia, watched the proceedings on public access from the clinic conference room. Earl's testimony was next, but it would make little difference. The inferences from the cross examination of Marshall would be all people would think about. All the promise of the treatment and vaccine would be dismissed. It would all fit with the assertion that the Hippocratins had manufactured the virus.

Patricia sat limply, head bowed and eyes closed. She said in a whisper, "They're going to win. Michael, everything we've worked for everything that Jacob stood for it's over. We've run out of time and options."

Michael was silent. Patricia looked at him but he said nothing staring ahead. Patricia moved toward him. On the screen, Earl was being sworn in. Suddenly Michael jumped up headed for the door. Looking back over his shoulder he said, "We may still have an option. Can you handle the clinic? I have something I need to do." Not waiting for an answer he headed out.

Michael found himself at the door of a typical old fashioned shotgun house near the river bend. The woman who answered the door showed both recognition and surprise. In the background he heard the vid broadcast of the court proceedings.

Afraid that she might close the door on him Michael spoke quickly, "Can I speak with you?"

Suzanne Hartstein, Darren Walter's assistant, and Jacob Rokoff's niece stood in the doorway, wearing sunglasses although it was rather dark in the house. That and her sniffling led Michael to guess that she had been crying.

"Suzanne, we need your help. I can see that you have been watching the proceedings and I'm sure you can see that everything that your uncle stood for is about to be destroyed. You helped Jacob before, and I was hoping that there might be something that you can tell us that will help us out of this mess."

She stepped back giving him room to enter, and removed her sunglasses. Her eyes were red confirming what Michael had suspected. She folded and unfolded the earpieces of the glasses, seemingly studying their construction. She still had not spoken.

Michael spoke softly, "I know that this is difficult, I know that you would be risking a lot, but we are running out of time. You are our last hope."

Finally she looked up and spoke. "I didn't know what to do. If you hadn't come by, I might have sat here while … But, I can't do this anymore. I can't be quiet." She folded the glasses and put them down. "Do you know how hard it has been?"

Michael was about to say something, but remembered Jacob's teaching. Always give the patient time to tell their story.

Suzanne began to fidget with her glasses again, "I tried not to take sides. My job. My uncle. It tore me up. Uncle Jacob was great about it. He never judged me and he never pushed me to get information about Med-Met. My bosses still don't know that he was my uncle."

Suzanne put her glasses firmly on the table. As they hit the table she seemed to take on a different tone. "I can't be quiet anymore. It's no longer about who provides the best healthcare. What they're doing is wrong."

Michael again waited but Suzanne was silent. Finally she walked to a bureau, opened the draw and took something out. She showed it to Michael who recognized it as a vid-recorder-chip. "Here, play this," she said pointing to the vid-player as she shoved it in Michael's hand.

Michael went to the vid-screen, switched off the court proceedings and inserted the chip.

For the next half-hour he watched in silence. Suzanne sat stonily beside him.

When it was over the screen went to dark, but he still sat staring at it. Suzanne, broke the silence, "So, you see why I couldn't stay on the sidelines anymore?"

Michael finally turned off the screen and faced Suzanne, "This is incredible. Can we use this?"

Suzanne nodded, "That's why I showed it to you."

"We need to get to the courthouse." He sent a quick message to Alex to let Mandel know that he was on his way to the courthouse with a surprise witness.

The crowd outside the courthouse had grown larger. Marshall's testimony had brought out more protestors convinced that the Hippocratins had created the virus. Michael and Suzanne had to push their way through. They could see Mandel pacing on the stairs.

Just as they reached the bottom of the stairs a hand grabbed Michael by the collar. "Hey ain't you Guidry?"

Michael shook his head and tried to break free which only tightened the collar around his neck. "Yeah, you're him. Look, its Guidry. He's one of them."

The crowd pushed toward Michael, he was separated from Suzanne who was able to move on to the stairs as the crowd converged on Michael. Michael felt like he was about to go down fearing he would be trampled. He could see Suzanne and Mandel, but they were unable to help him. He remembered that he had the chip and that he had to protect it.

He swung his fists wildly trying to create some space. The crowd fought back, he was hit in his back, his side, his head. As he began to topple the tight knot of the crowd loosened. A vagrant in tattered clothing roared into the mass of people screaming and pushing a hovering shopping cart. He rammed the cart left and right creating space between Michael and his attackers.

Just then courthouse guards, emerged with Mandel yelling at them and pointing. The guards began to clear the stairs opening a path for Michael. As Michael started for the stairs he turned to look back at his savior with the shopping cart. He was no longer screaming and seemed perfectly relaxed.

Michael thought he recognized the man and stared at him. The vagrant smiled and winked. It was then that Michael realized that the man in rags did not smell bad. He gave him a thumbs up, turned and ran up the stairs to Mandel, Suzanne stood nearby.

Mandel grabbed his shoulders, "Are you ok? My god, if it hadn't been for that whacko they would have torn you to pieces. Listen, if you have something give it to me quick. The judge only gave us a brief recess."

As they walked toward the courtroom Michael rapidly explained who Suzanne was, and what was on the vid-chip. The attorney smiled for the first time since lunch. "Ms. Hartstein, are you prepared to tell your story under oath, and substantiate the contents of this chip."

Taking off her hat, and squaring her shoulders she said, "I'm ready."

★ ★ ★

Michael waited with Suzanne outside the courtroom while the hearing was called to order.

The judge asked Barry if he had any additional witnesses to call. Barry looked at Darren Walters and said loudly, "Your honor I wish to call Suzanne Hartstein."

A bailiff signaled for Suzanne to enter the courtroom and move to the witness chair. As she came down the center aisle, the Med–Met attorney leaned over for a quick whispered conference with Darren. Michael was close enough to overhear Darren telling the lawyer that he couldn't think of any reason to object, he was confident in Suzanne's allegiance.

Suzanne was sworn in and Mandel took her through the usual opening questions. She gave her name, address, her profession. She explained that she had worked at Med–Met for eleven years, and that she was currently Executive Assistant to Darren Walters, Regional Director of Med–Met. He asked her about her responsibilities and she went through the scope of her work, including attending and recording meetings of the senior executive staff. The Med–Met team did not show any concern about the questions or her answers.

The give and take was proceeding quickly and developing a smooth rhythm, at that point Mandel changed the pace. He walked back to his table and picked up a piece of paper and appeared to study it. Holding the paper in front of him he approached Suzanne.

"Ms. Hartstein before we go further, I have an important question to ask you." Pointing to the Med–Met attorney, Mandel continued, "My opposing counsel has been diligent in eliciting associations between other witnesses we have presented, and the Hippocratin Society. Do you have any such relationships that we should be aware of?"

Suzanne, who had been looking down at her hands, straightened up and appeared to look directly at Wil, "Yes," pausing, "My uncle was Jacob Rokoff."

An audible rustling went through the room. Media picked furiously at hand held devices and whispered into mini-microphones.

Darren dropped the pen that he had been holding. Wil jumped up and yelled objection. The Med-Met attorney told Wil to sit down and addressed the judge, "Your honor we wish to object to this witness, we had no previous notice that she would be called."

"Overruled," the judge said, "If you had objection to the witness the appropriate time to express it would have been before she began her testimony." The noise and movement in the room was increasing, and the judge rapped his gavel calling for order and asking Mandel to continue. Darren furiously wrote notes and passed them to his attorney.

Mandel resumed, "Ms. Hartstein, you have said that one of your responsibilities was to attend executive meetings and keep a record of the proceedings."

"Yes."

"When was the last time you attended such a meeting?"

"Two days ago."

"Were matters relating to the search warrant of the Primate Center Laboratory discussed?"

"They were."

"Did you make a digital audio and visual recording of that meeting?"

"Yes, I did." Suzanne answered firmly.

The Med-Met attorney jumped up. "I object, the content of those meetings is private and should not be viewed."

Mandel responded, "Your honor the meeting in question was held at Med-Met. Med-Met is a publically traded company, which receives federal funding. In addition, all parties in attendance were aware that the meeting was being recorded and had agreed to that."

The judge shook his head as he looked to Darren. "Objection overruled. Mr. Mandel, please proceed."

Barry walked to his table and removed a small item from his briefcase. He brought it to Suzanne and asked her to identify it.

She looked at the markings on the item, "This is the vid-chip recording of the executive meeting of two days ago."

The Med–Met attorney again stood up and started to object. Barry interrupted, "Your honor we will of course agree to Med–Met having experts review the chip to verify its authenticity."

His opposing counsel sat back down and didn't pursue his objection. Barry took the chip and turned to the judge, "Your honor we would move to place this chip in evidence, and if it pleases the court, ask that it be viewed."

With the judge's permission a vid screen was activated and the chip inserted. The courtroom remained silent as they watched the events of the meeting two days earlier. Wil sank deeper into his chair as the playback continued. Darren grim faced stared straight ahead. Lacy had come into the courtroom just after Suzanne had been sworn in, and sat next to Michael holding his hand.

As the recording reached the portion where Darren said, *"The problem is our guilt, and what the Hippocratins know about it. We have hidden from the public the magnitude of this epidemic, and the huge numbers of people who have been sent for final treatment,"* the stirring in the courtroom resumed. As the recording of the meeting came to a conclusion an agitated Darren Walters was seen saying, *"I will personally castrate that little shit, Michael Guidry, and hang his balls on the wall over my desk."* The screen dissolved to a Med–Met logo with a date and time stamp. The decorum in the courtroom dissolved. Reporters were rushing from their seats to try and get advantageous positions for interviews. Hippocratin supporters were high-fiving, and hugging. Darren and Wil were arguing loudly with their attorney. The judge was banging his gavel and shouting for order.

Lacy looked up at Michael, he looked stunned. "He can't have them you know," she said with a mischievous smile.

Confused Michael asked, "Can't have what?"

Lacy looked around, as if to check whether anyone was looking at them. "These," she said as she gave his groin a playful squeeze, "They're mine."

CHAPTER
54

Three months later, Michael Guidry stood on the stage in front of the Med-Met facility. He scanned the large crowd recalling how Just a short time before he had worked here as a technician. It amazed him how much had happened. On stage with him were his colleagues, the physicians and students of the Hippocratin movement. Patricia Murphy now the senior physician and director of the New Orleans Hippocratins sat immediately to his left. Next to her sat Marshall Ellis, the 102 year old co-founder of the Hippocratins. Patricia and the others had unanimously decided Michael would be the main spokesperson today. His protests fell on deaf ears. They maintained that Michael had become the face of their organization. On his right was Georgi Chen, CEO of Chen Salvers and chairman of the Chen Foundation. To Chen's right sat two very uncomfortable former Med-Met executives.

With a signal from the Vid-crew, Michael stepped to the podium. "Good morning, my name is Michael Guidry. I am here this morning representing my fellow students and physicians of the Hippocratin Medical Society. I also wish to acknowledge my good friend, and our benefactor Mr. Georgi Chen," he nodded toward Georgi.

"This past year has been a trying and painful one for all of us. I do not think any of us has not been touched by the devastating viral epidemic. We all have lost loved ones. For me it has been most personal as I lost my friend and mentor Jacob Rokoff.

"Through old-fashioned epidemiologic and medical research we learned the origin of the virus was a secret lunar laboratory. My colleagues then devised a treatment and developed a vaccine for the virus. The treatment has been successful in decreasing the fatality rate by approximately 90%. The vaccine is being distributed through our clinics nationally and shared on an international basis.

"We also learned of severe flaws in the Med-Met system. The system did not allow for the recognition of a heretofore unknown illness. This led to an unprecedented number of people being assigned to euthanasia. The Med-Met algorithm calculated the cost of caring for these individuals and whether it exceeded their economic worth. If cost exceeded worth they were sent to their deaths. We know many of them would have survived given a chance. To compound matters Med-Met covered up the extent of the epidemic. They actively attempted to place the blame for the illness on the Hippocratins. Their harassment interfered with our efforts to find a cure. It is hard to calculate the number of additional lives that might have been saved."

The crowd stirred and the former Med-Met officials grew increasingly uneasy. Michael continued, "Out of disaster can come change. I would like to introduce my friend, Georgi Chen. He will make an announcement signaling a new era in medicine."

Georgi came to the podium, shook Michael's hand and spoke to the audience. "As you are aware, the government has ordered the dissolution of Med-Met's monopoly in healthcare, and the selling off of its assets. My father's will created a Foundation to promote and advance Hippocratin medicine. The Foundation is well endowed and has been successful in its investments. I am pleased to announce that the Foundation has purchased the assets of the New Orleans Regional Med-Met Center. The Hippocratin organization under the direction of Dr. Patricia Murphy will assume operation of the facility.

We will also begin to recruit a faculty and construct the syllabus for the Jacob Rokoff College of Medicine. This will be the first school to teach medicine in the last fifty years."

Michael returned to the microphone, as the crowd applauded Georgi's announcement. "Thank you Georgi. With much gratitude I accept this offer on behalf of my colleagues. I want to make it clear there will be changes. I do not want to give the impression everything that was the old Med-Met must be scrapped. Technology in itself is not evil, but it must be used correctly. There needs to be a human element in charge of the technology. Starting tomorrow our physicians will join with the staff at Med-Met to return the human element to medical care. Before this happens a few changes need to be made.

"First, the place needs a new name. If you look up at the Med-Met sign we will take care of that now." Michael uncovered a panel of buttons on the podium. He pushed the first and the Med-Met name was gone. With a second push of the button a new name appeared, *The Sara Anson Medical Center.*

"Next, we need to eliminate the worst aspect of what Med-Met was. I would like to ask Dr. Marshall Ellis and Mr. Vernon Biggs to join me."

The centagenarian rose from his seat, and a very large man came up the stairs and onto the stage. Michael continued, "I believe you all know Dr. Ellis. Mr. Biggs has been Med-Met's chief computer engineer. Mr. Biggs if you would."

Biggs came to podium and pressed another button which raised a large vid-screen behind the stage. With the second push a complicated mathematical formula appeared on the screen.

Michael addressed Biggs, "What are we looking at?"

"The algorithm. The one that calculates who lives and who dies."

"And you have arranged it so the algorithm can be eliminated permanently?"

"Yes, all it takes is for someone to push the red button on the podium."

Michael gestured to Dr. Ellis, "Sir, would you do the honors."

The frail scientist approached the podium. He stood straight and looked at the audience with clear green eyes. "For Jacob," he said as he pushed the button. The algorithm melted from the screen and was gone.

EPILOGUE

Michael again played with the small box in his jacket pocket. With his fingers he cautiously flipped the lid open and touched the cool facets of the diamond. Lacy, Alex and Georgi kept up a lively dinner conversation. Although the restaurant was lovely, and the food delicious, Michael remained relatively quiet and picked at his food. He concentrated on what he had planned for after dinner, when he and Lacy would be alone and he would ask her to marry him.

Michael was startled by Georgi snapping his fingers right in front of Michael's nose. "Hello, anybody home?" Georgi said and they all laughed as Michael focused on his friends.

"I'm sorry, I was distracted. There's a lot going on at the clinic. In the six months since we took over the flow of patients has increased significantly. There are also all the things we have to get done if we are going to admit our first medical class in the fall." All of this was true, but not the real reason for his lack of attention.

"Well, give it a rest for a few minutes," Georgi said, "I have some news to share."

The first thing that went through Michael's mind was that Georgi was going to announce that he and Alex were engaged, and that would take away some of the thunder when he proposed later that night.

Georgi smiled, "We're going back to the moon. The government has authorized a new expedition, with a primary objective of a full examination of Infinity. They want us to see what we can learn about what they were doing, and why. More importantly they think we may be able to learn from their biological work, and bring you back some more treatments and vaccines."

"That's fantastic," Lacy said. "Who's going, and when do you leave?"

"Chen Salvors will have the contract, and I will lead the expedition," Georgi told her. "In addition to my staff, Justin Reiser will be going. He is essential in that he is the only living person who has the biologics that will allow entry into Corridor A. Alex will head security, and Earl Carter will come as scientific and medical officer."

Michael felt a bit jealous that Earl would go, but he realized that Earl was a more accomplished scientist, and that his own role was to make sure the clinic and med school stayed on track.

They toasted the mission. Georgi looked across at Lacy and Michael, "We do have a need for one more member of the team. The government feels that there is a lot to be learned about the disaster. They want to have a better understanding of how much warning people had, and how they reacted. In the same way that excavation of Pompeii revealed a lot about the events immediately surrounding the eruption of Vesuvius, we may be able to learn a lot from more study of Sheppard City. So..." Georgi paused. "We have been authorized to bring a trained disasterologist with us." Looking at Lacy he asked, "Interested?"

Michael looked at Lacy. He expected her to be shaking her head and declining the offer. They had a good thing going, they were happy. It would be insane to run off to the moon, with all the risks involved. Instead he saw that she was nodding, had a huge smile and her eyes were opened wide.

She turned to him, "Oh Michael, isn't this wonderful? Everyone in my field would kill for an opportunity like this. You have the clinic and the med school, and now I have this. It is so awesome." She leaned over and kissed him.

He mustered a brave smile and agreed that it was wonderful as he pushed the ring box further down in his pocket.